BLACKMAIL BEHIND THE BARRACKS

MARGARET DRAKE

BEHIND THE BARRACKS

by:

MARGARET DRAKE

WORKBOOK PRESS LLC
187 E Warm Springs Rd,
Suite B285, Las Vegas, NV 89119, USA

Website:	https://workbookpress.com/
Hotline:	1-888-818-4856
Email:	admin@workbookpress.com

Ordering Information:
Quantity sales. Special discounts are available on quantity purchases by corporations, associations, and others. For details, contact the publisher at the address above.

ISBN-13:   978-1-955459-16-7 (Paperback Version)
             978-1-955459-17-4 (Digital Version)

REV. DATE: 24.03.2021

Previous novels by this author:

(2019) ABAYA www.amazon.com

(2011) *Haole Wife* www.iUniverse.com.

(2009) *Haole Teacher* www.iUniverse.com.

(2008) *Homesteading Woman* www.iUniverse.com.
Lincoln, NE

(2005) *Sanatorium Girl* www.iUniverse.com.
Lincoln, NE.

(2004) *The Disappearing Patient. A novel about an occupational therapist* www.iUniverse.com. Lincoln, NE.

(2003) *Reconstructing Soldiers: An Occupational Therapist in WWI* www.iUniverse.com. Lincoln, NE.

Memoire:

(2010) *A US Feminist in Saudi Arabia: 1980-1982.* www.iUniverse.com

Website:
http://www.margaretdrake.com

Table of Contents

The language in this book, for the most part is not in vernacular as that mode is too hard to decipher for many readers not familiar with Southern dialects or Hawaiian Pidgin. The hints at dialects and Pidgin Hawaiian English are made only to give a clue to their use. A Hawaiian glossary is on page 298 for those words. Some terms such as "Jap" and "nigger" which are considered offensive now, were commonly used in the 1940's.

The language and vocabulary used in the WWII Era may seem sexist or racist to our modern ears, but for the authenticity of the story, it is necessary.

All characters are fictional except for some government officials, and Miss Norris and Edith Aynes who indeed were real women of that era.

Acknowledgements

There are so many people to thanks for their contributions to this story.

Sam Yabuno gave me the idea for this book when he told me of his experiences as a small boy selling newspapers to soldiers in the military hospital in Mountain View, Hawaii during World War II. He read the first draft for accuracy of the setting.

Chuck Yogi provided other interesting stories of the Mountain View plantation days before World War II.

Akira Yamamoto and Ken Honuma long-time residents of Hawaii Island provided background information.

Jeanette Waits RN of Mississippi Nurses Association Historical Section provided help on information about nursing schools of the era.

My oldest sister Jean Bruning was in the Army Cadet Training Program but the war ended before she could be deployed. She told me about her experiences with training in that era such as nude sunbathing on the roof of her Des Moines training hospital and the attempts of the fly-boys from the nearby Army Air Corp camp to fly low over the hospital to view the naked sunbathers.

Sgt. Michael Westen, an Iraqi vet of Hilo, whom I sat by on the Honolulu to Hilo leg of a flight, explained the insignia for Army sergeants.

My cousin Barbara Murray and her husband Bob who grew up in a Chicago suburb gave me descriptions and information about WWII in that city.

Dr. Alberta Lindsay, recently deceased, a WAVE stationed on Hawaii Island during WWII advised about protocol for women in the WWII military.

My male relatives contributed to my deficit of military knowledge. Nephew Merle Goodell helped me understand beach and tide conditions as well as Hawaiian lifestyles. Nephew Dwane Goodell authenticated my details of a soldier going AWOL. Nephew Roger Goodell who had been in the Army advised on proper Army vocabulary. Cousin Darrell De Witt gave me information about the military of that era.

Coffee farmer Jimmy Decalio described the Punalu`u Beach he remembered from childhood.

Barbara Dunn and Martha Hoverson verified details about Volcano House of that era. Barbara also provided the author's photograph.

Lt. Col. USAF (ret.) JoAnn Bienvenu provided facts on the roles of military nurses.

Ashley Vargas, clerk at the J Hara Store, informed me of the WWII Era name of the store.

Millie Masa Uchima a former Mt. View teacher and Hilo Union School Librarian, as well as her exercise class friends, Sue Toyama, Teddy Mukai, Millie Katoka and Mary Chan, described many authentic details of that era.

Advice on the black experience came from my former colleague Dr. Tonya Taylor and my long-time friend Arthur Spears. Another colleague, Patty Barnett provided information on life in the South.

And thanks to my friend and neighbor, Mary Strong, who edited this manuscript however all errors are the author's.

CHAPTER 1

The Ward, Summer 1944

I adjusted my eyes to the dim interior as I followed Nurse Captain Sullivan inside the door of Section Eight Barracks, the psychiatric unit in Mountain View, Hawaii Island. The first thing I saw was the rows of beds on either side of this barracks style building. Most of the men's pale faces turned toward the sound of the door opening. However, several did not change their posture where they sat or lay on their single metal hospital beds, but appeared slack and apathetic to happenings in the world around them. Some of the men wore their uniforms but most had on Government Issue hospital pajamas. The haze of cigarette smoke made it difficult to discern more details.

The nurse at the other end of the barracks from the entrance door rose from behind her small desk and came around and down the aisle between the low metal arches on the foot-ends of the beds. Against the semi-darkness of the rainy day, the nurse was a bright image from her white shoes, white stockings and uniform to her crisp winged nurse's cap.

"Lieutenant Wagner, I want to introduce you to our newest staff member, Lieutenant Clara Brett. Miss Brett is an occupational therapist. She is also a nurse. She has just moved into the empty bed in Lieutenant Sisco's section in the nurses' cottage," Nurse Sullivan said.

I sensed tension between the two women. Nurse Wagner did not offer her hand to me but rather lowered her head ever so slightly as greeting. I suspected she was afraid of collecting germs off my hand. Her nurse's cap was secured to her recently permed brown hair. She had a sour expression on her otherwise pretty face. Tension is what her face held as she said, "Welcome, Lieutenant Brett. These men definitely need to get occupied!" She smirked as she turned and surveyed the faces of the men. Several of the men looked down or away from her.

One dark-haired man though, seemed undaunted by her apparent scorn of her patients. He stood and said, "Well Miss Brett, I expect you've got your work cut out for you, trying to make this bunch get up and get busy, if that's what you are supposed to do." He mirrored Nurse Wagner's smirk. "But I am ready," he blustered as he flexed his biceps. "How about getting me some engines to repair?"

His accent which I associated with New Yorkers sounded aggressive to my southern ears. I already began to expect he would not be easy to deal with. But then working with the patients during my training at Walter Reed Hospital had not been a tea party either. I had not joined the War Effort in order to be a slacker. I expected my job to be a challenge. But this room full of male psychiatric patients looked like they would be as demanding as I could wish.

Some of the patients obviously were not well washed with not much attention to grooming. Several of them had beards of more than two or three day's growth. I wondered why these Army nurses allowed this. Most of the patients did not seem to exhibit the behaviors that I had learned were signs of severe disturbance, like talking to themselves or batting at unseen things around their heads, but many looked beaten down, fearful and jumpy. I realized I would need to take time to get to know them individually. Looking at the few who dared to look back at me, I remembered my training, to keep a smiling but non-committal face.

As I passed within an inch of the face of a red-headed man lying with his head near the foot of his bed, I heard him in sotto voce say, "Hubba hubba!" It was obviously directed at me.

Giving myself a moment to arrange the proper expression, I ignored him and turned to follow Captain Sullivan toward the door.

However, apparently his voice had been audible to Captain Sullivan as she exclaimed, "Sergeant

Erickson, show some respect to Lieutenant Brett. The brig is not nearly as comfortable as this barracks."

From his position on the bed he casually saluted both women and muttered, "Sorry!"

Captain Sullivan was older, perhaps almost forty years old. Though she presented a no-nonsense approach, she seemed to have an accepting personality, apparently treating almost everyone as if they were making their best effort. This made me feel more secure and better equipped to face whatever came up.

Memories of the first time I stepped into the psychiatric ward at Walter Reed Hospital flooded my mind. Actually, these memories were reassuring. I had eventually come to feel quite comfortable to befriend the men, some of whom had suffered from their memories of the shooting and clubbing of Bonus Marchers in 1932. Some of these men had been in the Walter Reed Hospital Psychiatric back ward for more than five years. Their families would not have them back.

Some veterans of WWI had protested the delay of the payment of their certificates for the World War Adjusted Compensation Act of 1924. During the recent past Depression, they needed the money as they were unemployed and felt they could not wait to redeem them at the 1945 date. They camped near the White House in Washington D. C. until General Douglas MacArthur's infantry and cavalry drove them out. They were the "Bonus Marchers."

Captain Sullivan gave me a tour of the hospital building and grounds, then she turned me over to a corpsman to guide me up the hill to where the dining room, the surgery, the regular hospital barracks and the cottage where I would bunk with the nurses, dietician and the physical therapist. We followed a recently widen gravel trail up the hill, all the while using our Army issue umbrellas to push aside from our faces the huge fern fronds which dripped with the same rain which fell on our umbrellas. The trail passed a graveyard which seemed bleak and overgrown in this drizzle.

I let my mind slip back over my journey from Selma, Alabama to this exotic island of Hawaii. How had a little "black" girl advanced to a 2nd lieutenant's rank?

CHAPTER 2

From Where?

Working as a Negro maid in Alabama in 1936 meant that I was subject to the whims of Mrs. Creston, my White boss lady. She was less onerous than many White ladies who hired Negro maids in Selma. Nonetheless, she still observed most rules of segregation. I cooked the meals but was not allowed to eat with the family. I was trusted to take the children to Sunday school by myself, but not allowed to sit in the church service while I awaited them. Had the other church members not known that I was Mrs. Creston's maid, they would probably have thought me just a visiting Cuban or Mexican until I spoke. My skin was fair and my darkish red-brown hair was of the loose ringlet variety. I wore it pulled back into a bun low on my neck. The contour of my lips and nose was not protuberant in the stereotypical way of many Negroes. My greenish eyes were what I later learned were called hazel. Had I dressed like the other white women in the Baptist Church, I would probably have been welcomed. But in Selma, Alabama, a drop of Negro blood meant you were all Negro. Everybody knew who was a Negro and who was white unless you were a newcomer, so there was no possibility of me "passing" for anything else in this Deep South town.

As a little girl of perhaps six-years-old, I remember going with Mamma to the Greens' house when she was their cleaning maid. I watched how the little golden girl with the long yellow curls was treated by Mamma. Everything this little girl wanted, my mamma gave her or sweet talked her out of it by saying she would have to ask her mother, Mrs. Green. In contrast, at home when I asked for the same things that the "golden girl" requested, a quick swat would send me into a defensive crouch. When the little girl called my mamma "Nigger woman!" Mamma didn't even blink. I vowed then I would never let anyone treat me that way.

Mamma was a coffee and cream colored woman. I was more the color of light biscuit crusts. As soon as I was curious about it, I asked Mamma why I was a different color. She just snorted and walked away saying, "Mistah boss take what he want!" To a six year old, that was no answer I could understand.

Later when I was just thirteen, Aunt Beulah, while giving me a warning lecture about sex, told me the story of Mamma's rape while she had been working in the red-headed banker's house. It took me some more time to figure out that the banker was my sire, but I never thought of him as my father. He never took any responsibility for me. Some other children I knew whose fathers had been white business men in the town, and while never publicly acknowledging their black offspring, often did provide some financial support to the women whom they had impregnated. The red-headed banker never had any contact with us at all, as far as I knew. My mother quit her job there at the banker's house after he refused to acknowledge me and to pay any maintenance. This was the story according to Aunt Beulah but as the years progressed and as I learned more about human relations in the South, I wondered if she had been fired when his wife found out about me. I was my mother's only child, I think. She never discussed such things with me. Later, she got a job as a housekeeper at the Greens' and later yet in the white Vaughn Hospital. It felt like justice to learn that that man's bank failed during the early depression and he and his family had to move back to his family's plantation in the country.

Mother never had any real boyfriends that I recall. In retrospect, it may have been a reaction to her rape and to our situation. Or she may have simply hidden this from me. Consequently, I avoided contact with most men except teachers and my mother's brother Uncle Edgar. I suppose I was sexually retarded. Protecting myself predominated over teenage hormones.

By fifteen years of age, I had such a shell about

me, never allowing myself to get too close to any of these other "miscegenated" children. Aunt Beulah died when I was sixteen so I had no other confidante. I became a loner. I isolated myself from my peers at school and at church. Because I had the lightest skin of any of my classmates, I was often taunted, which pushed me further away from them. They called me "Yellow Girl" or "Ghost" or "Cream Pie."

There had been no help from the black Baptist Church. I had found no truth in the staccato verbal message from the Negro preacher, Brother Williams. He would build up his message and volume then subsequently lower his voice until the last words drifted away no matter how I struggled to hear them. It just took too much effort to sit in the pew and try to understand the message that came from the pulpit. Besides he never spoke to the conflicts I felt about my two races and the stigmatization and degradation of the colored part and consequently my life sentence to exist in that degraded group. Rather, he spoke about forgiveness and salvation in the hereafter.

After these realizations, I began to plot an escape from the "colored" world. Any person who lived in a Southern town or village could see that white people got a better life in almost any realm: money, houses, automobiles, jobs, schools, theater seats and clothing. When I looked the way I looked, with my fair skin and red-brown ringlets, why should I not enjoy those benefits, too? My scheme began by recognizing that I would not want to attend any of the cheaper, "easier to gain entrance" traditional Negro Colleges. I would have to go to North, because in any other Southern state, it would be immediately recognized that the Knox High School from which I would "graduate" was a "Negro" school. It only went to tenth grade. Probably, I would first have to go to some northern high school to get my diploma. I began immediately to apply myself harder to my studies so I could raise my grades in this Knox Negro High School and make myself a more desirable applicant to a northern college. This concentration on my studies further separated me from my Negro peers. When, however, the music teacher occasionally sat down at the piano and banged out a dance tune, I would usually join my classmates in trying out the new dance-steps.

I so wished I could enter the Selma Carnegie Library to look at the special book about colleges but the librarian knew that I was "colored." What I needed to know, was in one of those "reference" books on a special shelf that could not be checked out. Sometimes, I would get my one white girlfriend, Harriet Ruffinson to check out a book for me, but since this was a "reference" book, I could not ask Harriet to help me. She and I were almost the same color. Harriet volunteered after school in the Vaughn Hospital and I met her once while taking something to my mother at work. I did not enter by the front door which was under a portico held up by four white Aeolian capitals. Of course at that time, I did not know which category of classic capital it was. I learned this later in an art class for occupational therapists. Negroes like me entered in the backdoor of the hospital to do their jobs.

Sympathetic white girls were few and far between, but Harriet, coming from New England, was befuddled by the rules about Negroes using libraries and parks.

Her father had been hired by the Roosevelt Administration to oversee construction of the New Deal financed public buildings. He was a Democrat, but not the kind of Democrat they were used to in Selma. So while I had considered asking Harriet to look in the book about colleges for me, the logistics of asking her to look for specific schools of which I knew very little seemed too complicated. Besides, she might inadvertently spill my plans to someone else.

Not long thereafter, my mother learned of a job mopping the marble floor in the library. With her help, I secured the job and after the library closed at 5 PM on school days, I began my mopping. This opportunity to enter the white library felt like a godsend.

I did not want to quit my job at the Creston's as I was saving my money for college. Also, I wanted to be able to see Harriet when I took the Creston children to Sunday school. I negotiated with Mrs. Creston to arrive later after mopping and to work later till all the children were in bed. I told her I was trying to save money to go to a Negro college. Mrs. Creston seemed sympathetic to my aspirations though her skepticism was not well concealed. None-the-less, I felt my previous hard work had built her trust in me. Many white women would meet such a request by firing the maid as there were many unemployed Negro girls looking for work during these hard times. I worked even harder for Mrs. Creston when I was at her Church Street mansion.

I would rush home from school and find something to eat if there was something in our meager cupboard. My mother and I lived in a "shotgun" house where all the doors, from the front door into the front room, from the front room into the kitchen through our shared bedroom and out the back door into the alley which would allow someone to shoot straight back through all the doors, hence the name "shotgun" style house. The kitchen contained a rickety table in the middle and some orange crates stacked against the wall under the back window. Outside the back door was the water pump from which we brought the water inside the house for cooking, cleaning or bathing. Nobody in our neighborhood had running water inside their small houses. Mother tried as much as possible to bring leftovers from the hospital kitchen. She was friends with the Negro cooks there. We bought as little as possible at the grocery where we had to wait until all the white customers were served, so frequently, our cupboard was bare. Between the house and the alley were the pump, the outhouse and a small strip of garden. When there was nothing in else in the house to eat, there were always "greens." Sometimes I brought home leftovers from the Creston's dinner-table but that was not always convenient or available for me after I began to mop the library floors. The other black servants usually ate the leftovers or took them before I got there.

At first, the librarian, Miss Cash, who was just slightly lighter skinned than me, would not lock the door and leave until I was done mopping the floors and emptying the mop-bucket in the alley behind the library. However, after a few months she began to relax her observation over my work and even began to allow me to finish while she went to the butcher or the grocer. She would come back and lock up after her own shopping and my mopping. The second time she did this, I was able while she was away, to locate the college reference book on the shelves though I did not have time to take it out and examine it. But finding it was a triumph!

Additionally, I took advantage during these hours in the library to listen to how white people spoke. I recognized that their speech was slightly different from that in my neighborhood so I studied what they said and how they said it. At home in bed, I would practice speaking like them. Sometimes, when I went to the grocery store, while waiting for white people to be served first by the grocer behind the counter, I would listen to their conversations and sometimes, the storekeeper had the radio on so

I could listen to white people talking there, too. I would go home and practice mimicking what I had heard, trying to sound "white." I did not recognize yet that Southern whites sounded different from Northern whites' speech.

Gradually, I worked at building the librarian's trust in me. I offered to do errands for her, or to carry her bags if she had more than one and if it were still daylight. It was not safe for a colored girl to walk in her white neighborhood after dark. Actually, it was not safe for me to walk alone in my own colored neighborhood as some one of the men on the corner would call out that I looked old enough to "have my cherry taken" or similar utterances that showed that they thought I was ripe for sexual harvesting and that they would be glad to do it. The men who called out to me in my Negro neighborhood implied that I thought I was too white for them and that they should "teach me a lesson." One said, "You're mighty fine to be on this corner alone." They told me I was acting "too white" and should be brought down a notch or two by learning how good sex was with a Negro like them. I was disgusted by their gutter talk but did my best to avoid them and to ignore them if compelled to hear their uncivil comments.

I was not about to allow myself to be burdened with a Negro child which could be the outcome of such an attack. If I wanted to start being "white" the first thing was to escape this segregated town without being tied down with a colored child. I knew of other colored girls who had left their children with their mother's in order to find work in the North, but they did not look almost white like I did.

CHAPTER 3

Discovering A Way

I had never known a person who left the Negro world and entered the white world. When I thought about it, it was understandable. Most families from whom somebody might have left to "pass" would never know for sure where their lost family member had gone as that person would not want the family to track them down and perhaps betray them. The "passer" would try to leave without leaving clues to their location. Also, most Negroes in Selma were too dark-skinned to be able to "pass" even for Italians or Lebanese. If their skin didn't give them away, their hair or their speech would.

In a variety store especially for Negros, I read in one of the few magazines for Negros, a book review of Black No More, which was a novel by George Schuyler, about a young Negro doctor who went to Germany and learned from his own research how to make Negros become white. Of course, such a radical book would not be found in the "whites only" Carnegie Library in Selma. I saved my money, and sent away for this book. It seemed to take months for the book to come to Selma but it finally arrived. My mother could read very little as her own schooling had been less than three years long. She could write her name and my name but other written language hardly registered with her, so I did not think about her worrying about what I was reading. There was no need to hide it as she would then know it was not one of my school books and wonder what it was. I just kept it with my other books. For school, I covered all my books with newspaper and told my classmates it was to keep them clean. They might make fun of my fastidious ways, but they did not challenge it by trying to rip the covers off. Most of our books were in pretty bad shape anyway, as they were the books from the white A. G. Parrish High School that they passed on to our school when they got new ones.

In this novel Black No More, the main character, Max Disher, got in line to be the first Negro to receive treatment to become white in America. Subsequently, he began to see almost all American Negroes taking the treatment and becoming white and then all white people distrusting everyone, fearing that every other white person was a former Negro. This book had a great impact on me and helped me to understand the aspirations to become white in order to avoid the penalties of being Negro.

By the middle 1930s, I had heard, like almost every other Negro, about the flying ace, Charles Anderson from Pennsylvania who had tried to pass to get into the Pennsylvania National Guard. He was discovered to be Negro and was kicked out. He tried again to gain entrance to an aviation school by passing as white at a time when most aviators refused to train colored pilots, only to have his racial background again revealed. His story had mostly been passed orally, but a few of the Negro newspapers in the North reported it. None of the white stores in Selma would sell the Negro newspapers from the North. But occasionally, a traveler would bring one on the train and leave it when he or she got off. Uncle Edgar, the porter would recover it and it would be passed around among literate Negroes until it fell apart. Charles Anderson's story had been reported in the Pittsburgh Courier. The newspaper, Chicago Defender could occasionally be seen in Selma and the California Eagle from Los Angeles was seen even more rarely. They seldom passed through my teenage hands. I had just been lucky to see the one in the Courier about the aspiring pilot, Charles Anderson. His story, rather than discouraging me, made me plot every kind of situation that could rise for a Negro passing into the white world. Besides, I was much lighter skinned than he appeared to be in his photos.

During my surreptitious searching in the college reference book as well as in a government book about possible occupations, I discovered something called occupational therapy. It looked interesting to me because it used simple ways like crocheting, knitting or wood-carving to help people recover from illness. I remembered Aunt Beulah sitting in bed crocheting before she died. She told me it made her feel peaceful. If it helped her to be so occupied, it probably helped many others, too, I thought. Realizing this, I became aware of how inactivity, which was rare in the Negro community of Selma, made people whiny, dependent and sad. I felt better when I was busy. I liked making people feel good. Occupational therapy seemed to combine these ideas, keeping active to feel good. This idea inspired me to keep on toward my future career goal.

The education for this fairly new medical vocation, was to be had in only a scarce few colleges or universities, almost all in the North; Boston, New York, Philadelphia, Baltimore, Chicago or St. Louis. Almost all of them required two years of experience in nursing or teaching before being allowed to start the training. I looked on the map in the big atlas on the table near the dictionaries. St. Louis looked the closest but I had heard that Missouri was not friendly to some southerners. I needed to go far enough north to avoid the fear that people would be unable to distinguish my Negro inflections from other southern speech. Though I practiced talking "white" whenever I could, I knew that these southern whites talked differently than northern whites. St. Louis was just too close to the South.

I asked, Miss Alcorn, the Negro home economics teacher, if she had ever heard of "occupational therapy." She told me that she had visited one of her friends in the tuberculosis sanatorium in Magee, Mississippi. There they had a white occupational therapy department and her Negro friend who had tuberculosis had described how she could get materials there in the white occupational therapy department to take and use in the Negro Infirmary which housed the colored patients at the Sanatorium. This Negro patient, who was her friend, could not work in the occupational therapy department when white patients were present, but the therapist was most generous with her if the white patients were gone. The tuberculosis afflicted friend had even given my teacher an embroidered doily that she had made with cloth and embroidery floss that she got from occupational therapy. I wondered about the color of this Negro patient's skin color. Miss Alcorn's skin tone was just a few shades darker than mine, perhaps like sweet tea, but more obviously "Negro" than me.

This segregation story reinforced my decision to figure out a way to become "white." If I stayed where people knew I was Negro, I would be deprived of more than half of the world, the libraries, the good schools, the best hospitals and even the occupational therapy departments.

I inquired of the teacher Miss Alcorn, for every shred of information she could provide me about occupational therapy. Finally, after all my pestering, she promised to take me with her if she ever saved enough money again to take the train to Magee to visit her friend in the Mississippi Sanatorium before the friend recovered and returned to her South Mississippi home. I was determined to take the price of a ticket out of my little cache that I hid under a floorboard beneath my sleeping mattress which lay on the floor of the shared bedroom of me and my mother. Even though we kept the house locked when Mother and I were away, I still worried that some desperate person, and there were many desperate person in these days of the depression, would break in and steal my small savings.

I wished that I could figure out how to go to the Mississippi Sanatorium by myself and see if I could pass for white, because if I went with Miss Alcorn, I would be branded as Negro. My first effort was to get Miss Alcorn to tell me about the train route she took to get to the Sanatorium. She was eager to tell me about her travels. She boarded the train at Selma's Louisville & Nashville Station. There was no mention of having to ride the "colored car" because we both knew that was inevitable in Alabama and in Mississippi. From Selma, she went to York, Alabama, where the trained stopped but she did not have to get off to change trains. The train went on to Meridian just on the other side of the state line in Mississippi. In Meridian, she did have wait for an hour to change trains to one that went south to Laurel. At Laurel, she again changed trains to go back northeast to Magee, Mississippi. She had made the mistake of getting off in Magee and had to walk three miles through the country to the Sanatorium. If she had known, she could have stayed on the train for the last three miles, but she was reluctant to talk to any of the strangers on the train as they were mostly men she distrusted. They looked like "players" she said and feared they would try to tempt her with immoral suggestions.

When she returned, she was able to flag down the train coming southeast from Jackson. It always stopped at the Sanatorium if the railroad flag was up by the train tracks. Miss Alcorn's aunt lived in Laurel so when she got there, she walked to her aunt's little home and stayed overnight, sleeping on the kitchen floor wrapped in a blanket before starting her route back to Selma. The kitchen floor in her aunt's home was far preferable to sleeping on the rickety wooden bench in the "colored" waiting room at the Laurel train station. Miss Alcorn confided that she knew she would never get a wink of sleep in the colored waiting room as it was dirty and often frequented by drunks and men of ill repute. She did not define "ill repute" but we both knew she meant pimps.

In addition to continuing to pump Miss Alcorn for every detail of her trip, I made a plan to go to L & N Station in Selma and learn how it would be possible to escape from the colored waiting room and reappear in the white waiting room without being identified. My mother's brother, Uncle Edgar worked as a porter at Selma L & N Train Station. He was obviously a Negro with nut brown colored skin and the typical stereotypical facial features. I wondered why he and mother were so different but had observed this phenomenon in many Negro families; differing skin colors for each child. I knew Uncle Edgar would discourage me from lurking around the train station as it was a well-known fact that that was where both white and black men went to find prostitutes. So I enticed my mother to send me to give him an invitation to bring his family for Sunday dinner. That was the only day of the week in which my mother could be free of cleaning at the Vaughn Hospital. I agreed to help mother prepare the biscuits, peel the potatoes, dig some yams in the back yard and also cut some greens for her to cook. She was surprised to have me offer all this help as she usually complained that it was like "pulling teeth" to get me away from my books to help in our little house. She was so glad of the help and happy to visit with her brother who was equally busy earning money for his family, that she did not question my motives but instead credited it to my increasing maturity.

Uncle Edgar was surprised to see me at L & N Station. He sounded slightly irritated when he asked, "What yuh doin' heah, girl?" Because I had no father that anybody acknowledged, Uncle Edgar felt he was somewhat responsible for me.

He, like my mother, could barely read except

for what was necessary for him to decipher train schedules or the labels on luggage, so my mother's message to him was verbal. "Hi, Uncle Edgar," I said sweetly, hoping to disarm him before he could shoo me away. "Mamma wants you and Aunt Phyllis and kids to come to dinner on Sunday. She says we haven't seen you for so long and that inviting you to dinner was the best way to get you to come." I was aware of how my speech had begun to emulate the white people that I listened to while cleaning the library. I wondered if Uncle Edgar was aware of it too, but he seemed oblivious. Then I realized that he heard all kinds of speech here in the train station, though he continued to talk like a Selma Negro. For the rest of our conversation, I slipped back into this vernacular as well.

"Well, Gal, let me think if I be working or not on Sunday." He scratched under his porter's hat while he considered. Because he had a fair salary compared to most Negro men in Selma, his wife, Aunt Phyllis did not have to go out to work. She was able to stay at home and care for their six children. This was a rare situation for Negro women in Selma. Their children were all younger than me so I made little effort to spend time with them. They were also much darker skinned than me. Everybody in my family, including Uncle Edgar, was darker, I thought.

Uncle Edgar and Aunt Phyllis did come for Sunday dinner. It was a rare occasion, as feeding their whole family was a considerable stretch for our meager food budget. However, six children was a rather average family size in Selma at that time. Mother and I overspent our usual purchases at the butcher shop where we had to wait in line behind all the white customers. Mother knew that Aunt Phyllis thought she was a "fallen woman" for having a white man's child and not being married, to boot. This was part of the reason we seldom got together as Mother had told me that she felt Aunt Phyllis didn't respect her.

Mother got two chickens which she cut up, dipped in cornmeal batter and pan-fried in lard. We used our own collard greens and yams but mother bought butter for the biscuits. This was a real treat. For dessert she bought canned peaches for cobbler. She sent me out to stop the colored milk man and get some thick cream to pour over the cobbler. We did not get milk delivery as it was too costly. When we wanted milk, she just sent me out to catch him on his dawn-break trip before he got to the white neighborhood. He got his cream and milk from a dairy on the east edge of Selma which meant he drove his wagon through colored town before he got to Broad Street where the mansions of the whites started.

We were both exhausted by the time Uncle Edgar and Aunt Phyllis's brood arrived at our small house. We filled our plates in the kitchen where the food was placed on the cleared off work table. We all ate with our plates in our laps as mother and I did not have a dining room table. My mother brought home chipped and cracked plates discarded from the hospital but we still did not have enough for this many, so the smallest children and I ate off metal pie plates. Our seats were an assortment of chairs discarded from the white homes where we had worked or empty apple and orange crates retrieved from the back of the grocery store. I made it a point to seat myself as close as possible to Uncle Edgar so I could question him about his job at the depot, surreptitiously slipping in questions to help me find out what I needed to achieve my goal. I pushed down any feelings of betrayal of the family in order to efficiently collect as many facts about the operation of the train station as I could.

"How did you first get your job at the depot, Uncle Edgar?" I opened with an innocuous question, I thought.

"Well, when I was wanting to attend Knox Academy, Mammy and Pappy didn't have no money for tuition. So I decided to find work. I just went around asking anybody who looked kind if they had any work for me. I was just a little fellah, maybe eight years old, 'bout the same age as my Amos, there." He gestured toward one of his boys. "I stay this side of Broad Street. One day, Miz Scully, the Negro teacher, she pays me to dig up her garden. I did such a good job, she told some friends and fore yah knew it; I was digging up all the gardens on Range Street."

I interrupted his monologue to offer him more yams and greens. The two chickens had already been totally devoured by then with the bones saved in the black stewpot to make soup. "So how did you get the job as a porter?"

"Well, I was such a hard worker, when they was alookin' for somebody to clean the toilets, Miz Scully she suggested me. By then I was about Alvin's age." He gestured toward his older son, a dark-skinned boy. Then he went on, "I won't talk about that while we're eatin', but I did that nasty job for about five years before Old Man Buck died and I was ready. They knew I was a good worker so they took me on for the porter job. That was right before this Depression hit. Been there ever since!"

I led Uncle Edgar to talk about the daily schedule at the L & N Station by asking "What time do you start work?" I followed up with questions about which directions the trains came from and what kind of travelers were on each line. Then I began to question him about the line which went to York, Alabama and over into Meridian, Mississippi. Though he had never ridden the line, he knew all the conductors and had heard their stories. I inquired about what was the busiest time of the week as I figured that would be the best time to slip from the colored waiting room to the white waiting room in Meridian. The time of the greatest confusion would be the time when I might not draw particular attention.

"Well, Gal, now that they got the draft, there aplenty uh young fellahs comin' though on their way to Army training." Congress had enacted the Selective Service Act on September 16, 1940, creating the first peacetime draft.

Finally my mother interrupted grumpily, "You planning on working for the railroad after tenth grade, Lula? Let's serve up the cobbler." We served that in the chipped and cracked cups Mother brought home from the hospital.

Late in the afternoon, Aunt Phyllis and Uncle Edgar left with their brood in tow. I was left to look at the washtub full of dirty plates and cups and spoons as Mother went to bed exhausted.

CHAPTER 4

White Names, Black Names

Besides the Negro speech, anyone who lived in Dallas County, Alabama, knew from a person's last name whether they were black or white, except in the case of those Negro families whose slave ancestors had taken their former master's name after emancipation. When reading the local newspaper, if it said Williams or Kynard, it could be the name of either a black or a white person. But many names were known to be either only Negro such as Washington or Spears or to be only for a white person with names like Pettus or Mallory. These subtle distinctions were known only to people who had lived in Dallas County, Alabama most of their lives.

I decided to change my name from Tallulah Beulah

Norris which my mother had named me after the famous actress and after her sister Beulah. The rhyming sound seemed "too Negro" to me so I began introducing myself as Lula rather than using both given names as some southerners commonly did. My mother thought it was cute so she began to call me "Lula", too. After some contemplation, I decided that I should choose a Swedish or Norwegian last name when I became white in order to make people think I was from people of northern Europe. It would not be much of a difference when I eventually would change my first name to Clara. Lula, Clara, Lula, Clara.

In the children's section of the library I saw a lovely book illustrated by a British artist, Molly Brett. That last name, Brett, seemed to me to have a good simple sound, but also rather aristocratic. I began to believe that the further I put myself from my background, the less likely anyone would suspect. So I decided to borrow the English artist's last name. Clara Brett sounded to me almost like a movie star; Clara Bow, May West, or Mary Pickford. It was from Clara Bow that I got my idea for that name. I had never attended the movies but I had seen the movie posters with Clara Bow. The nickel entry for movies, plus the mandate that I would climb the outside stairway to the "nigger gallery" deterred me from even trying to see the movies that came to the Walton Theater.

Later when I learned of the racist Major General George Brett who was opposing the training facility for the Tuskegee aviators, I almost decided to abandon this name and find another. But by 1940 I had aligned my persona with the name Brett and it seemed too hard to change.

In my private journal which I kept with my cache of dollar bills, I began to call myself Clara Brett. I then realized I would somehow need documents to show my new name when I tried to enroll in a northern high school. When Miss Alcorn, who trusted me, sent me to the storage room for more cornmeal for the home economics cooking class, I decided to take this rare opportunity to snoop, to examine what the shed contained. I felt a small guilt at subverting her trust but my goal of making a new identity overwhelmed any sense of committing a wrong.

There on a wooden shelf on the other side of the shed from the home economics food supplies, I saw an unopened labeled brown package of blank report-cards. I realized I would never have a better chance to change my name. I took a hairpin out of my hair and carefully lifted the brown tape that partially sealed the brown paper package. Carefully I replaced the hairpin so my hair would not fall, as it was smoother than the coarse nappy hair of most of my classmates. I did not want to bring attention to myself by having my hair loose, particularly right now. Also, hairpins cost money. I was careful to account for the ones my mother lent to me. I lifted off the blank report card from the top of the pile and slipped it inside my blouse as I did not have my notebook with me. After graduation at the end of tenth grade, I planned that I would copy my real report-card unto this one with my new name. Then when I arrived in the North to finish high school, I would have my new name.

The cornmeal and other kinds of flour were stored in covered barrels left over from Prohibition times. This way of storage was to keep out the rodents. I had to almost stand on my head to reach the metal scoop to get the cornmeal in the bottom of the barrel. Clutching the bucket of cornmeal in one hand, with the other, I held the blank report card to keep it from falling out down between my skirt waistband and my panties.

I had to pass by the roofed shelter where Mr. Brown, the industrial arts teacher was showing the boys how to disassemble an engine. This shelter was simply a corrugated metal roof supported with pine poles over eight feet tall. The heat was radiating out from under this structure where I could see the boys sweating through their shirts.

As I passed by Woodrow Minter, the other pale skinned student in the tenth grade class called out to me, "What are you hiding there under your blouse?" I ignored him as I found him rather sly and devious so I scurried back up the wooden steps into the school building.

When I got back to the kitchen area where the class listened to Miss Alcorn give instructions for making corn pudding, I carefully sat the bucket on the table behind her, keeping my back to the class, I slipped the blank card under some newspapers placed there to catch cooking drips, once the actual recipe preparation started. I began to ostentatiously slap at my clothes as if to rid myself of corn dust. I finished by taking the newspaper covering the blank card and the card and carrying it to my seat at the side using it to slap dust away as I walked. Surreptitiously,

I slipped the card under my notebook and used the newspaper to wipe the cornmeal dust off my shoes. I, like my most of my classmates, had only one pair of shoes and it was necessary to keep them clean for all occasions. Many elementary school students did not have shoes at all, but by the time of high school, most Negro students had found some way to get shoes, even if it was by inheriting those of older brothers or sisters. I knew of some people my age who would have liked to come to Knox High School, but their inability to find a way to get shoes kept them away. They were too embarrassed to come, though the colored high school did not have a rule that required shoes.

Soon enough many of these young men would be issued shoes by the Army or the Navy. However, though Germany had already invaded Poland, Denmark, the Netherlands, Belgium and France, and the bombing of London had started, these events felt far away from the problems of continuing poverty in Alabama. Most Negro homes did not have a radio; nor did they receive the home-delivered newspaper. It was easy to ignore the warfare in Europe, and the coming war in Africa and the Pacific.

CHAPTER 5

The Hospital

In the spring of 1940, as I approached "graduation" from Knox High, mother began to be tired more often and to be unable to do her job at the Vaughn Hospital. She persuaded Miss Lanner, the white director of nurses to allow me to do her job for her on Saturdays and some days when the teacher let us go early. I had gone there often enough to meet my mother that I was acquainted with much of what she did. It felt degrading to me to be emptying and washing out chamber pots and scrubbing toilets, but I loved my mother and if she could do it, I could do it. Now I had three after school jobs; one the Crestons' mansion, one at the library and one at the Vaughn. I scrambled to do it all but as I was young and strong, I was able to do it all for a time and Mother and I needed the money. I kept my wages from the library and the Crestons, but gave the money from the Vaughn to her. They paid me only about two thirds of what they paid her, "because I was just a girl," the head housekeeper said. We were grateful for that though, because Mother had more and more days when she could barely drag herself out of bed, let alone push a bucket and mop for several hours. No one at the Vaughn Hospital asked me if there was anything they could do to help my mother. But I did not expect it.

Aunt Phyllis occasionally came to visit Mother after I went to their house especially to ask her to come, but she and mother did not particularly like each other and she came only to please Uncle Edgar. So most of Mother's care devolved on me.

Miss Alcorn took it upon herself to acquaint the Negro girls in her homemaking class with the possible places in which they might find a better class of employment after "graduation." We took field trips to Good Samaritan Hospital and to the YMCA and even though girls could not join the latter, we could work there. Miss Alcorn considered that it was a good place to work unlike most other institutions in Selma where the only work for Negro girls was with the mop. The YMCA had a Negro girl working on the switchboard. You couldn't see her from the entrance, but if you walked into the director's office, there she was in her little glass cubbyhole. Somehow, she managed to keep her voice from sounding Negro on the telephone. This fascinated and inspired me.

During our last year at Knox High School, both boys and girls were taken on field trips to acquaint us with the kind of work that Negroes could do in Dallas County, Alabama. The boys in our class went to visit the WPA (Works Progress Administration) camp outside town and the work site on Franklin Street where they were building a community center. We had several preparatory classes led by Mr. Brown and Miss Alcorn to prepare us for work.

My light skinned classmate, Woodrow Minter asked in one class session, "Why can the WPA men work together without being segregated but in the WPA camp, the Negroes sleep separated from the white men?"

"Mr. Minton, if you want to stay alive in Dallas County, you will keep those questions to yourself," responded Mr. Brown, the shop teacher.

Most of us in the class could have anticipated the answer though we seldom talked outright about such issues in our classes at Knox School. After Mr. Brown's answer, the subject was dropped.

When we ten home-economics girls from Knox High went to the Good Samaritan Hospital, we were allowed to enter the front door unlike we would have been able to do at the white Vaughn Hospital. Miss Alcorn led us to the hallway under the main stairs. The only hospital in which I had been before was the Vaughn where mother worked and where I helped when I was free. This Negro hospital was much smaller than the Vaughn Hospital, though still clean and neat. Miss Alcorn introduced us to Miss Mamie Norris, the graduate nurse from Tuskegee

Institute. Though she had the same last name as me, we were not related that I knew of.

Miss Norris had a presence that was very impressive to us "home-ec. girls." She wore a sparkling white uniform which buttoned down the front with white buttons and a nurse's pin on her dress lapel. Her shoes and cotton stockings were also white. She wore a white winged nurse's cap. Against her dark skinned face and hands, the contrast was startling. I had never seen a colored nurse except the untrained ones who occasionally hired themselves out as private duty nurses or wet-nurses. Miss Norris demanded that each girl step forward and introduce herself. Then she asked what plans the student had for after "graduation."

When it was my turn, I commented upon our common last name of Norris. She smiled ever so slightly but otherwise ignored this commonality. I told her, "I am interested in occupational therapy and I wonder if you have such a position in the Good Samaritan Hospital."

"While I have heard of this vocation, I personally do not know anyone in such a position. Where did you learn of it?" she asked in her strong clear voice which still sounded Negro but very dignified, like Miss Alcorn's.

I gave Miss Alcorn as much credit as I could while responding, as she was standing there waiting for Miss Norris's judgment on her home-ec. girls. These two educated Negro women were good friends in their Baptist church, as Miss Alcorn had explained to us while she was telling us how to behave on this field trip. I said, being aware of enunciating clearly, "I learned of it from Miss Alcorn who described occupational therapy at the Mississippi Sanatorium. I have also looked it up in the 'occupations' book after I have finished my work duties at the Carnegie Library."

"And young lady, what do you do at the Carnegie Library?" she ask, knowing full well that Negroes were not allowed to use the books in the white library.

Though I felt some embarrassment, I knew that Miss Alcorn would expose any slight embroidery of the truth, so I answered; "I am a housekeeper after school." I felt the word "housekeeper" was more pleasing than a "floor-mopper."

Before either woman could respond, I went on, "I saw a book on the shelf one day and just happened to flip through it to see if occupational therapy was there, and it was. I learned where I can study to be an occupational therapist."

"Do you know any Negro occupational therapists?" Miss Norris asked in her very professional voice. I suspected it could be quite a severe voice if she were displeased.

"No, Mam," I responded quickly. "Do you know any I could talk to?"

"Young Lady," she said again. She had a way

of saying this that kept me knowing I was just a beginner in life and not to be sassy. "I have never had the pleasure of meeting any occupational therapist, let alone a Negro occupational therapist."

Miss Norris led us on a tour of the surgery/delivery room which was empty. However, we did see a couple of little brown babies in baskets on shelves in the former pantry between the former dining room and the former kitchen which had become the surgery. The former dining room had been made into a ward room with four beds. Two beds were unoccupied. There were two women in beds side-by-side talking together. I vaguely recognized them but did not remember their names. Most of the women in my neighborhood called the midwife and did not come to the hospital. There was a generous bathroom at the end of the hallway on each floor of this former residence. It had once been a luxury home in this now Negro section of Selma.

Before we left, Miss Norris informed us, looking especially at me I felt, that "Nursing is a very honorable profession. Though the training is hard, there are many good jobs in hospitals for nurses. I know you girls have usually only seen private home nurses, but hospital jobs that require a diploma are much better. I invite you to come back for another visit to Good Samaritan." I never went back.

CHAPTER 6

Time For Goodbyes

Shortly thereafter, it was time for our tenth grade graduation from Knox High School. The field trips had been an attempt by Miss Alcorn to help us find proper employment so we would not end up hustling for the pimps at the L&N Station. I realized that this would be the best time for me to make my move away from Selma, but Mother got sicker and sicker. I came home from either school or from work at the Vaughn, the Creston's, or the Library to find Aunt Phyllis sitting watching my mother, or helping her to the outhouse. It was a shame that somebody who really didn't like my mother, as was evident from Aunt Phyllis, had to take care of her. I wished that I felt like I could leave school and quit my jobs to care for her, but Mother would not hear of it. Besides, we needed the money.

Uncle Edgar began to stop by daily on his way to and from the train station. Brother Williams or his wife, Sister Eulalie from the Baptist Church, began to stop by more often as well. The Brother spent a good deal of time praying with my mother. Somehow, I ignored the meaning of all this increased attention to my mother for her illness.

Graduation Day came and Mother was too sick to attend, but asked me to sit down and have a talk with her. She was gaunt and gray looking, lying on the mattress on the floor. Because she could not afford to go to the doctor, we did not know what was causing her to be ill. I sat down on the floor next to her on the mattress. She slowly took her hand out from under the quilt that her own mother had made and took my hand. I was impatient to be up and getting ready for the graduation ceremony, to take my bath, to heat the iron to smooth over the dress I had sewed by myself in home economics class to wear under the graduation gown. I restrained myself from showing my impatience.

"My little Lula! Mother ain't got much more time on this earth. I want you to have a good life, but I ain't gonna be here to guide you much longer." She stopped and coughed into a rag. I felt the heat and tension in her hand. My impulse was to ask her if we needed to have this talk now or could it wait until after the graduation ceremony but I held my tongue as she seemed so in earnest.

"There ain't no one I kin asks to care fo' you, some other body dat that I kin turn you over to and sides, you be eighteen soon. So I jist want make sure you find good friends and not let yourself be tricked by bad people." Her eyes were dry but her face was in an expression of deep intensity, looking into my eyes from where her head lay on the tarnished pillow cover.

Gradually, I began to realize what she was saying to me, that she was dying and I must live on my own. I already had my plans to flee Selma and find my own life, but I did not want it to be because of her life ending. Her earnestness reminded me of what she had overcome in her life and how lucky I was to have had her as my mother, despite the slaps and seeming lack of affection. She had done what she thought would make me into a good and independent person in this segregated city. Though she had never felt "educated", she saw to it that I paid attention to my books and teachers. It was a shame that she was too sick to be able to attend and enjoy my graduation from Knox High School. Though I felt the press of time for getting ready to get to the ceremonies, I held myself in check.

I no longer talked in the Selma dialect and I was aware of my different way of speaking as I said, "Mother, I am so sorry you cannot be there to see me receive my tenth grade diploma, but I am sure you are going to get better and when I graduate from college, you will surely be with me then."

"My little Lula, I wish that gonna to be true, but your mother hain't much more time for this ol' world, I know." She paused and seemed to gather

her strength to go on in a more cheerful tone, "I be there in spirit, be proud of my girl. I want you to remember that when you feel confused about what to do, go and find an older woman to be your friend and to advise you. Not just any woman, but a good woman, a church woman!" Her hand fell to the pillow as if she had spent all her energy talking. The lids on her eyes drooped and she seemed to slip off into sleep.

I bent and kissed her cheek as I slipped away from the mattress to finish getting ready. I had to lay a quilt over the kitchen table, take the iron from where I had it heating on the back of the wood cookstove, to iron it on the table. The dress I had finally finished just a few days ago was of pale lavender dotted Swiss cloth. It had short puff sleeves, a "V" neckline and buttoned all the way down the front to the hem with mother-of-pearl buttons which I had found in Aunt Beulah's button jar that we had inherited when she died. She had been a formidable dressmaker, even designing dresses for white ladies. I could not afford to buy eyelet for ruffles, but I was still very proud of this dress as it was the biggest sewing project I had ever finished. As soon as I had finished taking my sponge bath by the dishpan on the stove, I dropped the half-buttoned dress over my head, brushed my curls and added the ribbon band I had made from scraps of the dotted Swiss. Then I went into our bedroom, if a room with only mattresses and no bed can be called a bedroom, to show myself to my mother. Her eyes were still closed and she did not move when I whispered "Mother, do you want to see my dress?" Knowing the time was short, I left without waking her. I hurried to Mabry Street and rushed into the back door of the room that served as the auditorium where everyone was already lined up to march in to sit on the stage. I took my graduation gown from one of the hangers on a rope between two large nails on the wall. It was the last one on the rope. I slipped it over my head and grabbed one of the mortar board hats from the box on the floor.

There were so few in our class, we all could sit on the stage with our teachers. We were lined up alphabetically and since the name "Norris" is midway in the alphabet, which is where I was placed, between Woodrow Minter and Alvina Ruffinson. Miss Alcorn saw me slip in and came over to chastise me for being late as she had told us to be here at least half an hour before. I listened meekly to her scolding as I straightened the cap on my head and placed the tassel properly. My classmates were watching this chastisement with approval as I had so often been the one they called "Teacher's Pet." They had also called me so many less acceptable names like "Nilla Wafer", "Wax Candle" or "Peachy" since I was so much lighter skinned than they were. They never called me names in front of teachers as they would be soundly punished if discovered doing so, even on the day of graduation. They never dared to call Minter such names as he was just a tiny shade darker than me. However, he was also a target of darker skinned students' jibs about light-skin. Though Walter was considered a better student than me, I knew that he often cut corners and cheated. In fact he had taken ideas from me and presented them as his own, never crediting me for them. I kept as far away from him as it was possible to do in a class of near forty people. Because of my shame about my family origins, I seldom sought to know the family situations of my classmates.

Suddenly, the principal was calling for silence as "Pomp & Circumstance" began to be heard from the piano down in front of the stage. First the faculty marched out and took their seats followed by our alphabetized class. There was also one white school board member who represented the rest of the white board and he walked out beside the principal. I couldn't help but compare the color of my skin to his. It was the same. Perhaps I was even lighter. Later, I felt how shallow a thought this was comparing my skin to his, when I remembered the importance of this day.

On each of our seats was a sheet of paper showing the program:

Knox High School Graduation May 16, 1941

Processional "Pomp and Circumstance"

"The Star Spangled Banner" sung while standing by all present

Invocation by Brother Isaiah Williams

Welcome by the principal Mr. Ezra Stokes

Congratulations by the board member Mr. Alston Pitts

Poem "Be Strong" by Maltbie Davenport Babcock recited by

Salutatorian, Tallulah Beulah Norris

Valedictory by Woodrow Minter

The Keynote Speech by Mr. James Chestnut

Awards presented by Mr. Stokes and the faculty

Presentation of Diplomas by Mr. Stokes

Recessional

Reception following in the Home Economics Kitchen

After I recited my short poem, "Be Strong", I relaxed and sat back to enjoy the rest of the ceremony. It was such a short poem and we had all had to memorize it in our 9th grade literature class. I wondered if I were the only one who still remembered the words. Many times I had practiced it while walking to school or work. The words were as familiar to me as a frequently sung song.

I had attended graduation of the previous class so I took it all with aplomb until Miss Alcorn stood and called me to the podium to receive the "High Expectations" award. This award had not been given the year before so I was completely surprised as were my classmates. Miss Alcorn explained that the teachers had felt that I had a brilliant future ahead of me; therefore I deserved the award even though I was only the Salutatorian, not the Valedictorian.

I felt a hard twinge of guilt knowing that I would be leaving Selma and that anything I achieved would not resound to members of the colored community. My intended achievement was to be in the white world. It would not reflect back onto the efforts of my teachers at black Knox High School. None-the-less, I gratefully accepted this acknowledgement of my abilities and effort. I walked back to my seat in the back row of the stage as the applause subsided. Receiving the diploma was anti-climatic after receiving the award. I saw Uncle Edgar sitting in the back row of the auditorium. He slipped away as the Recessional started. I realized that he had sneaked away from work to see the first one in his family get a diploma, even if it was only for tenth grade.

I noticed the various parents who came to congratulate their children. Most of the parents were alone, having had to slip away from their work for this occasion as it would be unusual for a white employer to think graduation from Knox High School worth time off from work. It was the first time I ever saw Woodrow Minter's mother. She was a little darker skinned than he was. Her pride in her boy was very apparent.

One of the teachers retrieved our graduation gowns and caps from us as we exited the stage, to be stored for next year. They were hand-me-downs from the white high school, but still they were all we had so it was necessary to keep them as well as possible.

I left the reception as soon as I could politely do so as I wanted to share my diploma and award with Mother, but before I could leave I had to receive more congratulations from the faculty. Finally, I left nearly running down Mabry Street despite the already 90 degree heat. I tried to remember to keep some dignity as I was wearing my lovely dotted Swiss dress. Bursting through our front door, I called out, "Mother, I got an award." There was no answer, so I went in and knelt by the mattress. She lay in the same position I had last seen her. Her body had already turned cold. I dropped the award certificate beside her and flung myself on her body, convulsed by tears of unbelief.

CHAPTER 7

Colored Funeral

Uncle Edgar took over planning for the burial of his sister. He arranged for Brother Williams to officiate at the funeral and burial. Mother's body stayed there in our house, though Uncle Edgar and the preacher carried her out to the sagging sofa in our front room. I cleaned this small room as best I could. Her body could not be kept above ground for long as the May heat in Central Alabama was too hot to allow that. In fact by the next day, Saturday, I could already smell some putrefaction. Aunt Phyllis brought over a big bouquet of roses from her yard and from her neighbors. But even roses in the South, have their aromas fade quickly in the heat. We tried splashing cologne on the dress Aunt Phyllis and I had dressed her in but the smell of death still lurked. By Sunday after the regular service, when congregation members came to carry her body to the black cemetery, it was pervasive.

We could not afford a coffin so the pallbearers put her body on a wide pine board and covered it with a clean sheet. I dried off the stems of the roses which were already dropping petals and laid them on top of the sheet. I followed the pallbearers as they walked to the church. A number of choir members walked in front singing, "Swing Low, Sweet Chariot, Comin' for to carry me home." Aunt Phyllis and Uncle Edgar walked beside me. Their children followed in the next row of mourners. Some of the other Negro workers from the Vaughn Hospital also followed the procession from our house to the church. Miss Alcorn and the teacher with whom she lived were back some twenty feet from me in the procession. I felt the only emotional warmth that day as I did the unorthodox thing of waving to her.

Since the street between our house and the church was not near the business district, the only thing that relieved the view of shabby small houses similar to our own was the railroad track. Once in the church, I was led by Deacon Brown to the front row and seated between Uncle Edgar and Aunt Phyllis. Brother Williams mounted the platform which held the pulpit. He immediately began to lead in singing "Oh, Mary, Don't You Weep, Don't you Mourn." The choir filed past Mother's body on the board supported by two sawhorses and took their seats on the platform behind Brother Williams. A number of the rose petals had scattered on the sheet during the walk from our house to the church. Aunt Phyllis reached over and took my hand which made me tense up as I knew she didn't like Mother and I suspected she didn't like me either. She was probably glad to be relieved of Mother's care. I had overheard her discussing with Uncle Edgar whether or not they would have to take me in now.

Brother Williams started to pray. I had wondered why he called himself Brother instead of Reverend like the white preacher did. I never remembered to ask Mother and now that opportunity was gone. I felt guilty to be thinking such thoughts when I should be thinking of Mother. I had not cried since I first discovered her cold body, but now as the Brother prayed, I lowered my chin to my chest to keep from sobbing aloud. Tears streaked down my face and I was reluctant to raise my handkerchief to wipe them. I had to wear my dotted Swiss graduation dress as I had no black dresses.

"Let us pray to our Jesus to reach down his hand from heaven and lift Sister Norris up to join him. Though she, like all of us have been a sinner, Sister Norris tried her very best to overcome her sin, to be forgiven of her sin, and to live a life that Jesus would approve. Jesus, bring our sinning hearts to you on this sad morning. Sister Norris is leaving her little daughter Tallulah with us for guidance. Please Lord, help us to show her your way. Let us lead her in the right path. Let us guard her from evil. Let us shield her from the Devil. Let us instruct her in your ways, Oh, Lord! Let us not be weak in guiding her on the right road to achieve Heaven."

Then Brother Williams asked the head pallbearer to come forward and fold the sheet back so we could see Mother's face.

He continued his prayer as the head pallbearer complied with his request, carefully folding the sheet between Mother's chin and the bouquet of roses. Brother Williams's voice began to rise and the congregation began to respond with "Yes, Lord," every time he stopped to take a breath. In the background, the choir began to sing "Heav'n, Heav'n" almost in rhythm with the preacher's words and the congregation's response. Some of the congregation had raised both hands and were waving them in rhythm. Aunt Phyllis dropped my hand and joined in the waving. The choir switched into singing "Sometimes I Feel like a Motherless Child." This did not particularly cheer me up though I felt sure the choir director intended it to. When they came to the phrase "a long way from home" I thought this song may have some relevance after all as I was feeling more and more like fleeing, though it made me anticipate some of the loneliness I would feel as I went away to strange places.

Brother Williams continued to alternate between preaching at us to get a good relationship with the Lord and then to pray as if he had the only special telephone line to the Lord but he would allow us to listen in to his privileged communication. Between prayers and preaching the choir sang, sometimes starting the song during his prayer or preaching to provide a background to his words. The familiarity of this kind of worship should have offered some comfort but on this day, it made me just eager to finish so I could cry alone.

The choir sang: "Go Down Moses", "Ev'ry Time I Feel the Spirit", "Steal Away to Jesus", "They Crucified My Lord", "Roll Jordan, Roll", "Deep River", "Oh, Heaven Is One Beautiful Place, I Know", and "He's Got the Whole World in His Hands."

Finally, the preacher stopped and led down the aisle with the pallbearers, us and the congregation following down the street to Live Oak Cemetery to the section for poor Negroes. A grave had already been dug. The pall bearers slid the board on which Mother's body lay into the end of the grave and slowly let her body with the sheet slide off the board as they lift the board out slantwise. They had not waited for anyone to give any last kisses to the corpse. It was apparent that everyone was eager to get out of this May heat. Brother Williams did ask Uncle Edgar and me to come forward to the edge of the hole and throw in some clods of dirt. It felt like desecration to throw dirt on my beautiful mother, but I couldn't see her as the sheet had somehow kept her covered there on the dirt in the bottom of the hole.

CHAPTER 8

Flight

We walked back to the church where food covered the three crude picnic tables behind the church building. It seemed to be an offering to the family and congregation as a consolation prize for what they had lost. On most Sundays, one or another of the children's Sunday school classes took turns having their lessons on those same rough lumber tables, but on this day, the tables had been covered with discarded sheets from Vaughn Hospital. The food offerings were sufficient enough to cover any permanent stains that the Negro laundresses had been unable to scrub out before they were discarded.

I was inclined not to eat but out of politeness, I filled a plate and stood by the table playing with the fork. I planned to find a convenient bush or tree behind which to discard it when people began to gather their casserole dishes or greasy platters. "People spoke to me in funeral platitudes to which I responded in kind: "Thank you for your thoughts and prayers", "Mother would be so pleased that you came to bid her goodbye" and "Yes, I shall certainly ask if I need help."

As I spoke thus, I began to realize that this very moment was the one in which fleeing would be easiest and less anticipated by anyone concerned, especially Uncle Edgar or Miss Alcorn. Those two seemed to me to be the only ones who would worry and fret when they discovered that I had disappeared.

Miss Alcorn usually left town soon after graduation to take the classes required to maintain her teaching credential. Consequently, I surmised that she would leave almost immediately, and that she had only stayed these three days because of Mother's funeral. Uncle Edgar was due back at work as soon as he could leave here. Because of Mother's final illness, he had already been absent too many days to suit the white station master. Stories of slaves fleeing came to my mind and reminded me that the ones who were successful in flight, never told anyone of their plans.

Then it occurred to me that if I hurried, I could gather my things and leave on the train before Uncle Edgar could take his family home, change into his uniform and get back to the station. There was just one mid-day train at 2 PM on Sunday for preachers traveling between churches and visitors who must be back at work on Monday morning in some other city. I moved away from the table and dumped the contents of my plate into a cloth that I had taken from the table. It had undoubtedly covered the dish someone had brought to share. They would miss it when they gathered their things to go home, but I needed it. I knew I would need this food later, even if I did not feel hungry now. I walked back to the table and slipped the empty plate down between some dishes. After thanking Brother and Sister Williams and promising Aunt Phyllis to come over as soon as I got my things from our old house, I rapidly retraced my steps to the front of the house. She had extracted the promise from me. I agreed just to avoid having her interfere with my plan.

Because I had no suitcase in which to put my few possessions, I found a cornmeal sack printed with a small flower design. I slipped my new diploma and the two report cards, my final one and the one I had stolen from the shed inside my geography textbook that I had purposely failed to return as I felt the maps might be of assistance in finding my new home. The last thing I did was take the little ash shovel from near the stove and pried up the floorboard to recover my cache of money. I had used a metal baking soda can to hold it. I did not bother to count it as I felt it would take too much time, but I knew it was more than fifteen dollars. The can went into the sack as well. The only bar of soap from the house came next. I piled my other dress, white ankle stockings and panties on top along with my other pair of shoes. I kept my brown hat on my head, the same hat, my only hat which I had worn to the burial of Mother. The cloth with the food lay atop my shoes so it would not get grease on my clothing, I hoped.

After a look around our humble little house to make sure I did not leave anything important, I slipped out the back and down the alley before turning toward the railway station. It was the hottest part of the day, so I felt sure most people would be napping. I met no one until I neared the station where a few passengers straggled in under the shadow of the platform roof. I felt nervous as I had never before ridden a train, but I had seen others do it often enough when I visited Uncle Edgar while at work. Getting the ticket, which cost $1.25 from Selma to York, was easier than I thought. The white ticket seller did not even look at me, a simple Negro girl.

My tension also was in anticipation of the plan I had to change from colored to white in York. I remembered what Miss Alcorn had told me about her travels. I borrowed trouble and began to plan and worry about this process as I hid, hoping to be invisible, behind a large Negro man, undoubtedly a preacher. I pulled my brown felt hat with one simple tan ribbon as far down as I could to cover my face and hair without looking ridiculous. Soon a Negro family with three children joined the line to await the "Colored" car. They made me feel like I was more camouflaged. I tried to act as if I were with them so if Uncle Edgar asked about a single girl, people would not remember me. I knew that my disappearance would be a relief to Aunt Phyllis. There would be no search for me.

The train whistle which I had heard every single day I could remember made me jump this time when it blew as it came from the direction of Montgomery. The engine rolled past. I paid attention to which cars had the "Colored" sign by the door so I could slip on with as little attention paid to me as possible. The tall Negro seemed to know where he was supposed to go and the family behind me seemed acquainted with what to expect so I just sandwiched myself between them. I knew Uncle Edgar would question all his coworkers asking if they had seen me when eventually he realized I was really gone, but he would not discover I was gone until he went home after his shift and Aunt Phyllis would report that I had not arrived as I had promised. She would be glad rather than sorry that I had not turned up to stay with them. By then I would be across the state line into Mississippi. I would be white.

CHAPTER 9

From Black into White

The family with the three children squeezed themselves into four seats, two on each side of the aisle. An older tired looking Negro woman sat immediately behind them on the window seat facing the houses near the station. The seat beside her on the aisle was vacant. I politely bent and asked, "Is this seat available?"

She barely looked at me as she nodded "Yes," and went back to studying the view from the window.

I quickly slipped into the seat, clutching my cornmeal sack to my chest. I quickly assessed the woman beside me and decided I did not want her to remember me in case anyone should ask her later. Therefore I did not speak to her further. She seemed tired enough to be glad of the quiet, except for the noise of the bustle of people getting settled in their seats. I decided to keep my possessions in my lap to partially hide me and also to avoid calling attention to myself by struggling to put them in the narrow space left above my seat in the luggage shelf. One of the men might attempt to help me and that would draw further attention.

As the train began to move, I saw Miss Alcorn come out the station door toward the platform where the train going toward Montgomery would soon be arriving and departing. My guess was that she was heading to Tuskegee Institute for the summer school for teachers' recertification. She carried her leatherette suitcase openly, unlike me trying to hide myself and my cornmeal sack. I felt some nostalgia as I remembered her exemplary role in my life.

Though I realized she would be unable to see me through the dirt on the window of the Colored Car, still I turned away from the window facing the station. I wanted there to be absolutely no chance of being seen going away from Selma. It would not take long for Miss Alcorn to realize that my queries about her trip to Sanatorium, Mississippi, had not been disinterested. With her rectitude, Miss Alcorn would certainly judge this to be disrespect for my mother and her recent death.

While I had lived my life in Selma, I had seldom been outside of the city limits. Travel was too costly and my mother's relatives were too scattered to have inspired visits to them. Also, as I considered it, Mother had probably felt shame about her situation despite it being not of her own doing. She would have avoided situations where she was compelled to explain my existence.

As the train went west into the county, I was fascinated to see the countryside. I had lived so near it but knew little of it, except that some of my classmates had migrated to Selma from the nearby cotton fields. At this time of year, I saw cotton fields in all stages of work; being plowed by mules, being planted with a machine behind a mule, being hoed by colored men and women, being harvested by colored men and women dragging huge cotton sacks behind them as they moved down between the rows. Each field was in a different stage of growth or harvest. The cotton depot on the river in Selma took on new meaning in my mind as I realized from where those bales had come. Mother had mentioned cotton picking and cotton sacks, but it had always been something from which to flee, something she did not want to discuss further. She had discouraged me from learning about that hard labor as if knowing about it would somehow bring it into our lives. Now I wondered how many things I had never learned about my mother. If I could I would ask her why she did not want me to know about these people who lived and worked so close to Selma. Tears came into my eyes as I considered the possibilities. Crying would certainly draw attention so I closed my eyes and concentrated on suppressing these feelings.

When I opened my eyes, it was because there was a change in the sound of the train on the tracks.

The train was crossing a bridge. I heard the father of the children telling them it was the Cahaba River. Shortly thereafter the train stopped briefly at a station called Marion Junction. Another Negro man dressed like a preacher got on the train there but no one got off. Soon after without stopping, we went by a small station building with a sign with the name "Browns" on it. Selma began to seem like a sophisticated city compared to the small towns the train passed through. These little settlements had one line of buildings which looked to be covered with cotton lint; Uniontown, Faunsdale, Gallion. Demopolis more closely matched Selma in size and apparent importance. The trees along the side of the tracks had Spanish moss hanging down from the lower branches. Here I learned by listening to the man in the seat in front of me that we had crossed the Black Warrior River. I was tempted to take out my geography book to see if I could position myself on the map, but I realized such an act might cause other passengers to want to see the maps thus drawing attention to myself, so I suppressed this desire.

Despite my intention to avoid being noticed, a Negro man sitting on the other side of the aisle across from me insisted on trying to engage me in conversation. When I ignored his questions about who I was and where I was going, he began to make remarks under his breath about his guess that I was probably a woman "up to no good since I was traveling alone." I turned toward my seat mate, the older woman and asked her to talk to me in order to discourage the man from trying to converse with me. I wondered how he knew I was traveling alone and hoped by engaging my seatmate in conversation; he might think I was with her. However, I soon realized she was hard of hearing. I had tried to whisper to her and she did not respond. So I touched her arm and facing her, spoke softly, "Please talk to me so that man will leave me alone."

In quite a loud voice, she said, "You'll have to talk louder because I can't hear anything on this train."

I just shook my head at her and decided the best thing would be to act like I was asleep, while still keeping alert in case my harasser did anything else. Shortly, I responded to the fatigue which had lurked beneath the surface from my long tiring day.

I awoke as the train was slowing at York. Apparently the rackety-rackety of the train had finally lulled me to sleep. My cornmeal bag had slipped to the floor at my feet. I jerked myself up gripping my bag as I pulled it into my lap again. The conductor announced that there would be half an hour layover in York. Before I went to buy my ticket to Meridian, I decided to tell the conductor of the man who was harassing me. I knew from Uncle Edgar that conductors were often given charge of young females traveling alone to protect them from just such a situation. This conductor nodded sympathetically to my request, eyeing the harasser with an appraising look. I hoped he would never meet Uncle Edgar and tell him about encountering me.

As soon as I descended from the "Colored" car, I entered the station to study the board which announced departures and arrivals. I looked at the station clock over the board and it said nearly six o'clock. I found the "Colored" women's toilet and quickly used it before returning to the train fearing to lose my seat. The family had disembarked so I was able to move forward into their window seat. The older woman with whom I had shared a seat had also disembarked here, but I wanted to be as close to the door as I could so I could have as much time as possible for my change-over to becoming a white woman when we arrived in Meridian because York was too small for me to be inconspicuous. I also wanted to put more distance between myself and the man who had tried to start a conversation with me. The conductor was good as his word and stood near my new seat observing the man I had indicated. I had no further attention from him after that, but I knew I had drawn attention to myself.

As the evening began to close down over the forest beside the tracks and the day's heat began to cool off, I tried formulating in my mind how I would switch. I knew from Uncle Edgar that the "White" cars were in the back of the train, so I decided I would disembark as quickly as I could, remove and discard my hat which had flattened down my red-brown curls. I would walk back to where white passengers were getting off the train and insert myself into a crowd and enter the station with them. I would try to find a white woman entering the "White" women's toilet and follow her in.

As the train slowed down for Meridian I prepared to leap off. I made my exit as soon as the train came to a stop, and checked to make sure no one was watching me as I stepped over the train coupling and went toward the station, walking quickly on the gravel on the other side of the train cars. I had not seen any white women getting off the train. It was too late for most respectable white women to be traveling. When I came to the last space where the car was coupled to the caboose, after checking to see if I were observed, I stepped over the coupling to the platform facing the station and headed toward the lobby. It was full dark outside now. There was one dim light over the door between the platform and the waiting room door. Inside were the doors to the "Colored" and "White" women's restrooms.

Unfortunately, there were no white women for me to follow into the "White" restroom. Instead, I instinctively went into the "Colored" toilet wondering how I might get into the "White" restroom unnoticed. Nearly stumbling over a mop and bucket, the solution came to me: as a Negro cleaning woman, I would not be questioned about going into the "White" restroom to clean. Clutching my bag under one arm, I grabbed the bucket and mop with the other and exited the "Colored" women's restroom and walked boldly into the "White" woman's restroom. No one seemed to be paying attention.

As I expected, at this time of night, few women were traveling. I was the sole occupant of the "White" women's restroom. After looking at the layout of the toilets and sink, I quickly turned off the switch to the electric light bulb which hung down in the middle of the room. A small light showed through the transom over the door. It was enough for me to see by to change to my other dress. I quickly combed my curls up onto the top of my head and secured them with some combs I had retrieved from near my mother's little cracked mirror. My instinct was to discard my lavender dress and brown hat, but my frugality and awareness of my future needs for clothing in a new place where they would not be recognized won out. Further, I realized a discarded dress and hat in a "White" women's toilet would inspire questions. Consequently, I turned the cornmeal sack inside out so it looked like a nearly white pillow cover and stuffed them into it along with my other possessions retrieved from our shotgun house. I had saved the white cloth holding the food after I finished eating it so I partially covered the bag with this cloth despite some grease stains, thus further obscuring the inside-out cornmeal sack. I pushed the mop and bucket into the corner near the sink. I knew some poor Negro girl would get a tongue lashing for leaving the mop and bucket in the white women's toilet. I was sorry but it was necessary. Then I cracked the door and saw that the "White" waiting room was empty so I quickly slipped into a seat as far from the light as possible and began to study the departure/arrival board. I was finally white.

Memory of my mother and her recent passing gave me some small guilt about the triumphant feeling I had for entering the white race at last.

CHAPTER 10

Being White

For a few moments, I squeezed my eyes shut and relished my success. Despite months of practicing being white in private, the reality of now being white in public took a little getting used to. I soon realized I must look at the departure board in order to know when the train for Jackson would leave.

In the poor light of the Meridian station, I was able to see that there would be no more trains west until morning. The station clock pointed to eleven o'clock. I prepared to spend the night, barricaded by my cornmeal bag in the corner of the white waiting room until the first train of the morning at 6 AM. As all the other travelers who disembarked, had disappeared, the white man in the ticket cage and I were the only occupants of the station. I decided to see if I could be allowed to purchase my ticket to Jackson and thus perhaps strike up a conversation. Perhaps I could interest him in my welfare as a lone white woman traveling alone so I could sleep or doze in some assurance of not being bedeviled by bad men during the night.

Remembering to sound white, I spoke my first words as that race. "Sir, shall I purchase my ticket for the 6 AM Jackson train now?" I asked the sleepy agent behind the barred arch in the ticket cage.

Rousing himself, he looked at me skeptically and asked, "Why is a young lady like you traveling alone?"

I made up the first story that came into my mind." I must reach Memphis before my brother leaves for the Army. He wrote that he must be in Texas by June first. That's just a few days away. I do not want to take any chances to miss him."

"Well young lady," the agent's voice becoming more fatherly and solicitous, "Way I figure it you should be in Memphis by midnight tomorrow. That gives you at least a week before your brother has to be in Texas. Where's he going?" His voice sounded almost envious now.

The first name that came into my head was one that I had heard the boys in my class mention. "Fort Sam Houston," I replied.

"Oh, well, it will take him two days if he's on a troop train to get there from Memphis. You'll have plenty of time to see him." By now I almost believed the lie I was telling. I guessed that the white agent, who looked in this shadow light, was about forty years old. However, I was a novice at trying to guess the age of white men as I had been kept far from them most of my young life.

"Young lady, you just sit down here in front of this ticket office and I'll keep an eye out on you tonight. Wouldn't want your brother to miss seeing his pretty little sister." He did not actually leer but there was a tone in his voice that acknowledged my vulnerability. I wondered why he worried about my brother seeing me rather than the danger that might befall me, but I put this aside in the grateful feeling I had for his promise of protection. I wondered if he would be able to keep awake or awaken quickly enough were I to call for his help.

The night, thankfully, passed uneventfully. I awaken with the dawn and entered the white women's toilet to wash my face and relieve myself. As I came out, the night agent was explaining my plight to his daytime replacement. I was glad my ticket was already in my possession so I did not have to speak with the white day agent. The whistle of a train came from the east and I quickly walked out to the platform to see where the white passenger cars would stop.

My skin felt almost like a new skin on my body, no longer the fair-skinned Negro, but a white person in a white skin. Though my anxiety was not all gone, still I felt that the likelihood of discovery of my deception was tiny. I figured I would be long gone from Memphis before anyone trying to find me was able to ask the white Meridian night agent about the girl traveling alone. Besides, they would be asking for a Negro girl or more probably "A nigger girl."

I found the white car and boarded with nobody paying me any attention. I was able to find a seat beside a woman holding a baby. I would have liked to sit by a window, both for the breeze and for the view, but sitting by another woman seemed the wisest. During the three-hour ride to Sanatorium, I held the baby while she went to the toilet or stood while she used my seat to lay the baby on for diaper changing. She was so involved with the baby, who looked to me to be about six months old, that she did not try to engage me in conversation, nor I to converse with her. She did thank me for my help though. When she disembarked at Sanatorium, I realized she must be visiting someone there. The shame of having a family member or friend with tuberculosis probably kept her from talking to me, thus risking rejection. I wondered if it were the baby's father who was the patient, but did not ask as there was not time before the train was moving and she disappeared as she turned up the hill from the small station building.

When the train arrived in Jackson around noon, I got off with my inside-out cornmeal bag and decided I must find something to use as a suitcase. The whitish bag would mark me as a poor person. I had discarded the cloth that held the food in the Meridian white women's restroom.

I had been without food for almost twelve hours and my stomach grumbled. Before leaving the train station to look for something to eat, I examined the departure board above the ticket window. The train from New Orleans to Memphis would depart at 2 PM. That would give me plenty of time to find food and resolve my suitcase problem.

I walked out onto Capitol Street and began to walk east. Soon I came to the F. W. Woolworth Store. My first impulse was to not enter but then I remembered I was white and I could go anywhere I wanted. I entered and walked around. It was the first time I could remember not thinking of how long I would have to wait behind all the white shoppers in order to make a purchase. On a display shelf near the rear of the store, I found some leatherette suitcases and tapestry valises. The smallest of the valises would hold all my small possessions. It was one dollar. I hated to spend so much as I still needed to buy my ticket to Memphis and from Memphis to – who knows where? I would decide when I arrived in Memphis. But at least I would look like a believable traveler with a real grip rather than a cornmeal sack.

CHAPTER 11

Memphis to Chicago

When I disembarked the train at Memphis, Tennessee, after nervously using the white women's restroom, I felt tired and dirty from my two days of travel so I went to the ticket window and asked for directions to the YWCA. I had heard from various women on the train from Jackson that it was a good place for white women to stay safely. Perhaps one night there with a bath would make me feel better.

"291 South Second Street," the agent said without even looking up at me. I realized he must get this request often. He gave a gesture with his hand to point the direction to walk.

"Thank you, sir," I said automatically despite his lack of attention. Before leaving, I looked at the departure board to discover what places I could get to from Memphis. There was a train leaving for Chicago in just a few minutes. Rather than squander my money on a room at the YWCA, I made a spurof-the-moment decision to buy a ticket for Chicago and get as far away from Selma as I could before my money ran out. I knew many Negroes from Selma who had gone to Chicago for a better life. There was a bit of anxiety about perhaps meeting one of them and having them notice me, but I was a grown up white lady now and unlikely to meet Negros who would recognize me. So I used more than I wanted of my dwindling cache of dollars to buy the ticket. Then I used a quarter to buy some apples and boiled eggs from a Negro woman selling them from an unpainted child's wagon on the platform.

I awoke as the train stopped in Kankakee. I had never heard of this city before so I slipped the geography book out of my new grip to see how close we were to Chicago. It looked like about 50 miles. The blank report card and my award certificate were snugly in between two pages near the back of the book I noticed as I replaced it in the bottom of the bag under my lavender dress. I waited until the train pulled out of the station before going to the toilet in the end of the car. Suddenly, I wondered if the car was still called a "White" car. I was in the North now. As we approached the city, I could see the tall buildings. The windows reflected the sun as it lowered in the west.

The vastness of the railroad station in Chicago was almost over whelming. I stood amazed as I noted the number of boarding platforms. People were coming and going from all different directions.

Uniformed railroad workers scurried here and there with luggage trolleys, arms full of suitcases and hat boxes, as well as those with clipboards in their hands directing passengers to their destinations. Many of the men were also in military uniforms. At Union Station, I asked the conductor who helped me off the train how to find the YWCA. He directed me to the Lawson Hotel, 30 West Chicago Avenue. I remembered gratefully how Uncle Edgar had sometimes explained to me about his work. It gave me more confidence in navigating even this huge train station. A little guilt crept into my thoughts about Uncle Edgar knowing that he was probably very worried about me.

The lobby was of such grandeur! The columns and high arched ceiling with glass were in such contrast to the Selma station that I stood inside the lobby speechless for several minutes.

In the main lobby, there was a large bulletin board near the exit. In addition to the one reminding young men to register for the draft, there were notice posters asking for Red Cross Volunteers and also ones for high school graduates to apply for the nursing school at Grant Hospital at 2225 N. Lincoln or at Augustana Hospital at the corner of Lincoln and Cleveland Streets. Both schools offered board and room and pocket money. This was a hopeful sign, I thought as I had barely enough money left to pay to share a room at the YWCA. I memorized this information about the nursing schools so I would not have to walk the more than twenty-five blocks back to the Union Station if I decided to apply for one of them. It also reminded me that I must take care to make sure my blank report card had survived the trip in between the pages of the old geography book. Both requests for nursing student supplications specified high school graduation. Each poster specified that an applicant must be between eighteen and forty years old. I was only sixteen years old, but I could make the date on the report card say that I had graduated last year.

I exited Union Station unto Canal Street. Apparently the conductor was used to having young women ask for the YWCA. He had given me exact directions about going three blocks north on Canal to Washington. Take a right on Washington and go left at La Salle Street. At Chicago Avenue go left or west and look for the Lawson Hotel. Hurriedly I made my way and followed his directions precisely to find the hotel as it would soon be dark. The tall buildings loomed above and I occasionally glanced up, but my fear of looking like an ignorant bumpkin made me keep my eyes mostly straight ahead. I was glad my bag was not too heavy now. The geography book was the heaviest thing in it after I had eaten all the food I bought in Memphis. My stomach told me it was time to eat.

Remembering that I was white, I marched determinedly into the desk by the front door and rang the bell sitting on the corner. A middle aged woman ducked her head around the corner and asked me to, "Please wait a moment." As I waited, I looked around the spacious lobby. A group of girls huddled around a radio in the corner. I wondered if I could afford to stay at such a place. However, behind the desk a painted board announced the prices of rooms. A woman's dormitory room with four beds would cost fifty cents per night. Breakfast was included. I reached and felt the coins in my pocket and realized I could pay for four nights before I would have no money left. I decided to take this opportunity and use these four days to decide whether to apply for a nursing school or throw myself on someone's charity. Tonight, I would just have to be hungry.

CHAPTER 12

YWCA

The manager of the YWCA hotel gave me a key to a room on the fourth floor. She said there was one empty bed there. I could have that one for four days. After handing over my money, I realized I had only a few coins left in my pocket.

It was my first time to ride in an elevator. The young lady operating it closed the door after us and then closed the accordion bars before pressing the button. The jerkiness of the elevator made my stomach a little queasy since it had been empty so long. When the elevator stopped on the fourth floor, the young lady pointed down the hall to direct me to the room. I passed a bathroom room and took note of its location on my way to room #410.

When I pushed open the door to room #410, I could see that there were two sets of bunk-beds. Someone was apparently asleep in the bottom bunk behind the door. I could see that the one above had sheets and a blanket and towel stacked on it. The two beds on the other side of the door were both made up with sheets and blanket and both suitcases were underneath the bottom bunk. A window between the beds was open and I could see the buildings across West Chicago Avenue as well as hear the traffic in the street below. I supposed that was why the occupant of the lower bunk had not awakened when I came in. I tried to be as quiet as possible but it was apparent that the noise of the street overrode any noise I might make. I laid my bag on the top bunk behind the door and removed my toothbrush and the other set of underclothes. My first destination was the bathroom. After more than two days on the train, I was ready to wash off the travel dust.

As the person in the lower bunk was still quite asleep when I returned, I decided to avoid awakening her by making up my bed. Being as quiet as possible in changing clothes after my bath, I went down to the lobby to explore the other amenities of the YWCA hotel. It was quite dark now, or I would have toured the neighborhood, but my fear of the city compelled me to keep myself safe inside. I wondered what would have happened had I not found the hotel and been able to pay the price. I supposed I would have spent the night on a bench in the train station again.

There in the lobby was another bulletin board. It held the same posters about nursing schools as the ones I had seen in Union Station. Several young ladies were seated around a table playing dominoes. I stood and watched the game from a distance. The group that had been listening to the radio had disappeared and the radio was turned off. Since we had never been able to afford a radio, the only times I had ever heard one was in the grocery store while waiting to be served. I wondered if I could join that group of girls the next time they listened. The magic of listening to stories was something I had seldom experienced except for the few times a teacher would read aloud to our class. Stories were what I had gleaned from books. Our little high school library had a sparse few volumes and I had read them all.

One young lady from the domino table gestured and invited me to sit down in the only empty chair. This was a camaraderie to which I was not accustomed. In my Selma neighborhood and also in the only Negro high school except for Selma College, we were all too busy working or studying to have time for friendship, or at least that was how it seemed to me, perhaps it was because I was an only child. If I had had sisters, maybe close friendship would have come more naturally. Also, since I was whiter than most Negro girls, I may have been rejected out of jealousy. Sometimes I had felt like only half a person in that world of Negroes.

I took the seat and quietly watched the game. I had never played Dominoes, though some of the older Negro men had played it with handmade wooden tiles on a bench near the Negro variety store in Selma. The dominoes these young women played with were white like ivory.

The next morning after a night of deep sleep to compensate me for my two nights traveling without a mattress to sleep on, I went to breakfast first. Having been without anything but water for twenty-four hours, I ate everything offered on the table. There was oatmeal with raisins, coffee and real cream, applesauce muffins, scrambled eggs and fried steak. Meat for breakfast was a new experience for me but I devoured it all.

Thus fortified, I headed out through the lobby and decided to walk further up the famed La Salle Street. The famous Moody Bible Institute dominated that intersection in Chicago. As I progressed north, I saw a sign for the Henrotin Hospital. I counted six floors of windows. Again, I could not help but compare it to the hospitals in Selma. Since I was here, I decided to be brave in this big city and I walked into the lobby to have a look. There was no one behind the desk near the entrance door. I stood there pivoting on my heels as I waited and examined the hospital lobby. Finally, a thirtyish looking woman in a nurse's uniform came through a door and headed for the stairs at the back of the lobby. She was so preoccupied; she did not even look at me so I called out, "Hello, can I ask a question?"

She slowed her steps but did not stop as she

turned to me, "Yes, how can I help you?"

I hurried toward her afraid I might lose her if I didn't move quickly enough." I am trying to learn if there is nurses' training in this hospital."

That brought her to a stop and she came toward me." Yes we do have a nurses' program. Are you interested in becoming a nurse?" Suddenly she was more solicitous.

"Yes, I am staying at the YWCA. I am trying to discover if I am qualified to become a nurse." Then I remembered that I had not yet filled out the blank report card and that I must lie about having a four-year high school diploma.

"Let me take you to Miss Hall. She is the head of our nurses' training. Her office is upstairs near the back of the second floor." She gestured for me to follow her.

Despite not having any proof of my education, I decided to use this experience to see how one gets to be a nurse since it seemed to be obligatory for becoming an occupational therapist. I certainly did not want to be a teacher and knew that people who ran schools were more likely to discover I had only finished tenth grade even if I had wanted to become a teacher in order to be qualified to be an occupational therapist. I preferred nursing, to be like Miss Norris, so I followed her.

Her pace on the stairs increased again and I rushed to follow her up and down the central hallway to the back. She knocked on the door beneath the sign that said "Head of Nurses' Training." This nurse guiding me seemed preoccupied again and looked at a paper in her hand as we waited.

"Yes, come in," there came a rather business-like female voice.

The first nurse twisted the knob and pushed the door open for me, "Miss Hall, I have a young woman here who is interested in nurses' training."

"Please bring her in."

The first nurse gestured me in, did not enter, and closed the door after me, obviously eager to be back at whatever task I had distracted her from. I covertly examined the woman behind the desk who had arisen upon my entrance. She was not tall, but still her posture made her imposing. She wore her uniform and cap as if she were the head of the hospital.

"Have a seat" she said as she gestured toward the only other chair in the tiny office. She seated herself again and watched me as I did the same to her. "Now tell me about wanting to be a nurse," she ordered, but before I could start, she went on "Tell me some about yourself."

CHAPTER 13

Nurses' Training

I had been so preoccupied with becoming a white person, that I had not thought what story I would tell except that I was a graduate of Knox High School. So I started with the first thing that came into my mind, remembering to "talk white." "I want to become a nurse because I knew a nurse and she inspired me." I made myself remember to introduce myself as Clara Brett. It was the first time I had used the name with anyone but myself except for registering at the YWCA.

"Well, Miss Brett, I need to know your qualifications. Where did you attend high school? We are starting a class next Monday, June second. If you are qualified, I will see about enrolling you in our training. Before we go any further I will need to see some proof of your high school education." She had her hands folded on the desk blotter on her desk but it felt like she was ready to spring back to her work the moment I satisfied her requirements.

"I am staying at the YWCA at the Lawson Hotel. I just was out taking a walk when I saw the hospital and decided to come in and inquire about nurses training. I was not expecting to have an interview this morning. I have my high school senior report card in the hotel," I lied.

"Well, bring it in tomorrow morning and we can talk more and if I am satisfied with your qualification, I'll enroll you." She seemed over eager to be back to the task I had interrupted.

It was that easy. When I got back to the Lawson Hotel, I went to the bulletin board and looked again at the posters for both the Grant and the Augustana Hospitals. It would be necessary to get busy on that report card if I was to have it for the Henrotin Hospital or for talking to nurses at other hospital if that didn't work out.

There was a small desk at the end of the corridor. I decided it was private enough to sit at to make this false document. I asked for two sheets of paper at the desk in the lobby. Using my best penmanship, on a blank piece of paper I practiced writing the report card so I would not make any mistakes when I did the final version. I planned to use the second sheet to cover up my work if anyone came to talk to me.

Most of the courses in Knox High School for

Negroes were to train us to work well for white bosses. I knew that in the white high school they had different classes from those we had. So I thought carefully what those classes might be before starting to establish my educational history, English Literature, Algebra, Biology, World History. These were some of the requirements I remembered reading in the reference book about colleges.

The front of the report card was imprinted with the name Knox High School but the rest was blank; a line for the date, the year, the student's name and the grade. Inside were columns for the four semi-semester reporting periods and sections for the different courses. I gave myself some "B's" though in reality I would have gotten all "A's" in Knox High School. I was a better student than Woodrow Minter, the valedictorian because he had often intimidated other students into doing his work for him, so it meant his grades were higher than mine but I knew I was the best student in our class.

After I was satisfied with my fake educational career, I carefully copied it with blue ink on to the blank card. Using a different style of handwriting, I signed Mr. Ezra Stokes' name on the line for the principal.

The next morning, I arrived promptly for my appointment with Miss Hall. By then I had gotten my story of myself straight. My explanation was that I had only my report card because I had mounted my diploma in a frame and left it on my wall at home for my mother. This explanation seemed to satisfy her. Actually, the diploma said I had graduated from 10th grade. When Ms Hall told me that I would work twelve hour shifts six days a week, sleep in a dormitory with the other students, and have my meals in the staff dining-room, and be paid three dollars spending money each week, I agreed.

After I told the woman at the Lawson Hotel that I was enrolled in the nurse's training at the Henrotin Hospital, she allowed me to stay two more days on credit.

For the next five months, I worked hard but no harder than I had worked at the Carnegie Library and the Vaughn Hospital and at my studies in Selma. I made friends with the other girls in the dorm and overcame the feeling of discomfort at being in such close proximity to whites. There was a tall blond girl, Glenda, on the same shift as me and we developed a kind of friendship. She was a farm girl from Northeast Iowa who wanted another life than just as a farmer's wife. It was my first opportunity to ask the many questions I had about how to act, not as a white person, but as a southerner in the north. I was careful to conceal my own former Negro self, always couching my questions to Glenda as a southern white girl's quest for knowledge of a new place, a new home in the north. We seldom had many hours together to just chat as we were tending patients, attending lectures or sleeping. I did come to enjoy with her some of the friendship I had missed as an only child and as and almost white girl in a Negro community and school. However, I wondered if when a person must erase a whole segment of their being, it is really friendship.

I did every dirty job that my nursing instructors gave me. I worked on the surgery unit, the medical unit, the obstetric unit, the recovery unit. I did not pay tuition but I certainly earned this education by the hours that I spent doing back-breaking patient care; lifting and rolling patients, bathing patients, dipping out food from the kettles delivered to the various units, carrying trays, feeding patients, refreshing water pitchers from a huge can of pure water which I pulled from ward to ward in a children's wagon. But the food was plentiful at the hospital as it was not affected as severely when food rationing for private citizens was started.

We had several hours of lecture each day in addition to our work shifts. Lectures were on anatomy, medication, wound care, sterilizing tools, infections, hypodermics, and different categories of disease. If the doctor had an obstetric emergency surgery delivery, we could be wakened from sleep to come down and scrub to assist him.

Homesickness did sadden me during my first months there. The hospital work kept me so busy I hardly had time to ruminate on folks in Selma. In the few hours in which I had freedom from hospital obligations, I discovered a newspaper store on State

Street near the Loop which sold The Selma Times-Journal. This newspaper did not include news of the Negro community to any extent, but I was able to read some about my old home. Sometimes, I was able to see the Tuskegee News but that was the only paper about Negros in Alabama that I could find in the shop.

Then on December 7, the Japanese bombed Pearl Harbor. I was working on the obstetric unit and was standing beside one of my nursing teachers holding the tray with the forceps on it when one of my classmates ran in and whispered the news to both of us. The new mother was sedated so much she could not have heard us had she tried. My teacher and I both held our nursely calm as we watched the doctor extract the infant, leaving great blue bruises on its misshapen head. After cleaning up the mother and baby and wheeling the baby away to the nursery, I was able to find other classmates in the alcove that served as our break-room to discuss the bombing attack. Some of the other nursing students in our class lived at home in Chicago so they did not get to participate in our dormitory discussions. Few of us students got the same break times. However, the emotions aroused by being actually "at war" made us seek each other out more often.

For a few days, though we continued with our patient care, most nursing classes consisted of discussion of the war, and war injuries rather than our planned curriculum. Eventually, we were taken in small groups on field trips to the Veterans' Hospital to see the kinds of patients that were being cared for there even though all the victims of Pearl Harbor were far from being brought back to the United States yet.

"Blackout" mandates appeared on every bulletin board and in every newspaper. Though Chicago was not near either coast where the enemy's bombs were expected, the city was also under national defense laws which required as few lights as possible at night for fear we would make a good target.

The Women's Army Auxiliary Corp first known as WAACs became the Women's Army Corp know as WACs, in 1942. Recruiters from the Army Nurse Corp came to talk with the students in our class to think about joining them upon graduation. This recruiter, who was a nurse, was embarrassed to tell us we could not be an officer like the WACs could be. The other women's services, WAVES or Women Accepted for Volunteer Emergency Service, and SPARS for women in the Coast Guard came to visit as well. They could be commissioned officers. This dilemma of having our training unappreciated by our government if we joined the Army nursing corp. was a bitter pill to swallow. We were more than halfway through our training then when we realized we would not receive the status of other enlisted service women. This was my first awakening to inequities other than race. We expressed much indignation during our discussions in the dormitory and in our classes.

Our teachers encouraged us to think of the good we could do rather than the privilege denied us.

No occupational therapist came to speak to us because they had no official status at all in the armed services. Some occupational therapists volunteered for the Red Cross, but they were not treated as professionals. I still yearned to be an occupational therapist though there seemed no avenue to be one as I was halfway through my nursing courses. Then they passed the Nurse Training Act in 1943 for the cadet nurses' training programs.

Finally, in May 1944, I graduated from the Henrotin Nursing Diploma Program. By this time, the Army had learned its lesson and now commissioned trained nurses as officers. I kept on working for the Henrotin Hospital simply changing from my student nurse uniform to a regular nurse's uniform.

On Christmas Eve 1944, the bill for drafting of nurses was written. We nurses all expected that we would have to register just like men being drafted, but the bill did not pass until after Germany surrendered.

CHAPTER 14

Special Programs

After graduation from nursing school in 1944, I had begun to explore some of the special programs the Army was organizing, knowing that nursing had never been my ultimate goal. One program that particularly interested me was a twelve-month emergency training program for someone already a nurse to become an occupational therapist. Finally I could achieve my dream. Since I was now a nurse, I sought out the Army office where I could apply to enroll in this program, but the enlistment process was so daunting. There would be a long waiting period as I put my life on hold while the Army made up its mind. If chosen I would have to undergo basic training before actually entering the emergency training program.

Everyone wanted to be included in the effort to defend our country. If a person was not working in a defense plant or as a neighborhood civil defense warden, or as a farmer, or planning to join the armed forces, they could feel the scorn of many other citizens. We all feared the Nazi monsters and Prime Minister Tojo's minions. The level of patriotism was whipped up in newspapers, radio programs and bulletin boards. The whole country seemed headed the same direction, to defeat the Axis powers. I, like almost everyone else I met, felt a compulsion to do something for my country. There was urgency about becoming part of the effort to overcome our enemies.

Since the Carnegie Library in Selma had been such a resource for me, my immediate thought was to go and see what I could learn in a library. Though libraries in Chicago did not prohibit Negroes from entering as they did in Selma, neither were they encouraged. It still took me some time to accustom myself to the freedom to enter without expecting to wash the floors. When I had spare time from my nursing work at Henrotin Hospital, I visited the closest public library which was on Division Street. I read the bulletin board where there was a paper announcing a lecture at the Newberry Library by a speaker from the Civil Service. Newberry Library was closer to the hospital but it was a private library. However, they contributed to the war effort by allowing their meeting rooms to be used by the government for recruitment sessions. I discovered that the lecture by the recruiter from the Civil Service about their various service sections was at a time when I was scheduled to work in the hospital.

After bemoaning this in the break area, one of the other nurses who had graduated with me from the nurses training offered to exchange shifts with me.

The room was almost full when I arrived so I took a seat in the middle of the back row on the left side. The room was mostly women older than me. I was nineteen now. Most of those seated in the back row with me were Negroes. Several made deferential gestures as I sat down. I was reminded of my hidden racial background and immediately tried to assume the attitude of preferential treatment for my whiter skin. I was barely seated when the white male Civil Service representative introduced himself as Mr. Eckert and began to exhort us about joining the war effort by participating through Civil Service. He was very good looking in his uniform with his carefully trimmed blond hair. It seemed that almost everyone wore a uniform now and seemed proud of it. People, especially men, out of uniform were suspect. The representative explained that previously many civil defense workers had been conscientious objectors but this was no longer the case in the current army. Women were needed as nurses, as occupational therapists, for agriculture, for metal salvage and in the civil air patrol. Even though the government anticipated the end of the war in Europe, "manpower" was still needed. After he had made his selling points, we were requested to stand to ask our questions. I noticed that men were called upon first. Each time he finished answering a question, I stood up, in my nurse's uniform in the back row, but until everyone else had been called upon he did not call on me. I realized later that he probably thought I was a Negro like everyone else in the back row and that is why he called on me last. I was torn between the indignity that I personally felt from him and, the humiliation of my fellow Negroes, whom I had left to live a better life.

A few people left during the question period and I feared he might close the session without calling on me but finally, he said, "Woman in the back row, this will be the last question."

"Sir," I said, falling into old habitual deferential way with white men, but carefully speaking with my best "white" language, I said, "I am interested in working as an occupational therapist. I am already a graduate diploma nurse. Have you positions for such as myself?"

He was obviously surprised by my question. Other questions had mostly been about locations, wages and housing, nothing as specific as mine. "The Civil Service has just authorized consultant positions for occupational therapists." He went on to explain that, "Occupational therapists are categorized as 'sub-professionals', thus receiving no commission. You'd have to buy your uniform, pay rent for housing and pay for your meals unlike physical therapists and dieticians who do receive commissions in the Army. Oh, they let occupational therapists live with the nurses, but they had to pay for everything unlike PTs and dieticians. So you would be better to join as a nurse."

He did not allow for more questions. Apparently the librarian had signaled to him that it was closing time and that the winter curfew was immanent though blackouts were now over.

I weighed my options as I hurried back to the hospital where I now lived in a room for just two nurses rather than the student dormitory. My roommate and I were on different shifts so I seldom saw her or had to worry about awakening her when I entered.

CHAPTER 15

Choosing

Should I join the Civil Service and ask for the OT training program or should I join the Army Nursing Corp and be paid like a nurse and just take my chances at getting a posting where I could do occupational therapy. Or perhaps I should enter the new Army twelve-month occupational therapy training program. The patriotic zeal was in the air around me. I knew I wanted to help our country defeat her enemies.

Since my roommate and I seldom had time to talk as we were either too hurried or too tired, I had no confidante to whom I could appeal. I was not a religious person or perhaps I might talk to my pastor. In Chicago, I had been too busy working or training to find time for a regular church. I wished for Miss Alcorn but she was lost forever to me, who was now a white person. My betrayal of the Negro race would make me a pariah in her eyes. I felt sure she would feel as if it would be like a rejection of all her good teaching.

One afternoon, my dorm-room classmate, Glenda, who had also stayed on at Henrotin Hospital and I had a rare chance to sunbath on the roof of the hospital when I had a chance to discuss my choices with her. We seldom had shifts together but when we did, we sunbathed in the nude. Glenda remarked on how much more quickly I tanned than she did.

This day, as I was describing my career situation and the possible choices I could make, a low-flying airplane buzzed right over where we lay on towels on the flat roof. I looked up and saw the Army Air Corp. insignia painted on the side of the plane and the pilot and co-pilot were leaning as far as possible toward the windshield ogling us. We scrambled for our clothes after first thrusting the towels over ourselves realizing these towels wouldn't cover much. That was the last time we sunbathed nude as we knew they would go right back to the airbase and tell all their buddies to come have a look. We had a good laugh together. However, we continued to sunbath in our one piece swim suits. We waved at the "fly-boys" when they swooped down for a look. And Glenda ceased to ask me about why I never sunburned as we seldom had time for such a frivolity anymore.

There was an Army recruiting station near City Hall on Washington Street. The next time I had a whole day off from work; I walked there and addressed the young man behind the desk, who wore the three stripes of a staff sergeant. By now almost everybody I knew had learned to identify the rank of men in uniform. He was quite surprised to see me and stuttered as he responded to my questions. "I th-th-th-ink y-y-y-ou n-n n-eed t-t-o g-g-g-o to the of-f-f-f-ice on Michigan Ave." I realized just my presence made him nervous since he lost his stutter as he became accustomed to my presence.

"Please, could you write the address down for me?" I asked. It was obvious he was unused to having women volunteers come into his recruiting station.

Persevering, I found the office on Michigan Avenue, filled out the long pink application form. I never expected that I would be boarding a train within two weeks for Washington D. C. and Walter Reed Hospital where I entered into the new emergency training program for occupational therapy for the Army Medical Department as a civilian volunteer. The Bolton Bill, passed in December 1943, specified commissioned status only for nurses, physical therapists and dieticians. As an occupational therapist, I could be paid, but would not be able to have a rank or advancement like the dieticians and the physical therapists had. Although, a registered nurse with the special occupational therapy training, I could still have officer rank. I had not been tempted by these two other Army professions open to women. Occupational therapy was what I wanted to do. I wanted to be able to help the men returning from the battle front remember their skills from before the war or to help them learn new skills appropriate to their disabilities.

I cleared my stuff out of our room and said goodbye to Glenda while promising to write often. The train trip east was completely different from the one when I had arrived in Chicago in May 1941. Now in 1944, I said my goodbyes to the other nurses and took the El to the Loop to board a train north to Fort Sheridan.

When I arrived, I stayed in a barracks room with a number of other nurses and a couple dieticians on their way east. Each morning we were rousted for exercises before being marched to breakfast at the officers' mess in a special dining area designated for females. We were fitted for one basic WAC uniform. Fitted may be an exaggeration since they came off a shelf of ready-mades. Each day a few more women arrived. Finally, when they had gathered enough of us, we were given the notice to board a troop train. I had had the experience of getting along with other female workers in the nursing dormitory at Henrotin Hospital so I was not as uncomfortable as some of the other barracks occupants for whom this was their first experience in congregate living. Before long we were becoming comrades who protected each other from wolf whistles of the men when we had to leave the barracks. During the 1930s, the term "comrades" had been poisoned by the communist hunters, but it most closely describes how close we became as we headed for the war. We all wanted to help win the war which had been going on three years already.

We females were given a car of our own at the end behind the cars full of men. The mess hall sent a canvas bag full of sandwiches, cookies and fruit for us to eat on the train. There was also a box of C Rations in case we ran out of the fresh food. As we went south through Chicago, each station we stopped at there was a mad scene of troops pushing to board. We were glad to be in our own car. Eventually, our car was attached to a troop train on the New York Central Railway. We slept upright in our seats during our two nights on the train. Few complained of the discomfort though we felt it. The sparely furnished passenger car sometimes swung from side to side making walking to the toilet difficult. The seats were hard, unpadded benches with an aisle down the middle. Since it was now almost summer, most of us just sat on our coats or sweaters to cushion ourselves against the wooden slates of the benches. The sixteen hours that it took from Union Station to Washington D. C. was extremely tiring but not as much as our future training would be.

Some of the girls had jumped off in Chicago Union Station and purchased The Chicago Tribune which they brought on board and took turns reading aloud. Meat rationing had just ended so there were notices about this change. U. S. Troops were on their way toward Rome, fighting their way up the Italian

Peninsula. A few of the girls had fiancés posted to the Mediterranean so they were particularly interested in the Italian front.

I had had only a few social encounters with men during my years in Chicago, because I was still too new at being a white girl to feel comfortable when white boys or men asked for my company. I certainly avoided colored men as evading being a Negro in the past had taken so much planning and energy that I could not risk that anyone think I was somehow associated with Negroes. Besides, I was usually so tired from my hospital work that I had no energy to be bored or to be tempted to seek a broader social life. I listened to these girls talking about their boyfriends and future husbands, trying to learn how it felt to have such a committed person to think about. I had nursed young men in the hospital who regularly made suggestive remarks to me. Part of our training had been on how to respond when men made such suggestions to us. I am grateful for this training. In Selma, the only interactions I had had with white men had been in my custodian role, not someone to speak to as an equal.

The woman sharing the seat with me near the back of the train car was also a nurse heading for physical therapy training at Walter Reed Hospital. Her name, Cassandra Amari, sounded so exotic. She was shorter than me and her skin was about the same color but her soft hair was black and curly. She told me she was Italian and from Chicago. As we traveled along through the countryside, we shared our anxieties about the new professions for which we were going to train.

I explained, "If I weren't already a nurse, and just trained as an occupational therapist I would not be able to have officer status. That seems kind of unfair to me since in the last war, occupational therapists and physical therapists had the same status."

"Well, I guess when so many men began to come back with amputations and such severe wounds, that they decided that now they wanted PTs immediately," Cassandra explained thoughtfully. "I enjoy nursing but after I visited a physical therapy department in the Ft. Sheridan Infirmary, I knew I would like that work better than bedside nursing. How about you? Why are you training in OT?"

Now I found it necessary to fabricate a story. I just couldn't bring myself to risk telling about Aunt Beulah and my research in the Carnegie Library. I might slip and somehow reveal that Aunt Beulah was Negro or that I was a floor mopper in the library that Negros couldn't enter otherwise. "Well, I went to a civil service lecture at the Newberry Library and the man described occupational therapy," I replied simply.

We began to feel more comfortable as we shared our stories; however, there was so much of my early life that I felt I could never share with another white person.

After we passed out of the Chicago area, turning toward the east around the tip of Lake Michigan, we began to see farmland from the windows, though the Lake was still visible from the windows on the north side of the car as we crossed into Indiana. Since it was a troop train, it did not stop at all the little towns through which it passed. However, it stopped at the South Bend Station for us to exit the train and get coffee and sandwiches at the nearby USO. It was late afternoon, our train having left Ft. Sheridan about noon.

The soldiers from the other cars seemed not to distinguish us from the USO girls. Dance music was playing from a Victrola in the corner of the huge room. Cakes, coffee and sandwiches were set up on a length of end-to-end sawhorse-tables covered with sheets. The men were confused about whether or not to be gentlemen and encourage us US Army women to go to the tables first or whether to rush toward the USO girls behind the tables in their eagerness to interact with females after several weeks of all male company. The USO girls were only too happy to dance with these soldiers who were starved for female company. Apparently were never enough USO girls to go around so the men also rushed to us Army nurse trainees and swept us out unto the dance floor in the middle of the room. Before too many minutes, the train whistle gave a warning hoot and bedlam ensued as we all rushed for our carriages, swallowing coffee and grabbing sandwiches for the trip.

CHAPTER 16

Washington

We stopped in Washington D. C. at the station nearest to Walter Reed Army Hospital. The small bit of marching we had done at Ft. Sheridan now became useful, as we were expected to march to the dormitory barracks on the hospital grounds. We women marched in front followed by the fellows from the other train cars. The police stopped the traffic in the streets and intersections as we marched. The weather was already warm and muggy. It began to sprinkle rain near the end of this march. We were all carrying our packs with our meager possessions that we had been allowed to bring. The civil service enrollees were directed to a different barracks from those of us who would be WACs.

After depositing our packs on our bunks, we were immediately marched off to the hospital cafeteria for a meal. It was good to eat something besides sandwiches and C Rations. Afterward, we gladly lay on our bunks after sitting up for almost thirty-six hours. The bunks were set against the two long barracks walls with the heads against the walls between the windows. Blackout curtains rolled down like window shades. The aisle between the bunks was about three feet wide between the foot ends.

I immediately discovered that Cassandra's bunk was just across the aisle from mine. In the few minutes between our heavy schedules, we sometimes put our heads at the foot of our bunks and whispered to each other across the aisle about our patients, our complaints and our anticipations for our future work. It was necessary to keep our voices down as someone was always trying to sleep in this barracks. Almost every one was suffering from fatigue from our heavy work and study schedule. In a room with twenty bunks, there was always some coughing or mild snoring, but a human voice had the power to awaken and irritate more than general noise it seemed. Cassandra and I were warned to "Shut up" more than once when we forgot to modulate our voices. She soon became "Cassie" as we knew each other better.

The next morning after we arrived, a stern looking Women's Army Corp Captain opened our door and shouted to us to "Roust out and bring your orders."

After a rushed breakfast of scrambled eggs, which I later learned were made from powdered eggs, and toast and coffee, we were herded into a basement room where shelves held stacks of uniforms. A half-wall divided the men's section from the smaller women's section. We stood in line awaiting our turn to be issued a nurse's uniform, stockings, shoes, undergarments and a nurses' WAC cap.

The training for the occupational therapists took place in the basement of one of the buildings toward the rear of the main hospital building. The nurses had enlisted in the Army, but a number of the others were civilian volunteers who were in a different category, as they were ineligible as occupational therapists to be officers. Most of these had been art teachers or social workers before volunteering for this emergency civil service occupational therapy program. A sort of hierarchy developed and we nurse occupational therapists knew we had more status.

In addition to regular morning calisthenics and running around the hospital grounds with a thirty pound pack, our curriculum included classes in woodworking, printing, art principles, ceramics, leather-work and about how men with disabilities could benefit from adaptations in these main crafts. The trainees who were not nurses had additional classes in anatomy and disease processes but no calisthenics or running. We all had further training in working with amputees since so many of the men who had returned from the battle fronts had lost a limb.

The nurses in the emergency training program were not allowed to have a lighter schedule than the civilian volunteers, though the nurses had already had anatomy and learned symptoms of the various diseases. When we were not in lectures or craft laboratories, we were assigned to work as nurses in the regular hospital or we trained in putting up pup tents, making stretchers from our own uniforms, or crawling on our stomachs across the parade grounds.

My first assignment was in the orthopedic ward. Here amputees were cared for and sent to the physical and occupational therapy clinics to have fittings or training for using their prostheses. When eventually our occupational therapy training allowed us to minimally participate in the regular OT clinic, I was already acquainted with many of the patients from having nursed them on that ward. Some of the other nurses in our group did their hospital shifts on the infectious disease and psychiatric wards. Eventually, about halfway through this year of training, I was reassigned to nursing on the psychiatric ward. I quickly discovered that this population, which included a great number of "battle fatigue" patients, was much more challenging than the patients with simply a missing limb.

Some of the psychiatric patients were immobilized by their war trauma. They sat quietly without expression and did not respond to suggestions for craft activities. Others were extremely sensitive to noise and would fall to the floor if a metal tool was dropped. Extreme irritability characterized many patients on this ward. Eventually, when they became more trusting of me and I became friendlier with some of these men, they described for me the horrors they could remember of the battlefield. I found when they were able to sit still and tell me of the noise, of the comrades they saw killed before their eyes, of the bombs and bullets that tore up the earth around them; they often became altogether calmer afterward.

During the last three months of my training, I was relieved of ward duty and spent all my time not in lectures and labs, but in the morning occupational therapy clinic with the amputees. There I taught various crafts on using special equipment. In the afternoons, I worked with the "battle fatigue" patients. Some evenings, I took advantage of the clinic sewing machine and made myself one civilian blue rayon gabardine suit like the ones advertised on the newspaper fashion page. It was on such an evening when the radio, which was on most of the time when anyone was in the clinic so we could get the war news, announced that the Allied invasion force had successfully landed on the beaches in Normandy and they were on their way toward Germany. For several days, this was the only topic of conversation for both patients and therapists.

At first I was more nervous about working with

amputees, fearful that I would not be able to figure out how to adapt machines or tools to allow them to complete a craft while wearing their prosthesis. Later, I discovered that the intricacies of the damaged mind are more puzzling than those of the body. The damaged body is so concrete: either it is partially absent, or will no longer work properly. With the mind, almost nothing visual tells the therapist what is required to help the soldier. However, I found the mysteries of the mind more compelling to me than damaged bodies.

With such a heavy schedule, we seldom had time to visit the sights of our Capitol, though one afternoon early in the fall when I had five hours off, I persuaded Cassie, the physical therapy student, to come with me. We got on the train in order to go to make the walk from the U. S. Capitol up Constitution Avenue to look at the White House. By the time we got there, it was time to find the other train station to return to Walter Reed Hospital to get some sleep before our next shift in the clinic.

CHAPTER 17

Hawaii

In summer 1944, I was finally posted along with a couple other nurses who had finished the emergency occupational therapy program. We went to Letterman Hospital in San Francisco to await shipment to hospitals in the Pacific. A few went to Alaska but most of us were sent to join the 148th General Hospital which was called a secret destination. On board the ship, we were required to attend calisthenics, other kinds of exercises for "on board" emergencies, amateur shows, and glee club when we were not hanging over the rail in seasickness. When we got to Honolulu, we were quartered in barracks which were really converted classrooms at old St. Louis College. We were given lessons in Hawaiian language. A hula dancer, who regularly performed with the Royal Hawaiian band, came and gave us a few hula lessons. I compared the tone of her skin to mine and decided hers was darker.

After about ten days, eight of us were commanded to board another smaller ship which took us to Hilo. I was the only occupational therapist. Cassandra had been assigned to this group too, along with six nurses and Wanda Lindley, the dietician. It had been in Honolulu just long enough for our bodies to readjust to being on land so we all had to endure seasickness over again, but that voyage was just overnight.

We arrived at mid-day. Trucks met us at the Wharf and we loaded into the back. As we drove up the narrow highway toward our new hospital in the school which had been requisitioned by the Army, it began to rain. The driver and his assistant with difficulty, found a place to pull off the narrow road and a canvas cover was installed over the truck bed where we sat on wooden benches with our grips on the floor. The road had almost no shoulder so the truck was half in the road and teetering on the edge of a rock ledge.

After an hour on the winding road between dense vegetation in the rain, the driver slowed and yelled out the window to us to look to our left and see the school house that was the first building which the Army had taken over for a hospital. Then he shifted and ground the gears to climb further up the hill through a village and stopped before some low cottages. Somehow, none of us were prepared for this kind of weather, so as the driver and his assistant handed us down, we ran down a gravel path to the tiny porch that covered the door of the nearest cottages. A woman in a nurse's First Lieutenant uniform beckoned us inside. By the time we had all gotten inside, the entryway floor was very wet. The lieutenant assigned us to bunks informing us that the cottages had recently been named Hale Koa, translated as "Brave Soldiers' House." The bunks were more spacious than those on the ship or the dormitory at St. Louis College. Cassie, the blond dietician Wanda and I were assigned to the bunks in the room furthest from the door since we had special assignments and were not likely to be called for emergency services for patients. Our other roommate was Lt. Sisco, a nurse, already in residence.

After drying ourselves off and stowing our bags under or near our bunks, we were issued umbrellas and led on a cement covered walkway to a bungalow for chow. Before we ate, Lt. Sisco led us on a tour of the house where the doctors had their own dining room, but all of the nurses, the dietician, and both of us, the physical and the occupational therapist also ate together in another dining room. We were the only ones in the dining room this time, as the other nurses would eat after their shifts. The food was very similar to what had been served to us in the mess-hall at Walter Reed Army Hospital. However, the cook had managed to get the nearby plantation manager to donate some fresh bananas.

The Army had also gotten some boxes of pineapples from the Island of Maui which had arrived on one of the inter-island ships that had also, like the school house, been taken over by the military. These two fruits were plentiful here and really porked up our otherwise repetitive meals of creamed dried beef on toast, canned meat, canned vegetables and the eternal mashed potatoes. I missed okra and yams, but I missed little else about Selma. My three years in Chicago had blurred but not erased some of my Selma memories.

As we fell into our bunks after the bumpy rainy trip in the back of the truck, Cassie said to me, "I don't know about this living out in the wilds of the jungle. I've only lived in cities before."

I started to blurt out, "This is almost like the Black Belt in Alabama." Then I remembered to edit my speech. I wondered when I would ever be done with the burden of always stifling my first impulse when I spoke with a friend. I wondered what Cassie and Wanda would say if they knew they were sleeping in the same room with a "black" woman. I had not participated in the talk much at Walter Reed about the "Black troops" but I had listened and knew that segregation was observed in the Army, except when Colored troops had a White officer, but even then, he slept in his own room, not with the Black men he trained and supervised.

Even though the various cities I had lived in during the last three years had been under "Black

Out" status, there were usually some level of low lights such as the unpainted lower half of car headlights so people driving and walking could find their way. Out here in the jungle, or at least that is what it felt like to most of us, the night was without light. Hawaii Island was still considered a possible bombing target and thus "blackout" was severely enforced. Country skies were blacker than the cities where I had been living for the past three years and despite blackouts and we were definitely out in the country. The windows had blackout curtains and hardly any light seeped in around the edges. The windows were open slightly on the bottom and during the night whenever I awoke, I could hear rain or wind whipping the nearby foliage. Despite the strangeness of these rain forest sounds, I slept soundly until the inevitable "Roust out."

CHAPTER 18

Mouuntain View

Promptly at 600 hours the next morning, Nurse Sullivan, Captain Sullivan as I came to call her, was the one to shout "Roust out, ladies." Over the next months, I came to know my commanding officer rather well. Practical Captain Sullivan was from Kansas. She had been a nurse for almost twenty years. As was common in the twenties, she had to fight with her mother in order to join the profession. Her mother had a bad opinion of nurses until Miss Sullivan persuaded her through stories of Florence Nightingale and the heroines of WWI of the nobleness of the calling.

"Lieutenant Brett, after breakfast, I will take you on a complete walking tour of the hospital. Better wear some galoshes over your white shoes. There are puddles everywhere. Lt. Amari, you come along, too."

We met Captain Sullivan outside the dining room

and we sluiced our way down the gravel path leading behind the corpsman's barracks and the cemetery. Captain Sullivan used her sturdy Government Issue umbrella to hold the huge fern fronds away from our faces as we splashed through accumulations of muddy water. The umbrella sometimes caught a rib on a frond threatening to collapse the umbrella.

Finally, when the hem of the skirt of my white nurse's uniform was quite soaked despite the black Government Issue rain slicker, we arrived at the wooden awning over the Section Eight Barracks doorway where this story started.

Immediately after our rain-soaked tour of the hospital grounds which had formerly been the Mountain View School, Captain Sullivan led us across a road and walked us up through the village center which included a bakery, a theatre, a post office and small shops. Close packed workers' cottages lined the other side of the road. I could hear the growl and rattle of a nearby train. Captain Sullivan pointed across a vacant lot crisscrossed with paths through the vegetation to the roof of the railroad station. Though few people were on the rainy road in the village, I became aware that most were oriental looking with a few Army uniforms scattered here and there.

Nurse Sullivan delivered us back to our cottage in time to join the others to tramp through the wet to the dining room for the mid-day meal. "Your first shift starts tonight at eleven, Lt. Brett. Private

Wilson will call for you about 10:30 PM to walk with you to Section Eight. A rule here is that nurses do not walk alone. A corpsman will always accompany you unless you are walking with another nurse. There are too many soldiers around here who haven't seen an American woman for a long time, so be careful!" With that she gave me an answering salute and started to disappear in the rain. After I became familiar with this camp, I frequently broke this rule about walking alone as an occupational therapist I could not always find someone to accompany me as my shift did not coincide with the nurses.

I protested, "I was sent to work as an occupational therapist and nobody was going to be awake to do crafts during the night shift."

She turned back. "I like all my nurses and other medical specialists to start out working a regular shift till they know the patients and the set-up here. Besides, the recreation room where you'll be doing crafts isn't quite cleared out for you yet. I read your 'Service Record Booklet' & '201 File' and I know you are also a nurse. So for a few nights you'll have to work as a regular nurse, not an occupational therapist."

Inwardly, I grumbled to myself about "Following orders." I also realized that much of the Army was "Taking Orders" whether or not I agreed with them. So with as good grace as I could force myself to express, I saluted and answered, "Yes, Ma'am!" Captain Sullivan did not seem to be aware if there was any tartness or sarcasm in my response or if she did, she ignored it.

After a noontime dinner of fried Spam, rice and canned corn, I returned with those not assigned to a shift and took the opportunity to divest myself of my dripping outer-wear and change into my pajamas. I tried to warm myself in my bunk and fell asleep before I knew it.

I awoke in the dark to a knock on the cottage door and a male voice shouting, "Lieutenant Brett, I'm here to escort you to Section Eight." I realized he dare not stick his head in this women's haven.

I swung my feet over and walked on the slightly damp feeling floor to the door, opened it a crack and whispered, "I'll be ready in a minute." I didn't want him shouting and waking up any of the other staff. I could not see as there were no lights outside either. Black out rules of course!

I dressed in the dark including my garter belt and white stockings. Some nurses wore slacks but since they had only been allowed in June, I had not had time to get ones that fit. I had plans to get some soon in the Post Exchange in Hilo.

The rain had stopped but the wet fern fronds still frequently flapped me in the face as we walked the same route I had gone with Captain Sullivan in the morning. Fortunately Private Wilson had a flashlight which he beamed on the ground in front of him. The path was only wide enough to walk single file so I kept my eyes on the ground between his legs following the small circle of light provided by the flashlight.

Private Wilson knocked on the Section Eight barracks door, and then swung it open for me to enter. He asked, "Would you like me to bring you some coffee?" Gratefully, I nodded my head indicating my acceptance, hoping he could see me in the dimness. The door closed behind me and I blinked to try to readjust my eyes to the dim light coming from a small lamp on the nurse's desk. Dour Nurse Wagner lifted her head off the desk and blinked to wake herself up. Slowly she stood up and opened a drawer to retrieve her purse. She picked up a clipboard and handed it to me silently indicating the list of patient names and bed numbers. She pointed to a bell on the wall which had a tag under it which read EMERGENCY BELL. "It will call the corpsman if necessary," she whispered. Then she silently closed the door after herself. She would be pretty if she'd just smile, I thought to myself.

I heard a few of the men move around on their bunks, turn over or sigh. It was too dark to see if any of them were really awake and watching me. I felt a little uncomfortable being unable to determine this. Beginning to examine the list which also had a column of abbreviations for each patient's diagnosis and another for their medications, I settled down behind the desk. About an hour later, Private Wilson returned with a thermos of coffee but no cream or sugar. I searched through the desk drawers and found a small jar of sugar. Not knowing to whom it belonged, I helped myself anyway, figuring it was all Government Issue.

Fortunately my first night here alone, except for Private Wilson, in this barracks of twenty sick men, passed uneventfully. Twelve hours later, after the corpsman and I had distributed breakfast from a covered food cart pushed over the rough gravelly walkway from the kitchen by another corpsmen, Nurse Wagner reappeared to relieve me. I was very glad to see her as I had not had the responsibility of dispensing medicine for some time and was glad she arrived in time to do it.

A different corpsman, a Private Stilley, was waiting outside with a Government Issue umbrella. I was grateful for his strong arm holding the heavy-weight umbrella over me as we trudged back up the hill to the nurses' cottage. He saluted me as he went on to his own barracks. It still took me somewhat aback to have white men saluting me. For sixteen years I had been black and I had only been white for three years.

CHAPTER 19

The Hospital on the Hill

My orientation to this Army Hospital in Mountain View was not a formal affair for me since I was the only occupational therapist-nurse. I learned incidentally that this hospital housed 300 patients and had sixty nurses. Many had the diagnosis of malaria while those in the Section 8 Psychiatric barracks most of which had "battle fatigue." The treatment for the mosquito diseases was just rest and good food while making sure that the patients drank plenty of water and juice. Aspirin was also used to reduce the fevers. The treatment for "battle fatigue" was what I was trying to figure out.

Much of my time would be spent in the recreation center as that is where the bicycle saw and pottery wheel would be set up. I also hoped to spend several hours a day seeing if I could get the "battle fatigue" patients occupied with worthwhile projects in their barracks.

I learned from the other nurses that Captain Sullivan had only been on the job as the director of nurses a coupled months. Previously, the famous Chief Nurse Edith Aynes had been transferred to Washington, DC to the Surgeon General's Office. Lieutenant Wagner had been the interim chief nurse until Captain Sullivan was assigned to the Hospital on the Hill," She was still figuring out what her role was expected to be with the constantly changing regulations regarding women in the service. Perhaps this was the reason for some of the hostility I felt between them on my first day's visit to Section Eight barracks.

A few days later Captain Sullivan notified me that I was relieved of my nursing duties so I could arrange for the opening of the recreation room where I was expected to get the patients to do occupational therapy crafts and games. I was thrilled to comply, to be relieved of the rather boring nighttime duty.

The clearing out of the recreation room advanced quickly as soon as I took it upon myself to go and watch and ask questions. I got the corpsmen to find some tables, chairs and work benches. A wooden container arrived with hand tools for woodworking, for gardening and for the parts to assemble for a bicycle saw, a bicycle pottery wheel and a bicycle drill. There were tools but no craft materials yet so I got permission to take the train with another nurse from the Mountain View Railroad Station to Hilo to shop for ingredients for white modeling clay, and firebricks for assembling a kiln and some seeds for gardening. The other nurse surveyed the drug and medical supplies available in the civilian drug stores; Shindo Drugs, Machida Drugs, Chock Chong Drugs, and Hilo Drugs this last which had the ones with which we were more familiar. We observed Nurse Sullivan's injunction to go in pairs, never go out alone. This was a good thing as the streets of Hilo had a number of leering service men.

One of the several blacksmiths helped me find the firebricks. The local woods such as koa, mango and ohia were plentiful though the bicycle saw found the ohia was so hard it was impervious to its blade.

Local merchants were glad to work with the Army. I made several visits to Beamer Hardware, Hilo Dry Goods, S. H. Kress, and a number of others. They were glad to run a tab for the Army. Everybody was trying to make some money in the seeming time of plenty with the presence of the military. I persuaded the Hawaiian woman at Lauhala Shop on Kamehameha Avenue on another occasions to teach me how to make the beautifully woven fans and hats. She eventually taught me how to harvest the leaves and prepare them for weaving. We were able to find the Post Exchange where I bought a rain cape to protect me from Mountain View's daily shower as the GI Issue umbrellas were heavy and cumbersome to use if I was carrying something to the recreation room. I also got my slacks.

I was eager to get started using the new bicycle potter's wheel so I wondered if there was a source of indigenous clay to be found on Hawaii Island. In each store I entered, I inquired if the merchant knew of a place to get potter's clay. Finally, in the Enseki Blacksmith Shop, I learned with difficulty as I tried to understand the Japanese man's pidgin English, that on Oahu Island, in the early 1930's, some clay had been discovered in the mountains, but on Hawaii Island, I would find only lava rock. As soon as I returned to the Hospital, I requested that some potter's clay be sent from San Francisco. Why had they sent a wheel without the clay? Oh, well, it was the Army way, I guess.

I asked for Cassandra Amari, the physical therapist to go with me after the first trip. Nurse Sullivan recommended that we request a jeep from the motor pool rather than using civilian transportation such as the train. The driver could substitute for a corpsman. That way we would not have to wait for delivery of any supplies I was able to sign for in Hilo. This seemed a good idea to me as we would not have to carry heavy supplies back on the train. I wished I had had the opportunity to learn to drive but instead I would have to rely on a driver from the motor pool. Cassandra did not drive either. They were very strict about us not going alone. While fraternization with enlisted men was forbidden, I had heard more than one nurse's tale of enlisted men threatening to hold women hostage unless they participated in sex.

Captain Sullivan sent a message to the motor pool for a driver to pick us up at the recreation room. It was a short walk down the hill from the nurses' barracks and since the rain had stopped, we walked quickly before another of Mt. View's unpredictable showers could catch us. As anticipated the jeep showed up almost as we reached the shelter of the small roof over the doorway, along with the rain.

We ran around to the passenger side of the jeep glad the canvas cover was already in place. I jumped in the back on a jump seat and Cassandra sat in the passenger seat. The rain on the roof of the jeep was so loud that I shouted to the private that we could start driving.

"Yes, ma'am," he shouted back as he thrust the vehicle into gear moving ahead jerkily. We bounced along the gravel finally rolling unto the hard top road. The noise slightly lessened but it was still too noisy to try to speak easily. I could see the soldier eyeing me in the mirror from under the Army cap pulled down as far as possible and sneaking looks at Cassandra from the corner of his eye, but steering the vehicle took most of his attention. Some of the rain blew sideways in upon us below the canvas, but the rain gradually decreased and disappeared altogether as we passed the Sako Store.

The driver reached behind the seat and tossed Cassandra a towel to wipe off her face and wet legs and shoes. She passed it back to me but I had not gotten as wet as she had. Finally the driver spoke,

"Where we goin' in Hilo? The paper order just said take a nurse shoppin' in Hilo."

This voice sounded familiar in the recesses of my mind. I looked up at the private. Slow recognition came to me. It was Woodrow Minter, our class Knox High School valedictorian driving this jeep. Our eyes met in the mirror but we both kept silent as the full import of recognizing each other as Negroes passing in our white mans' Army struggled with the recognition. Acknowledging each other could destroy both of us, no matter that Cassandra was my friend. I could never ask her to protect our secret even if she were willing which I did not know. Nonetheless, I was wild with curiosity to know how Woodrow had accomplished his disguise. I would be forced to be patient until another time to satisfy my desire to know how he ended up here. Memories of his devious ways in high school arose in my mind, but who was I to accuse him of deviousness?

As I exited the jeep upon returning to Mountain View, I allowed Cassandra to get out, before I turned back saying, "Please deliver these supplies to the recreation room. Did I drop my pencil?" and as I searched around the passenger seat, I dropped a note on the seat

"Sunday, meet me in the cemetery behind the ferns after breakfast."

CHAPTER 20

Fall 1944

The good news of the Allied takeover of the Island of Guam in August lifted everyone's spirits. It truly felt like we might be starting to win this war which had started in such ignominy at Pearl Harbor almost four years ago. We wondered if we might receive any patients from those battles who undoubtedly would be sent to Hawaii on their way back to America. Nursing reinforcements arrived from the United States.

Captain Sullivan sent orders that relieved me of all nursing duties in order to be able to dedicate myself full time to rehabilitation of patients. While I busied myself with initiating activities with patients in Section 8 and the Rec. Room, my mind was preoccupied with my wondering about Woodrow. Fortunately, I was learning about the various patients such as Arne Erickson. This diverted me from obsessing about Woodrow.

Arne was a soldier who had been one of the few who dared to look back at me that first day I had entered Section 8. Obviously, he was not as apathetic or fearful as his barracks mates as his "Hubba, hubba!" indicated. He was an aviation artist and a patient after the Battle of the Coral Sea, spring 1942. Arne was one of the some 2700 men rescued from the sea along with the captain's dog when the Japanese sank the aircraft carrier USS Lexington. He had watched several of the two-hundred-sixteen men who died during that battle as they expired. All his paintings and art materials had sunk in the sea. His diagnosis was "battle fatigue."

I had surprised him one day as he tried to slip his drawing under the bed-covers as I passed by his bunk. "OK, soldier," I addressed him, hiding my anxiety about challenging a patient. "What's that you are hiding under the sheet?"

Thus confronted, Arne sheepishly, drew out the sheet of paper. Guffaws resounded from the few non-sleeping or non-catatonic patients as I realized it was a cartoon of me with much enhanced breasts and derriere. Apparently he had been displaying it to the other patients while I bent over trying to show another patient a simple leather wallet lacing project that he could work on while sitting on his bunk.

I considered being outraged but knew that that was what these men would enjoy. So I simply said, "Why thank you Sergeant Erickson. I am complimented," as I handed the paper back to him. "You are good enough to be in the Red Ryder cartoon, or at least in Wash Tubbs." I knew the men passed these cartoons from the Hilo Tribune-Herald newspaper around amongst them.

This put the attention back on Arne as the men now guffawed in his direction. It was obvious to me that it would be in my best interest to use humor rather than anger or sarcasm with these suffering men.

Sunday morning came and as many as possible of the patients and staff who could attend church did so as there were so few diversions in this village. Several services were held as the church was so small. Some marines from the training camp down the hill on Kukui Road also attended services. A few brave soldiers went to the Buddhist Temple to sample this very different service. Despite the December 7, 1941 bombing of Pearl Harbor on Oahu, the temple had been allowed to continue to have services. The Chaplain held services in the recreation center. I had pushed tools and furniture out of the way for him last evening and had gotten the corpsman to arrange the chairs. We had left a space near the door for the wheelchair patients.

This meant that few people were around on this rare sunny day to see me go down to the Japanese Cemetery to meet Woodrow by the cluster of huge hapu`u tree ferns nears the southeast corner. I was not sure he had gotten the note as I had not looked back after I left the jeep and he had sent no communication to me. There was a cluster of the huge hapu`u tree ferns near the south east corner.

After breakfast, I went back to the nurses' cottages on this my one day off and watched until the other nurses were either sleeping or writing letters. I slipped out without saying goodbye or explaining where I was going. The back trail which had been well-cleared on both sides when the hospital was first opened in the school in spring of 1942. The abundant rain in Mountain View had caused all the greenery to grow up again along the sides of the gravel and mud trail. I carried an umbrella despite the rare sunshine. Occasionally I gave furtive looks behind and around me to make sure I was unobserved. Finally I went off the trail and slipped over the low rock wall to disappear behind the ferns. No one was there.

I feared that Woodrow might not know the location of this cemetery. Perhaps he thought I meant the Catholic Cemetery rather than the Japanese Cemetery as I had not specified. Not being sure what time he was served his breakfast, I decided to wait at least an hour. I checked the time on my nurse's watch pin. It was almost 830 hours. Despite the sunshine, there was no dry place to sit. I had a novel I was reading Blackbirds on the Lawn by Jane Norton, one of the year's new bestsellers. It had been left in the barracks. WACs had been allowed to wear slacks when Major Julia Flikke had been persuaded to allow it in 1943. Consequently, I wore slacks as often as possible now so I just squatted behind the ferns to read the novel while I waited.

I had pondered finding Woodrow here many times since I stepped out of the jeep. None the less, I was too nervous to really concentrate on the novel. I was nervous about being discovered here, especially as we females were not supposed to go off alone.

Suddenly, he pushed aside the huge fern leaves and appeared from down the hill. "Well, well, Lieutenant Brett, where did Lulu Norris go?"

I was startled because I had expected him to appear from up the hill. "Well, are you still called Minter? I had to change my name. Anybody from the South would know that Tallulah Beulah Norris was a Negro name."

He slipped into Dallas County vernacular as he said, "Nah, I'm still Woodrow Minter. Nobody in Los Angeles knew that Minters were all black in Dallas County. But ain't it strange, us two Niggras from Selma ending up here in Hawaii being white?" His sarcasm surprised me as I had never known him to be like that in high school, but we were never friends.

I had not particularly planned what I would say when we actually met. It seemed just most natural to ask, "I hope I can trust you to keep my race a secret from this white Army. Can we make a bargain to guard each other's secret?"

He mockingly saluted me, "Why Lieutenant Brett, you can trust me. Looks like we're both holding each other over a barrel! I guess we both have to trust each other."

Despite his smarty answer, I was kind of amazed that the well-mannered, though sneaky boy from Knox High School now seemed so worldly, well, not worldly exactly, but rather white trashy.

CHAPTER 21

The Woodrow's Story

"How did a nice Negro boy from Selma end up in this white man's Army?" I asked somewhat archly.

"Wa'll there, Nilla Wafer, how come you think you have the right to question me on passing?"

"Oh, come on, Woodrow; tell me how you were able to fool them. I'll tell if you will," I said closing the book.

"Looks like we're both holding this big lie over each other's heads, huh? Should we make a pact to protect each other's story?"

I was so curious about him and his situation, that I impulsively promised, "OK, I promise not to tell if you do, too. But what is your story?"

Woodrow squatted on his haunches near me just off the cemetery path. "Wa'll back in Selma you always kept to yourself so much I never knew much about you. I figured since you were lighter than me, you thought you were better than me. Course, since you're an officer, I guess you ARE better than me."

I stood up slowly, as my knees were not used to squatting. "Woodrow, you know we are not supposed to be associating anyway, so I guess all that 'rank' stuff is out the window now since we're breaking Army regulations. Let's just pretend we're meeting each other for the first time. Tell me about yourself as if we'd never met before, OK?"

I could almost see his mind considering whether or not to tell me the truth as the old sly expression I remembered from high school flitted across his face. But he realized I was watching him and he quickly remade his face into a mask of sincerity. "You want the version about my mulatto mamma or the one about my white grand-pappy?"

"Oh come-on, Woodrow, pretend you never met me before and tell me that one. I want to know how you got into this white man's Army."

"Well, Nilla Wafer, you remember Uniontown over in Perry County? My great grand-pappy was a white manager over there at Fairhope Plantation. He slept in the house when the master took the cotton to New Orleans or when he went off to fight the Civil War."

Since I knew so little about my white antecedents, I wondered how Woodrow knew all this about his. "How do you know who your white great grand-pappy was? My mother certainly never wanted to talk about my white relatives."

Woodrow went on, "Well, my great grandmamma was a house slave and she had four children with Seth Russell, my great-grand-pappy, the Fairhope manager."

We both knew that having children with the master was more prestigious than having them with the manager. If Woodrow really wanted to make-up a story I expect he would have said his great-grand-pappy was the master. This inclined me more to believe him. But I kept my counsel and encouraged him to go on by nodding my head in acknowledgement.

"After the civil war my great-grandmamma left the plantation and came to live in Selma where she got work as a cook. In those hard times after the war, she took up, according to my mamma, with one of those carpetbagger men who came from up North. They had one baby before he got driven off by the end of Reconstruction. That baby was my grandpa. According to Mama, he was about the same color as me." Woodrow said this with something like pride.

"So you are only a quadroon, aren't you Woodrow? You're almost white." I knew I was stepping on uncertain ground, saying this, as Negroes of Selma almost never talked about things like this with people they didn't know well. The ambiguity of our race was confusing, and I was envious that he could recount his ancestry where I could not. He bested me again like being the valedictorian when I had really deserved to be it.

"Grandpa met-up with a dark brown woman in Mobile while he was working on a cotton boat on the Tombigbee River. So Mamma's browner than me but lighter than her mamma. I never met my daddy. Mamma just told me stories about him. He worked on a ship that sailed all over the Gulf of Mexico and sometimes to South America. Sometimes he sailed up to Selma on the Alabama River. He was Spanish from Cuba and came to see my mamma every time he docked in Selma. That's why my skin is lighter than my mamma's."

I held my tongue but my immediate reaction was to wonder if his mother was a part-time prostitute in addition to being a cook. I tucked this bit of information back in my mind to explore at a later time. I don't remember anyone in Selma telling me about prostitutes as my mother was so strict about what she discussed with me. Since living in dormitories with nurses and other WAC girls, I had come to realize how isolated I had been as a child.

While this tracing of his bloodlines was interesting to me, I was also very aware that our being together here was against regulations so I wanted him to get on to the adventure of joining the white man's Army. "Tell me about how you fooled them to get in the Army," I encouraged.

"Mamma wanted me to go to Tuskegee Institute but I knew I would be branded 'black' forever if I did that. So as soon as I realized that, I decided I'd join the white man's army. I knew I'd have to be really white so I started sneaking some of my mother's Scott's Face Bleach and Beautifier."

I scrutinized him as he talked realizing that he was slightly darker than he had been at graduation but it was the kind of skin I had seen often here in Hawaii. He fit right in here on this island. I couldn't keep myself from breaking into his story to ask, "Haven't any of the other soldiers questioned you about it? "

"Nah! Lot's of these guys have tanned more here in Hawaii. They just figure I'm getting darker from the sun. I don't use skin whitener anymore. I'm afraid somebody might catch me at it."

I wondered aloud, "Which one of us has the most to lose if we get caught?"

He ignored my question and went on with his story. "I knew I couldn't join the Army there in Selma, and I couldn't get no jobs there in Dallas County. I knew if I tried to join the WPA (Works Progress Administration) in Alabama, I'd be sent to a Negro camp. So I decided to hop a train to California and join the WPA where they didn't know me. Lots of fellas had done that before and I'd met some. So I waited till the freight train to York came through about midnight. It slows right before the bridge, so I jumped on there."

"Maybe you'll have to finish your story another day. I'm afraid somebody's going to come down that path and find us," I interrupted.

"Well I'll tell this part quick: I got to join up with the WPA guys building the new hangar at the Oxford Airport in Ventura County, California. After Pearl Harbor was bombed almost all the fellas decided to join up. I did too and went to the army office in Oxnard in January. By then the hanger was all finished anyway."

"I want to get back to the barracks before somebody finds us, but I also want to hear about where the Army sent you. Where and when can we safely meet?" I asked.

"I'm helping with the stage settings at the Yamada Theater where the guys are practicing for that play 'As Husbands Go'. Maybe you could drop by the theater while they are practicing."

CHAPTER 22

Play Practice

Though practice for the play "As Husbands Go" had started before I arrived in Mountain View, I was expected to participate if not take charge. Play production was generally under the recreation responsibilities I had been assigned when Capt. Sullivan went over my duties as occupational therapist. I was expected to supervise the corpsmen who led recreation and games as well as to assure availability of crafts supplies and the allotment of materials to the patients for their projects. The plays fell under the jurisdiction of "recreation." I would be supervising white men. This turnabout required some soul searching in order to make myself assume the assertiveness necessary to give commands to them. So far I had worked mostly with women in this Army except for patients and they expected orders.

A young man who was a walking-wounded

patient had volunteered to direct the play. He had been in several plays in his high school. No one else had stepped forward after the Broadway actor Robert C. Bridgewater had been director of "The Galen Players" which is what they were called here at the Hospital on the Hill. Pvt. Bridgewater had been reassigned to Special Service where his acting skills could be more widely viewed. He became part of an important traveling drama troop for the Army. Our young replacement director, Earnest Owens, was doing his best following the professional actor.

Pvt. Owens had returned to the method of assigning all parts to the male patients or staff no matter whether or not they called for women. I learned that Pvt. Bridgewater had stopped that practice and assigned women the women's parts, but the nurses had difficulty getting away from their assigned shifts and the WACs who did the secretarial work in the various training camps nearby could seldom find the transportation necessary to attend all the play practices. The local Japanese-American or Hawaiian girls were not even considered for these parts. This situation certainly made me thoughtful considering my own origins, but right then I had too many other things to think about to dwell on it.

The Yamada Theater was in the Mt. View village on Volcano Highway by the grocery store. It had a high front wall facade more than two stories high. Over the entrance and ticket window, there was a roof supported by poles out over the wooden boardwalk. I stood my closed wet umbrella against the wall of the small lobby.

When I first entered the Yamada Theater, I was confronted with male soldiers dressed clownishly in women's clothes. Half of the cast for "As Husbands Go" was for female characters. Pvt. Owens had been unable to secure any female actresses for these parts so men were cast as women. My old classmate Woodrow was acting as prompter sitting in the front row with a script. He ignored me and slid down in the seat. Ignoring me, the only female there in a theater that held only about 70 seats, was hard to do.

"As Husbands Go" was a rather silly three-act comedy about two middle-aged Midwestern women, one a housewife and one a widow who had become entangled with lovers in Paris in the 1920's. The story revolved around deceiving the salt-of-the-earth husband of the irresolute wife upon their return to Dubuque. There were a number of scenes with mildly intimate caresses between the lovers and eventually between the husband and wife.

The young American service men treated these scenes with such silliness, that it detracted from following the plot. After sitting through one practice session, I stayed after it was finished and said to Pvt. Owens, "Private, perhaps I can help you get some women for those parts for Lucille and Emmie. Would it hurt the feelings of those fellows if we got some women to replace them?"

"Oh, no Lieutenant, I had to bribe them to take

those women's parts anyway. I'm already out the price of beer, but if we can find some women for those parts, I don't mind even if I still have to give them the food my mother sends next mail day, as I promised. I've already treated them to the beer."

"Well, Private, you talk to your cast and I'll talk to some of the women in the cottages. How many female characters are there?"

Owens counted on his fingers as he named the female characters; "Lucile, Emmie, Christine, Peggy and Katie, five. Do you think you can find five women?" he asked incredulous.

"I'll do my best. I bet the male actors would rather be whispering to and kissing female actresses instead of men don't you?" I was not sure I could get five but I felt sure I could at least get Cassie and Wanda. They usually didn't have to work the night shift, not working as nurses.

I sat down to watch the current play practice to learn about was still needed. I had had only bit parts in the few plays at Knox High School and they were directed by the principal Mr. Ezra Stokes. My after-school-jobs had prevented me from participating more than what was required for simple walk-on parts or as part of a chorus or crowd scene.

The males, playing the parts of Lucile and Emmie in Paris, were bursting out of the dresses they had squeezed over their uniforms. They stumbled through their lines in the first act. Their "European" lovers took advantage of their discomfort in the role of women and said their lines in sarcastic voices rather than caressingly as was called for in the script. Poor Pvt. Owens did not have the courage to correct their expression. I decided not to address this in front of his all-male cast members, rather asking him to come to the recreation center early the next day for a private discussion in the corner office I had arranged for myself with some strategically placed bookcases and the pool cue rack. For now, I requested Pvt. Owen to please accompany me to the hospital grounds as I was feeling somewhat leery of walking back alone after dark as there had been many men from the nearby camps as well as from the plantation lounging on the boardwalk as I had arrived.

I glanced at Pvt. Minter as I exited with Pvt. Owen close behind me. Our eyes met momentarily as he rose and hurried to hold the exit door to the lobby to open it for us. He managed to slip a note into my hand as I put up my hand to push the door further open. I did not read it then, but instead tucked it in my pocket to read later.

As I stepped out of the lobby into the misty air and turned on my flashlight, my ears were assaulted by the raucous shouts coming from up the street. I turned my head to look up the highway to discover where all this noise was coming.

"That's the gambling joint, the Planter's Store. We are not supposed to go there, but the officers never check to see if we do or not. I don't go as I prefer the theater and keeping my money," Pvt. Owen explained.

We headed up the hill on the other side of the roadway from the place where soldiers went to lose their money.

CHAPTER 23

I waited until I was inside the toilet before switching on my flashlight to read the note. It said:

Meet me behind the Japanese School on the rubbish dump side, Thursday 2100 hours.

It was not signed but that was not necessary since he had placed it in my hand. Thursday was night after tomorrow. I was not familiar with the area of the Japanese School which had been closed after the December 7, 1941 bombing of Pearl Harbor, so I took a walk with Cassie and Wanda after we finished our regular duties the next afternoon. I needed to get them alone anyway to try to persuade them to take parts in "As Husbands Go," I didn't have to tell them my real reason for needing to walk around the Japanese School. We walked up the Mamalahoa Highway which went on up above Mountain View toward the Volcano. We passed the post office, the Catholic Church and the various officers' cottages before turning into the next long overgrown driveway back to the Japanese School. It looked somewhat forlorn but it was obvious that someone was still taking care of the building. We were able to stroll around the whole T-shaped structure. I identified the place where I thought Woodrow meant to meet me the next night.

Beginning our trek back down the driveway toward the main road, I addressed my two prospective actresses, "Capt. Sullivan made me responsible for the drama part of recreation. I went over to visit the play practice last night. They have been using soldiers for the women's parts in the play they are practicing over in the Yamada Theater. The men look so silly and out of place playing women's parts. Could I persuade you girls to help me by taking a couple of the women's parts?"

They both laughed uproariously at the prospect of men in women's clothes. Cassie excitedly replied, "Oh, I think that would be fun. I got to be the Virgin Mary in the Christmas play at the Catholic School in Chicago."

Wanda surprised us both. "Back in high school, I was the main character in our operetta 'Jeannie with the Light Brown Hair'. I had to sing solos and dance. I even thought about trying to go to New York City and see if I could get a part in an Off-Broadway play but then the War happened so I just forgot about it."

"Well maybe you can use your talents now. That play 'As Husbands Go' could sure use your help." I had no idea these women had already had theater experience. Quickly, I secured their agreement to go with me to the Yamada Theater at as soon as supper was finished.

As the girls walked in with me, the men applauded and whistled their approval. The two fellows who had been playing the parts of Lucile and Emmie gave up the scripts without protest and took seats in the last row. Pvt. Owen was grateful to have some real females so there was not so much laughter at every word spoken by these two characters. There were still three men playing the parts of Emmie's daughter and the two maids. The two maids had only a few speaking lines so the practice was much easier this night.

As we closed up the theater on Wednesday night, I said to Pvt. Owens, "I wouldn't be able to attend the Thursday, tomorrow night, but Lt. Amari and Lt. Lindley will be here." I said their rank purposely so all the soldiers would remember to treat them respectfully.

He held out to each of them one of the mimeographed scripts with instructions, "Start learning your lines."

The following day after supper, I grabbed my flashlight even though it was still an hour or so before dark and went out the backdoor toward the trail that would lead up to the track toward the Japanese School. I was breaking two rules at once, walking alone without a partner and meeting with an enlisted soldier, but these were nothing to lying about my race. The first two might net me a reprimand but the latter would probably get me a dishonorable discharge. I carried my umbrella but fortunately it was not raining.

As I rounded the corner of the back of the Japanese School, I saw that Woodrow had not yet arrived. Leaning against the building out of sight of any passers-by, I wondered what he could possible think was urgent as to meet here on a weeknight. It was so quiet up here compared to the barracks and the mess-hall.

My ruminations ceased when I heard the grass rustle at his approach. He was still in uniform. He held out his hand to shake which I found unusual but took his hand none-the-less.

"Thanks for meeting me. I need your help." He jumped right into his explanation of the urgency of this meeting. "My boss Major Beving got a girl pregnant and he needs a nurse to help with an abortion."

I was speechless at this declaration. Through my mind went all the stories I had heard in nursing school of botched abortions. In fact I had had to care for a young woman who was septic from trying to abort herself with a knitting needle.

Because I did not respond, Woodrow went on, "I have to find someone and of course I thought of you. You're a nurse as well as an occupational therapist, yes?"

Still speechless, I nodded "yes."

"Well, we need to help each other. Major Beving learned from Captain Craig who went to Marion Military Institute that Knox High School was a Negro school. My 201 File has Knox High School in it. Major Beving threatened me with exposure as a Negro if I don't help him find a nurse to help with the abortion."

It took several moments for his dilemma and consequently mine to dawn on me. I was speechless again. I started to feel rage at him for involving me in this disgraceful affair. Couldn't those darned doctors who already had so many privileges solve their problems, especially sexual problems of their own making? But as I let these facts stir around in my brain, I realized I was caught as well as Woodrow. He didn't have to involve me but he was doing so. He was blackmailing me to help him help his rascal of a superior officer.

CHAPTER 24

Night Surgery

The next morning, a large wooden packing box arrived on the walkway in front of the recreation room building. It was full of occupational therapy supplies; leather and leather tools, the machinery parts to set up another bicycle saw, caning for chair seats, rolls of copper and tools for metal tooling, several hand-tools for woodwork, tools for gardening, 300 pounds of white potters' clay and also the parts for a kick wheel for pottery. Tucked in a small packet I almost overlooked were tubes of oil paint, a palette, rolls of unstretched painter's canvas and a bundle of artists' paint brushes.

I was overjoyed to finally receive something I could feel comfortable using with the patients. With the help of my corpsman, I got the materials and tools inside before the rain came. They were stacked around the bookcases and pool cue rack making getting in and out of my tiny office an obstacle course. After giving him instructions about how to more efficiently store the precious supplies, and how to assemble the bicycle saw and potter's wheel, I sorted through the packet of artist materials and chose some to take down to Sergeant Erickson in the Section 8 Building.

There had also been some spools of cord tucked around the other supplies. I took one spool along with me as I went down the gravel trail to Section 8 Building. There were so many things a person could do with simple cord; sailors' knots, string finger games, or macramé. I feared this last would seem too feminine for these soldiers but perhaps the French name was unfamiliar to them. I could try anyway.

When I went into Section 8 Barracks, most of the eyes turned toward the door and followed me as I walked down the central aisle. I could hear some sotto voce comments like "At last something to look at," or "Well, look who's here." A low whistle followed me.

I found the bed of Arne Erickson was empty. My eyes sought the nurse in charge but it was not Lt. Wagner. It was another young nurse who sat behind the small desk. I looked for her insignia before addressing her, "Lieutenant, where is Sergeant Erickson? I am the occupational therapist and I have some art materials for him?" Her name tag was too small for me to read her name.

"Sergeant Erickson took a tablet and pencils and

went out behind the building to try to draw the giant ferns. He was getting more and more rambunctious and teasing the other patients. I encouraged him to go outside. I'm keeping my eye on him."

I went out the front door as the back door was locked in case some of these psychiatric patients tried to escape. I found him sitting on an upturned bucket with the tablet on his right knee which was thrown up across his left knee. His rendition of the ferns with clouds behind was indeed pleasing though he folded the tablet-cover over it when he realized I was beside him.

"Sergeant Erickson, I received a shipment of art and craft supplies today. I was wondering if you might like to use these paints and charcoals." I held them out to him.

He looked at the supplies I held for almost a minute before reaching for them. "Where can I get some tools to stretch this canvas?" He pointed at the roll under my arm.

"I will talk to your doctor to request he give you a pass to come to the recreation room where the woodworking tools are so you can make a frame for stretching it."

"I haven't been away from the barracks at all until this afternoon. Somebody will have to show me the way to the recreation room. Besides I don't think they'll let a 'crazy' like me wander around without a keeper." He sounded bitter.

Knowing he was correct, I said, "Of course. What is your doctor's name?"

"Dr. Beving is my doctor," he replied.

My heart slipped down into my toes as I heard this name again. Woodrow had told me who had impregnated the nurse but not whether Dr. Beving would perform the abortion himself, but just the fact of his name being connected to blackmailing me into helping caused me anxiety. How could I address him about anything knowing that he was a lawbreaker to arrange for a woman to get an abortion?

"I'll see what I can do to get him to allow you to walk up to the recreation room." The Section Eight patients had to get permission to leave the barracks unlike the orthopedic and malaria patients. They also had to have someone accompany them.

* * *

I had changed out of my white uniform and donned a gray blouse and slacks and black oxfords in order to be invisible while walking up the hill. Woodrow met me near the corner of the recreation room at 2100 hours. Silently I followed him up across the road toward the surgery in the gymnasium. I focused my flashlight on the ground in front of me as Woodrow also did with his. This was the dark of the moon so there was no light, not even starlight to help us as the usual clouds of over Mountain View obscured the sky. The blackout curtains on the windows of the building did their job completely. Once we got near the gymnasium, I flicked off my flashlight and followed so close I was almost touching Woodrow.

I felt trepidation as I had not been taught about abortions in nursing classes. My only experience with this kind of situation was caring for the women who were hospitalized with septicemia after trying to cause their own abortions. I tried to remember what I had heard during gab-sessions in the nurses' dining room. We discussed the most gruesome afflictions of our patients. I also remembered whispered stories in Selma by the nurses at the white Vaughn Hospital. They ignored my presence for the most part so I had listened without fear of being scolded for eavesdropping.

We enter by the south door and even inside there was very little light. In the furthest corner of the gym, there was a shaded light hanging over the operating table. Captain Sullivan had showed me this building that first day when she walked me around the grounds but I had not been near the building since. Woodrow whispered that he was going to the motor pool to get a jeep to take the woman back to her bed after the operation. He silently closed the gymnasium door and I turned toward the light.

Some man was standing at the operating table with his back to me. He was applying an anesthesia mask to the person on the table. I got a whiff of the ether as I approached. He was dripping it on the mask and covering it with a sponge. Though I had not participated in surgery for a long time, I knew that what he was doing was usually a nurse's job.

I removed my WAC cape and laid it on a chair. I immediately went to the sink against the wall and carefully washed my hands. Then I approach the operating table from the other side looking up into the face of the doctor. He had his surgeon's mask hanging around his neck. I knew he should have had it over his mouth and nose but this whole thing was not done according to the rules, so why should he follow all the require protocols for surgery now?

He was tall with a clean-shaven face and a ring of grey-brown hair around his bald pate. He was dressed in street clothes with a white surgeon's gown over them. Without even introducing himself, he said, "Are you a nurse?" His voice was deep like a radio announcer.

"Yes," I replied, "but I haven't helped in surgery for at least a year." Since he had not introduced himself, I did not give my name either. My cape was the only part of my uniform I had worn so there was no way for him to identify me except by my face.

Calmly he said, "This isn't a complicated surgery. All I need you to do is to hand me the instruments when I ask for them, you know, just the regular nurse's job in surgery." His acceptance of my lack of any but basic nursing skills was plain in his tone.

With my foot against the table leg and my hand

covered with a washcloth, I pushed the small towel covered table with the instruments down to the foot-end of the operating table as per his instructions. I protected my clean hand with the washcloth to keep from contaminating it again as I stabilized the wobbly little instrument table. So far I had not even looked at the face of the woman on the table, mostly out of shame for her needing such a shameful operation.

"Put her legs up on the table with knees apart," he instructed me. As soon as I finished, I rushed over to the sink to wash my hands again. When I turned round I saw that he had already picked the curette off the instrument table and was reaching under the covering sheet. I dried my hand as I ran back to the table to pull the sheet back to ease his entry into her vagina with the surgical instrument.

She began to moan as he wielding the curette and he briskly said, "Put some more ether on that mask and hand me that emesis basin." He scrapped the bloody tissue into the basin. Then he took a syringe full of clear fluid and flushed the bloody residue into the basin.

I followed his instructions and the moaning ceased. When I replaced the sponge on the mask, I looked at the face it was covering and realized the woman was Lt. Wagner.

My shock almost made me exclaim out loud but my training took over and I forced myself to just do the doctor's bidding as his surgery nurse. I felt it would really not do for the doctor to know that I knew this patient on the table. I pretended indifference to the procedure as he packed the vagina to stop the uterine bleeding.

"Remove the mask from her face," he told me as he filled a syringe from a bottle of yellow liquid on the small table. I assumed that this was the famous "penicillin" though I had never seen it before because it had only been manufactured for the military since the war started. I had never had the opportunity to see it in the Henrotin Hospital.

"Now get one of those wheelchairs," he instructed and pointed to the darkened corner across the gymnasium.

I hear a motor vehicle pull up outside. Woodrow slipped in the door just as Lt. Wagner began to mutter.

"Come help me get her off the table and into this wheelchair," the doctor instructed Woodrow. "You hold the wheelchair," he said to me. To Woodrow he said, "Lift her carefully as I don't want her to start bleeding."

The two men carefully lifted her into the chair. She was still somewhat floppy. I held the door as Woodrow wheeled Lt. Wagner out. The doctor followed holding an umbrella over her as Woodrow guided the chair over the boardwalk where the boards sloped down to the gravel. He rushed to open the passenger door. The two men lifted the slowly awakening Lt. Wagner into the passenger seat. I ran back through the rain and grabbed my cape.

"Minter, do you think the two of you can get her back to her bed OK?" asked the doctor.

"Yes, Major Sykes, I can lift her by myself if necessary. The nurse can ride in the rumble seat."

"But Doctor, don't you want me to clean up the surgery before I leave?" I asked, remembering this usual duty of surgery nurses.

"No, just get this women home and into bed as fast as you can. Nurse, can you stay with her for a few hours to make sure she doesn't hemorrhage?"

I was already in so deep that I felt I couldn't refuse. I reluctantly answered "yes" as it was still so dark, he could not have seen me if I simply nodded my head.

"Send Pvt. Minter for me if she does, OK?" he said as he turned back toward the gymnasium. "Nobody else needs to know about this surgery."

I felt disgust with myself for being sworn to secrecy in this illegal operation instead of doing the patriotic work I felt proud of. I should have been caring for our brave troops and instead here I was helping the supercilious and cynical Lt. Wagner who seemed not to care about the troops it had seemed a few weeks ago when I first met her.

CHAPTER 25

Recovery

Lt. Wagner bunked in another cottage where most of the charge nurses lived. I had not been inside this cottage before; however, Pvt. Minter knew which one it was as he had picked her up before the abortion. He drove the jeep with the lights turned off as close to the front door as possible. Nurses on shift work can usually sleep through a lot but light in their eyes was not one of the things, at least not for me. While enforcement of "black out" was no longer as strict as it had been before the June bombing raids on Japan, it was a habit for most everyone in Hawaii, not just for the military.

I was glad I had not worn my white uniform, I thought as Woodrow and I sat planning while still seated in the jeep, how we would get her into her bed. She was slowly waking up but was not still fully conscious.

"I can pick her up and carry her in if you just

shine your flashlight on the ground and open the door for me," Woodrow directed.

"Do you know where her bed is from the front door?" I asked." I think all these cottages have more or less the same floor-plan," I explained.

"Well when I came to get her, I was told to signal her to come out by knocking on that window over there," he pointed toward the front window on the right side of the front door. "I suppose her bunk is in that room."

"Well, let's assume that her bunk is in there. Let me go in first and find the bunk and then I'll open the front door from inside to signal you that I've found it. Then you can pick her up and bring her right in," I suggested thinking to keep from awakening any nurses asleep inside.

With Woodrow's agreement, I opened the front door as silently as possible. Every door-hinge in Mountain View was a little rusty because of the almost daily rain, and even though the maintenance crews oiled the hinges frequently, there was still a small screech as I opened it. I decided to prop it open with a bucket that sat in the front entryway so the screech would not be repeated. Shining my flashlight on the floor I pushed open the door of the room that corresponded with where the front window should be. There were two bunks in this room both on the floor level and fortunately, both were empty. I showed my flashlight on the beds to try to determine which might be Lt. Wagner's but there was nothing there to identify which was hers. So I assumed that hers was closest to the window if she was supposed to have heard a knock as a signal to go out. I went into the bathroom across the hallway and grabbed several towels. These I spread these on the bunk by the window to catch blood if she started bleeding. I don't know how I knew to do that but common sense told me I guess.

I went to the open door and flashed my light once to Pvt. Minter to signal him to bring her in. I went out the front door in order to point the flashlight on the board path in front of him. As my eyes had finally accustomed themselves to the dark, I saw him struggle to get her blanket-wrapped body out of the passenger seat and hoist her up in his arms bending slightly backward to walk somewhat spraddle-legged up to the steps with her. The blanket fell half-off her body and almost dragged on the damp boardwalk. He swung side-ways through the door and followed me into the vacant bunk room. I grabbed the blanket and threw it back over her nude body. He tried to lower her easily to the bunk by the window, but because he was almost the same size as Lt. Wagner, he was unable to stop a slight fall unto the bed. I was immediately fearful that she would start to bleed. Lt. Wagner moaned as she hit the surface of the bed. I again tucked the blanket around her naked body.

"I'm getting out of here before somebody misses that jeep," Woodrow whispered to me.

I was too worried about whether or not the impact of her slight fall to the bed had started a hemorrhage to even acknowledge Woodrow's exit, though I heard him start the jeep engine and pull quietly away from the cottage.

I didn't think Nurse Wagner even recognized me yet as she was still too zonked on medication. She moaned slightly so I knew her pain was what mostly occupied her mind, besides it was still too dark to see facial features in this room. It was even too dark to see whether she had started bleeding on the towel.

I whispered, "Lt. Wagner, I'm going to check the towels and see if you are bleeding," as I pushed her slightly to roll toward the wall to get her on her side. So far there was no blood on the towels. I remembered that Major Sykes had packed her vagina with absorbent cotton which might catch most blood. So I covered her again with the blanket and went to her kit which lay on the floor and found a pajama top which I managed to put backwards on her under the blanket so she was not completely unclothed should anyone come in or the blanket get thrown off.

Then I took off my damp shoes and lay down on the other bunk against the inner wall. I feared rumpling someone else's bed but I was so tired from the strain. With my cape as cover, I tried to rest but not to go to sleep for fear of not awakening if Lt. Wagner tried to get up and fell. Also, I wanted to be able to jump up and slip out in case I heard anyone approaching from the outside. I lay there planning how I would roll off the bed, grabbing my shoes and being out in the hallway walking toward the backdoor in case someone came in the front. Change of shift was several hours away so I was somewhat relieved to know I could probably leave before the other nurses returned. My plan was to stay until Lt. Wagner was fully awake so I could be sure she would not bleed to death before hopefully having to reveal my identity. None-the-less, it was a long time since I had used the toilet so I swung off the bunk bed and padded into the hallway. I assumed all these newly-constructed cottages had the toilet more or less in the same place off the central hallway.

When I returned to Lt. Wagner's room, she was sitting up with her legs hanging over the side of the bunk. She whispered, "What's your name?"

I had hoped to avoid telling her, hoping she would never know I knew her secret, but thus confronted, I felt compelled to reply, "Lt. Brett, ma'am."

"Brett, I hope I can trust you not to tell anyone," she whispered. "My nursing career would be finished if Capt. Sullivan finds out."

Relieved to know she was awake enough to worry about that, I whispered, "Of course. I would never tell because I'd be in trouble, too. Are you well enough for me to leave?"

"Yes, it would be best if nobody ever finds out

you have been here. I'm well enough to look after myself. You go ahead and go to your cottage."

CHAPTER 26

Recreation

Despite having been awake until way past midnight, I was expected to open and supervise the recreation room at 8 o'clock after all the patients had had their breakfasts.

When I arrived at the cottage which served as our nurses' mess-hall, I found a letter beside my place. I had no one to whom I wrote regularly like most other nurses or hospital staffers had; however, I had put my name on a list for the Red Cross to receive letters from Girl Scout members in the United States. This letter from Elsie Johnson from Oak Park, Illinois seemed as if it had probably been copied from an example given by the Scout Leader;

Dear Lt. Brett,   June 6, 1944

> I am proud to be writing to such a patriotic woman as you.
>
> We are all working to defeat our

enemies, the Japs and the Nazis.

I am 13 years old. I will be going to high school in September. I like to read. I especially like Nancy Drew mysteries.

I have a brother who is almost old enough to join up. Our parents want him to finish high school first.

Please tell me about yourself.

Sincerely,

Elsie Johnson

Apparently this letter had arrived in a bunch sent to WAC nurses in Hawaii. It must have followed me around to finally find me here. I knew that all mail had to be censored and then sent in bunches as space was available on ships or planes. There had been such letters lying by several other nurses' places, too. I wondered what I could tell this girl about myself as I tucked the letter into my pocket. When would I find the time?

Being up all night had not affected my appetite. The food here was better than the food served to the nurses in mess-hall in Washington, D. C. We had butter for our bread and cream for our coffee which were not easily available to regular citizens at home in the United States.

I hurried down the hill to the Recreation Room

hoping to arrive before the patients. The corpsman, Pvt. Stilley had gotten there before me and opened the room. He had unlocked the case holding the pool cues and balls and the ping pong paddles and balls. Within minutes, the walking patients began to straggle in in bunches.

One of them immediately went to the piano and started banging out "Boogie Woogie Bugle Boy." Another soldier raised his hands to his face and began miming playing a bugle. I decided I'd best get some control here or I never would be able to later. So I put my hand on the shoulder of the boy at the piano and he slowly came to a stop at the end of the first chorus, at "Company B."

"Please could you all take a seat on those benches by the walls?" I asked in my most winning voice, forgetting that I outranked most of them and could have commanded them instead; however, I wanted the Recreation Room to be a comfortable place to be, not like a parade ground.

There was some low muttering but all complied except Arne Erickson who instead leaned against the door frame as if he were not actually in the same room with the other soldiers. I decided to ignore his passive-aggressive behavior. I had learned techniques for dealing with such defiance during my training at Walter Reed Army Hospital. Besides, his corpsman was right behind him out on the boardwalk smoking. Most of the patients here had jaundice or some less obvious infectious disease. A few sported bandages. They were not psychiatric patients like Arne.

Sometimes, I took craft materials to the patients in the Section 8 barracks but most of the time, I supervised crafts and games in the Recreation Room. I had arranged the Recreation Room into obvious sections; the pool table was near the cue ball cupboard.

The ping pong table was kitty-cornered from it in the other corner of the room. The tables for craft work were nearer my desk and the craft tool and materials cupboards. I had learned in Walter Reed Hospital to keep all cupboards locked except when tools were being used. The other corner had tables for card games and table games like carom and dominoes. Before my arrival here, the corpsmen had more or less let the patients do as they pleased. The room was terribly disorganized but I had sorted everything and I had labeled each section and each cupboard. I unlocked those cupboards as well before speaking: "Gentlemen, you know the rules. I went over them with you before. Please tell newcomers how to behave here. You may choose you recreation now." I felt if I called them "Gentlemen" instead of "Soldiers" I might get more cooperation and respect. So far, this seemed to be working.

Confusion reigned for five minutes while the soldiers sorted themselves into their recreation preference groups. Arne continued to lean against the door frame. I noticed that he had his art materials under his arm somewhat wrapped in newspaper. I continued to ignore him while I helped the patients who chose crafts to find the proper tools and materials for their projects, some of which they had started at a previous session.

I kept all the unfinished projects locked in the cupboard unless they did not require special tools. Those, the patients were allowed to carry their projects with them to the hospital barracks to continue work on their projects. Favorite craft items locked in the cupboard were leather tooled wallets or coin-purses to send to their girlfriends and fiancées at home. These projects required that they work on them with the special leather-tools here in the rec. room.

I had instructed the corpsmen to construct a rough shed roof over the back door for the bicycle saw and foot-operated pottery wheel which had been set up there on the board floor of this shelter. So far, I had not been able to get a patient to use either of them. I felt somewhat overwhelmed with all the different things I felt responsible for and decided I must train one of the corpsmen to supervise this area. These activities would be good for some of the men still recovering from jungle foot rot which afflicted some coming back from the Battle of the Philippine Sea or New Guinea or Saipan.

Arne must have gotten tired of standing because when I turned, I noticed he had found a seat on a bench near the door at the corner of the room with the pool table. He had laid the package of art materials on the bench beside him. Other patients did not sit near him. I wondered if this was because they were afraid of him, jealous of him having special skills they could never aspire to or was it because he was a Section Eight "battle fatigue" patient.

After scrutinizing all the activities to see that all patients were occupied or at least not distracting those who were, I went and sat on the bench near Arne. "Did you do any drawings?" I asked mildly.

He responded with a sort of smart-aleck tone, "Ain't much around here to draw!"

Well of course, we both knew that was not true. Everywhere I looked, seemed to offer extraordinary scenes. So I laughed as if he had made a joke. I could tell he wanted me to beg him to show me his work. I knew this would be bad for our future relationship so I said, "Well would you like me to set up a still-life project for you?" knowing that he would not find that interesting after drawing and painting war scenes.

He snorted with disgust, "What do you take me for, one of those studio artists that never paints anything real?" There was an undertone of angry contempt in his response.

"If you showed me what you'd done, I wouldn't have to guess," I answered rather coolly.

He contemplated this a few moments before unwrapping the tablet and charcoals. The top sheet was a recognizable portrait image of the young Japanese boy who came round selling the daily Hilo Tribune-Herald. The boy had visited the Section Eight building while I was there working on a project with one of the patients who could not get a pass to come to the recreation room. The boy had told us to call him "Tom" though we had learned that his Japanese name was Tadashi. I believe he thought we couldn't learn to say his Japanese name properly and also, it felt as if he were trying to distance himself from his Japanese heritage. Though by this time in the war, most of the Japanese-Hawaiian internees had been allowed to exit the internment camps in America, the stigma of being of the same ancestry as the enemy was strong.

"How about you sit over there and let me draw your picture?" Arne suggested knowing I would have to decline as I had a room full of men, probably thirty soldiers whom I was supposed to be supervising.

"Rather than give him the satisfaction of refusing him as he knew I must do, I said, "If you are willing to forego the noon meal, I'll be glad to sit still for you then. I could ask the corpsman to bring us some sandwiches." With that I arose and went to where the men were working on crafts or awaiting my help with their projects.

CHAPTER 27

Sitting

I instructed Pvt. Stilley to bring sandwiches back for us after he had finished his lunch in the mess. Fortunately it had ceased to drizzle in the morning and Arne found a spot on the north side of the recreation hall and dragged out two chairs. He seated me sideways so I was in profile against the north wall as he placed his own chair again further north of me and the building. The high noon sun caused a shadowless landscape so he avoided the problem by placing me under the north eave thus being all in shadow. He put his hand on top of my head on top of my white nurse cap and turned it to a position he preferred then went to his own chair.

"Can I talk while you draw?" I asked while maintaining the position in which he had placed my head.

Intent on his paper and charcoal he said, "If you can do it without moving your head, I suppose you can."

"Where were you born and raised?" I'm sure he knew I could find out this information from the medical record in the Section 8 Building but I wanted him to tell me. I very much wanted to turn and look at him as he answered, but he had set me in a position where I would be unable to see his facial expressions.

"I'm from Minnesota, a small town, but I took some art courses at the University. That's why I was inducted into the artists' corp."

Holding my head still, I said, "Oh, that's the reason I hear a different sort of accent from you. What exactly is that accent?"

"I suppose it's the Swedish accent. Most of the people in my town and nearby farms came from Sweden before 1900. How about you?"

I should have know that my question would stimulate such an inquiry and I hesitated a moment thinking what an appropriate answer would be to a patient to deter further inquiry." Oh, I just had a regular childhood. Tell me about your family," I coaxed.

"Don't move your head," he commanded. "My father was killed in a farm accident. Lightning scared the horses and they turned the hay wagon over on him. That happened when I was about six. My mother had a couple babies that died after I was born, but when my father died, we moved to town, she earned our living from laundry and sewing, and the charity of the Lutheran Church ladies." This last was said so I could almost hear the sneer I was sure was on his face.

Thinking of my own mother's struggles, I said, "Sounds like a hard life."

I tried to speak without moving the muscles in my face.

"Well, one good thing about it was that the town school was better than the country school. Mr. Nygaard, my 4th grade teacher saw that I liked to draw so he got me some colored pencils. That started me off." He stood up and came toward me. "Time to move your position so I can draw a different angle."

I stood up and he gripped my folding chair and set it facing his chair. With a gesture for me to be seated, he tipped my face to the angle he wanted. I felt a stirring as he touched my chin.

"Don't I even get to see the drawing you just did?" I asked.

"I'll show you later. I'm drawing as fast as I can because I know when noon mess is over, you'll have to go back to work in there, so let me just draw now. I'll show you later. Besides, I'll have to do some final shading before I show them to you."

Even as he spoke I saw the ambulatory patients filing out of the mess-hall head back our way.

I did not see the drawings until the next day when I went down to the Section 8 barracks to take some wood and a carving knife to another patient who claimed to have been a whittler in his rural southern home. I would have to get the nurse on duty to promise to lock up the knife after each whittling session. Working with these other fellows whose "southern cracker" accent reminded me of my changed race, offered me a challenge. Sometimes now in Hawaii, I was almost able to forget my deception.

Arne was lying back on his narrow hospital bed with his hands clasped behind his head of bushy red hair. The war news was being broadcast from a radio on the shelf by the nurse's desk. He was staring at the opposite wall and appeared not to register my presence so I went to the foot of his bed and asked, "Did you finish the drawings you did of me yesterday?"

"Oh, hello!" He reached under his bed where I could see he had constructed some temporary shelves. He handed me two sheets. The first was my recognizable profile with no apparent background. The second sheet with me facing front had a fanciful background nothing like the plain wall against which I had been sitting. He had made the background into a jungle of huge fern leaves and stalks with cloudy shadows which appeared to be fiendish faces hiding among cloudy mists.

I was taken aback by the setting he had drawn around my face and seated body. The contrast was shocking. I kept myself from gasping and studied the sheet silently until I thought of what to say.

"You certainly made an interesting background for the second drawing. Am I supposed to be hiding in the ferns?"

"Just my fantasy!" he said. "You never really told me anything about yourself, so I have to make it up."

CHAPTER 28

Road to Punalu'u Beach

Usually, by the time I got back up to the nurse's cottage I was ready to relax a little, but I was still catching up with the sleep I had lost from the night I assisted in the surgery. I wanted to lie down on my bunk for a little catnap before supper but Cassie came bouncing in almost shouting, "The doctors are arranging a beach trip and they want us to come. The hospital ship is taking about half our patients back to the United States tomorrow. The ship is already docked at Hilo Wharf. We get a little break before the next bunch of patients arrives."

I reluctantly opened one eye and yawned. "Tell me about it at supper," I pleaded.

"Oh, come on you slug-a-bed," she muttered as she lifted my feet off the bed. "Major Sykes asked for you specifically, Clara Brett. He said he'd arrange it with Captain Sullivan."

That brought me fully awake. If Major Sykes asked

for me, it meant he wasn't willing to completely erase the forbidden surgery from his mind. I was hoping to put that whole experience in the past. Didn't the doctor want to forget it too? Dismay filled me as I feared that helping with that illegal surgery might be something else that could be used to blackmail me.

"Come on. We don't get that many chances to see this island. Major Sykes is arranging for two cars from the motor pool and we can camp on the beach overnight. Do you have a swimming suit?"

I tried to delay by asking, "No, I don't have a swimming suit. When is this outing supposed to take place?"

"Tomorrow morning. I'll lend you one of my suits. I have two; I expected to be near the beach in Hawaii, where I could swim all the time. Major Sykes says it will take us about three hours to drive there so we should be there by noon. And we'll get back before dinner Sunday night," Cassie explained.

"Who else is going? Aren't you and Wanda due at play practice?" I questioned, struggling to figure out if there was any way I could avoid having to be in the presence of Dr. Sykes. As an occupational therapist now, I had little to do with the surgeons, unlike Cassie who had worked more closely with all the surgeons as she worked with their patients in physical therapy.

"You, me, Wanda and your roommate, Lt. Sisco.

I don't know her very well. Private Owens excused us from play practice. By the way, I learned today that Lt. Wagner has gotten a transfer back to San Francisco. I guess she thinks there are more eligible fellows at Fort Mason," Cassie smirked.

I focused on combing my hair and putting my uniform back on as I absorbed the information, that Lt. Wagner was leaving. At least I would not have to face her with the knowledge of her illegally terminated pregnancy.

"Do you know why she requested a transfer?" I asked keeping my face down as I buttoned up the front of my uniform.

"She just said she wanted to work in a bigger hospital with more of a variety of patients but she didn't explain any more than that. She'll go with the patients on the hospital ship back to the Coast," explained Cassie.

From this I determined that nobody but me among the nurses knew the real reason she was leaving but I wanted to have a chance to ask Woodrow if he knew she was leaving and why? This meant I would have to contrive a reason to talk to him since thankfully, our paths seldom crossed here at the Hospital on the Hill.

The next morning a convoy of trucks and ambulances started down the Mamalahoa Highway toward Hilo Harbor as soon after daybreak as the patients could be loaded. Several nurses accompanied them though we heard that there was already a contingent of nurses on the hospital ship, probably WAVES who we suspected thought that they were better than us. Navy nurses had a reputation of being strict disciplinarians.

As soon as the last vehicle in the convoy disappeared around the curve by the corpsman's barracks, a jeep driven by Dr. Sykes pulled up in front of the nurses' cottage.

He motioned for us to get in while explaining that Major Beving was driving the other jeep which pulled up behind his. Another man in the passenger seat leapt out and ushered Wanda and Lt. Sisco into the jump seats as Cassie and I stepped into the back of Major Sykes jeep. The front passenger seat of his jeep was occupied by Pvt. Stilley whom we discovered later was brought along to do the dirty work such as starting the campfire. Several bedrolls were stuffed back of the jump seats in both jeeps there beside the food hampers.

"You ladies bring your swimming suits?" asked Major Sykes abruptly as he swung the jeep around and headed up Volcano Road. The road was bumpy as the frequent rains washed holes in the gravel which was laid over the bare lava rock. It was already a very bumpy ride.

I was reluctant to even talk to him since he apparently thought he could order me around, and of course, him as a major and me only a second lieutenant, he could order me around. I let Cassie explain; "Lt. Brett borrowed one of my swimming suits. We brought some towels from our cottage."

Between the jolting of the jeep and the wind through the giant ferns and the scraggly ohia trees bordering the road, it was too noisy to carry on a conversation for which I was very grateful. Cassie and I sometimes pointed out especially interesting views to each other, but mostly, I gripped the side of the jeep to keep from being thrown out.

We arrived at the Volcano about noon. After noting the new Volcano House on our left at the edge of the crater, Major Sykes promised to stop there for a better look on the way back. Then we passed a field of columns of steam rising on our right. Major Sykes in the lead drove our little convoy of two vehicles. We stopped at a stone building in Kilauea Military Camp to get permission to go further into the national park which the military had more or less co-opted from the park people for the duration of the war. He came back out and drove to the edge of the crater. The view was breathtaking across this great abyss. Major Sykes ordered Pvt. Stilley to unroll a couple of the bedrolls and to lay out the lunch of sandwiches prepared and wrapped separately in one of the hampers.

Finally, Major Sykes introduced the fourth man. "This is Major Zukoski, another doctor. He is a specialist in tropical diseases and sure has his work cut out for him with these guys coming back from the South Seas. The major arrived just last week so I hope you'll let him know how lucky he is to be posted to the Hospital on the Hill. I think he is missing Birmingham, Alabama," he states to all us women.

Immediately, my defenses went up suspecting that even though he was from Birmingham, he could possibly detect small failures on my part to act completely white. I instantly became more vigilant. My mind switched immediately to my "proper English" mode.

For the first time, I got a really good look at Major Beving. Previous to this time, I had only seen his written order for patients in the Section 8 Building. Our paths had never physically crossed before. Dr. Beving was a slender, medium height man with short military cut blond hair under his cockily set Major's cap.

"This is Lt. Brett," Major Sykes introduced me to him. "You remember, I told you about her."

Major Beving examined me in a way that made me very uncomfortable. I wondered what Major Sykes had told him but decided to do as little as possible to draw attention to myself. He must know that I had helped in the abortion. I noticed that he slipped his wedding ring off his left hand and into his pocket. Aha, I thought, this is why he had to have Lt. Wagner get an abortion. Well, I had something on him, too, but it was unlikely I would be brave enough to use it against him.

We could hear the artillery practice from the training range on the other side of the crater. Except for that and the occasional plane landing at the Kilauea Landing Field on the south rim of the crater, we might have been hundreds of miles away from anything to do with the war. The doctors were wearing civilian clothes as were we girls. However, the olive colored Army jeeps and bedrolls belied our apparent civilian status.

I did my best to shield myself from attempts at flirting from the doctors by sticking to the other women like a leech. At a signal from Major Sykes, we women helped Pvt. Stilley re-roll the bedrolls and repack the hampers. As we descended from the Kilauea crater, the views were again breathtakingly spectacular. Cattle grazed on the downhill side of the road. This was a surprise as I thought the whole island was given over to the military. After an hour or so of the bone-jarring ride down the west side of Kilauea, we stopped to stretch our legs at the lane marked Kalapana Ranch. We did not drive in, but just stopped and refreshed ourselves with drinks from the hampers.

"A doctor I met in officer training is stationed in the Pahala Hospital," said Major Sykes as we neared the sign pointing up the hill to the village of worker houses. "I just want to stop and say hello," he said as he turned the jeep up the hill and parked next to the line of other Army vehicles beside the hospital building. The Army had taken over the plantation hospital in Pahala in 1942 when they took over so many other public buildings on Hawaii Island. Major Sykes soon came back as his colleague was on duty and had little time to talk. It was us girls' last opportunity to use a regular toilet before we camped on the beach.

We were soon back on the main road down the hill toward the ocean. About four in the afternoon, we arrived at a road which led to the left. Major Sykes slowed to make the turn on the narrow lane with no ditches that curved down toward the Pacific Ocean. Eventually, the two-wheel track opened out of the low forest unto a shelf of lava above the black sand beach. Unfortunately, there was another cluster of jeeps in the cleared area which served as a parking spot. Some Marines had gotten here before us. None-the-less, Major Sykes parked somewhat away from them, as far as the cleared space beneath the low forest would allow. We all disembarked and stretched our legs and wiggled to relieve our backs which had been jolted on the rugged road for the past few hours.

By late autumn 1944, many beaches which had had barbed-wire barriers to prevent invasion by land, had had this obstacle removed as Japan seemed to be retreating.

<h1 style="text-align:center">CHAPTER 29</h1>

At the Beach

"Why don't you girls go change into your bathing suits while we unload and set up a campsite?" suggested Major Sykes. This time he avoided making it sound like an order.

Cassie seemed braver than Wanda, Lt. Sisco or me. She grabbed the towels and our two black one-piece suits and headed back into the shrubs that made up the forest near where the jeeps were parked. We all followed her in different degrees of timidity. Though I shared a room with Lt. Sisco, I had never used her first name, so was somewhat uncomfortable saying it now. I had never even seen her naked though we had been sharing a room for over a month now. She asked me to hold up one of the towels to shield her from the girls as she changed into her bathing suit. I was tempted to peek around to see what she had been hiding all this month but felt it would be childish so I did as she asked and then reciprocated her request.

"I am surprised your bathing suit fits me since I must be at least a size larger than you," I said to Cassie.

Oh, well, I gained some weight before joining up. I was afraid they would say I was too light if I didn't, and not let me join. I gave you the old suit from when I weighed almost ten pounds more," she explained.

Our modesty was apparent when we all emerged from the haole koa thicket in a group with towels wrapped around us hiding our bathing suits. The afternoon sun beat down as we tiptoed across the smooth lava rock shelf above the sand. The rusting barbed wire which had previously covered the beach was half submerged in the water several feet from where the waves lapped now. Since its installation in 1941, it had been pulled in different directions by beach goers and by the waves.

Pvt. Stilley was completely occupied with preparing the campsite when we girls broke into the open beach area. The three doctors were over at the Marines' campfire. There were no women in the Marine group. All the men turned as they sensed we had emerged from the shrubbery. Because we were with the doctors, they refrained from the catcalls we were accustomed to from service men when off the base.

"These fellows were just telling us what they

knew about the liberation of Paris," explained Major Sykes as he came toward us. "It looks like we have Hitler on the run." Then he walked over to Pvt. Stilley to check on the progress of the campsite.

Before, I had often noticed while dressing in Medical Specialist School that Cassie's legs were about the same color as mine. They all looked white when we were in our uniforms. Consequently, I was not prepared when Major Zukoski said, "Looks like you've already been out in the sun." It sounded like he was giving me a compliment. I was still so unaccustomed to flirting that I did not have a ready answer to what I considered a rather personal remark.

Apparently, Major Sykes did not want Major Zukoski to spend too much time talking to me, so he called out, "Come and see the big turtle resting on the sand below the ledge of rock." I was glad to escape this Birmingham doctor and readily fled down toward the water feeling the heated smooth black rock beneath my feet.

It became obvious to me that the other doctors felt subordinate to Major Sykes as no one attempted to counter his suggestions or orders. Major Zukoski quickly turned his attention to Wanda.

Major Beving poured his charm on my roommate, Nurse Beatrice Sisco thus leaving Cassie to entertain herself. Part of me felt like I should warn Beatrice, but that would involve thinking up an explanation for how I knew of his bad character. She would just have to take care of herself. She could see the indented skin on his wedding ring finger for herself or perhaps she had also seen him take it off since she had been riding in his jeep.

Cassie seemed glad to be on her own and rushed down to the water's edge wading out to her waist. Just as she was about to thrust her arms and head into the water to swim out, a three-foot wave tumbled her back toward the beach. She stood up and shook herself looking out at the ocean which seemed to lunge back and forth like something live.

"Hey, take care! I don't want to have to explain why I brought back only three of you girls," shouted Major Sykes. Soon we had all followed Cassie into the water but with less bravery.

Major Sykes seemed to always be near by where I was splashing. I had never learned to swim, thus I stayed in the calm water close to the black sand. Also, I didn't want to get my hair wet, lest it curl up too tightly. I was aware of the major's presence nearby and it made me uncomfortable at the same time I observed how handsome he was in his swimming suit. A comparison of him anonymous in his surgeon's gown flitted through my mind. His height of over six feet showed off his the rim of dark wavy auburn hair around his pate and his chest full of curling dark hair. His swim trunks clung to his abdomen and privates. It embarrassed me to think of this though the coldness of the water did not allow an erection. Despite my inexperience with men generally, I had had enough experience as a nurse and an occupational therapist to have to have seen patients with erections. I was aware of the difference in how I was regarding Major Sykes. This is what embarrassed me, I realized.

"Can I call you Clara?" Major Sykes suddenly asked. Without waiting for my consent, he went on, "I'm going to swim out a little bit but I just wanted to be sure you are OK. You don't act like you have had much experience in the water."

Not wanting to explain why I simply replied, "No I didn't ever have the chance to learn." Putting the focus back on him, I asked, "Have you been a swimmer for long?"

"Oh, yes, I grew up by Lake Erie near Buffalo, New York. We always swam in the lake in summer."

Keeping the focus on him instead of me, I asked, "We, does that mean with your family or friends?"

"Both, I guess. I had a couple brothers and we always went, but in high school, I went with my friends." He suddenly looked self-conscious. I wondered what he was hiding that caused him to seem embarrassed.

I did not feel I was in a position to ask bluntly about his reaction so I said, "It must have been nice having brothers. Are they in the service, too?"

Glad to have the topic changed, he said, "I'll tell you when I get back. Right now I want to swim before the sun starts to set." He dove into the water before a wave could drag him toward the beach. He obvious felt quite at ease in these turbulent water of Punalu`u Harbor. I could hardly take my eyes off him as his vigorous strokes took him almost out of sight. I had some difficulty concentrating on what the others were saying until he stepped dripping out unto the black sand half an hour later.

I kept myself from obviously seeming preoccupied with him by walking to where Pvt. Stilley was tending a fire and whittling sticks for us to use later to cook our steaks over the fire. I wondered how they managed to get steaks. By bribing the cooks perhaps, I guessed. The others all seemed involved in water play near the edge of the harbor or in exploring our little bit of beach, except Cassie who had sat down on a rock and seemed to be writing. I guess she had decided enough of the waves.

Major Beving and Lt. Sisco had started a card game on one of the bedrolls. Major Zukoski and the dietician Wanda Lindley were looking through the hampers to see what was for supper. It just occurred to me then that Wanda must have had a hand in planning the meals for our outing. Maybe she was somehow able to get special food like steaks. However, I was sure it was not she who had provided the beer.

By this time of the late afternoon, everyone of our group had gotten back into their regular clothes as the afternoon wind was too cold for bathing suits.

The Marines had gathered up their gear and left the beach to us. I looked to see where Pvt. Stilley had put our bedrolls. He had grouped the women together and the men together, I supposed according to orders from Major Sykes. This was a relief to me.

After we had cooked and eaten our steaks and potatoes baked in the coals, Pvt. Stilley brought out his harmonica and I realized another reason Major Sykes had brought him along. I had no idea he was so talented. He seemed to know how to play all the popular songs; "When the Lights Go on Again All Over the World", "I'm Beginning to See the Light", "Juke Box Saturday Night", "Love Letters in the Sand", "A String of Pearls" and even "I'll Be Home for Christmas." When he started on "The Anniversary Waltz", Major Sykes stood up and reached down pulling me up into his arms and we danced there on the lava rock shelf above the glinting water. I was surprised but I did not resist and found I enjoyed being held in his arms. It was very romantic and before the waltz ended there were three couples dancing on the beach. Cassie sat with Pvt. Stilley and watched. I had had no idea Pvt. Stilley was so gifted and I silently vowed to engage him in some entertainment sessions for recreation for the patients. I realized I did not even know his first name.

Everyone was quiet after we sat down until Pvt. Stilley played "Don't Get around Much Anymore" and Major Sykes began to sing along in his rich baritone.

Soon every one was singing; "A Nightingale Sang in Berkeley Square", "One for My Baby", "Cruising down the River", "This is the Army Mr. Brown" and "I'll Be Loving You Always." This last song seemed to lead everyone into a somber mood and soon we scattered to wrap up in the blankets on our bedrolls.

Major Sykes asked me, "Would you like to take a walk down to the shore?"

He was so attractive that I was tempted but I feared he might bring up the illegal abortion so I made an excuse of being too tired.

He looked chagrined at my refusal but I turned and went toward the girls' bedrolls.

After we had all bedded down, we witnessed a canoe full of Hawaiians apparently returning from a fishing expedition as they noisily drew in and pulled their vessel up into one of the rough boathouse shelters further down the beach. They ignored our presence as they called out to each other and even sang as they trudged up the road with their nets

The next morning when I awoke with first light, there were only three of us clustered near the coconut trees where Pvt. Stilley had placed the girls' bedrolls. Being curious, I raised my head and discovered that Beatrice Sisco was not there. Oh, my God, I thought, I hope she hasn't put herself in the same position of Lt. Wagner. Knowing there was nothing I could do, I slipped back into my bedroll after answering the call of nature under a shrub up the hill. Soon, I heard the scuffling of a bedroll being dragged and realized she was back with us. It seemed none of the other girls were awake to notice her disappearance and reappearance.

Before we gathered our things into the jeeps, we all took another dip in the morning surf awhile the tide was out and we could see more of the beach.

CHAPTER 30

Return Up the Hill

The fog had rolled in as we dried off and packed our suits. Daylight had revealed on the hills and near the beach, small wooden homes of some Hawaiians. We had been oblivious to them the evening before, perhaps because they were nestled back into the kiawe thickets. Had I taken the walk with Major Sykes, we undoubtedly would have passed some on that trail. Our campfire had completely gone out during the night and rather than wait until Pvt. Stilley could rustle up some camp breakfast, Major Sykes decided that we should all eat just bread and butter and coffee from the thermos. He acted a bit more peremptory this morning. Perhaps he was not a morning person, I thought, or maybe he was angry we never took that walk.

Soon we were back in the bone-jarring jeeps which were so noisy that conversation was prohibitive. When we finally drove off, we went up unto a plateau of smooth rock beside the road where we stopped for an early lunch. Our bodies already stiff from the night on the ground, suffered further abuse from the jeep ride so we almost had to pull each other out of the vehicles. Major Sykes surveyed this flat spot and ordered Pvt. Stilley to gather some of the dead wood lying about. We were almost above the fog now but the air felt cool. Wind moved the low vegetation surrounding this barren desert scene. I felt sorry for Pvt. Stilley who seemed to have to do all the work so I yelled, "Come on, Cassie, let's help Pvt. Stilley get the wood."

This seemed to put Major Sykes into an even darker mood as he watched us gather quite a stack of fallen branches, while Pvt. Stilley dragged the hampers over toward the fire. The cook had sent boiled eggs so Wanda helped peel the eggs to make egg salad sandwiches. These along with apples and bananas made up our mid-morning lunch. Pvt. Stilley made fresh coffee on the fire. This livened us enough to embark on the last two-thirds of our beach and mountain outing.

I decided to wait until Beatrice Sisco and I had some privacy back in the nurse's cottage to warn her about Major Beving's womanizing without telling her how I knew this about him. It would have been hard to get her aside anyway as she seemed glued to Major Beving's side. I wondered if I should confide in Cassie about the illegal abortion and Major Beving's probable cause of Lt. Wagner's departure from the Hospital on the Hill. Cassie's Catholic upbringing seldom came into our conversation but I did not want to risk offending her and losing one of the friends I had developed. I knew she went to mass regularly but we had never discussed religion in a deep way as I had more or less stopped going to church after I left Selma. I knew very little about the Catholic religion except myths Baptists in Selma had repeated. Until I met Cassie, I'd never even talked to a Catholic that I knew of.

Major Zukoski and Wanda leaned against the back of one of the jeeps and talked about the challenges of the patients who had caught diseases in the jungles of Guadalcanal, New Guinea, and the Solomon Islands. These two seemed totally engrossed in discussing solutions for their patients.

Wanda wondered, "Do you know if any special diets that had been tried for diarrhea have worked?"

"That's your department! As for me, I find the drug Atabrine works best on almost all those jungle diseases these fellows bring back," he informed her. His mode was playful but not flirtatious. He wore his wedding ring without trying to hide it and was just enjoying a normal conversation with a woman, it seemed.

Wanda questioned Doctor Zukoski if there was any remedy she could supply from the kitchen for the poor buggers who had contracted schistosomiasis from wading in contaminated water while in the jungle.

"Well, I trust the new drugs mostly but the penicillin doesn't work on those protozoa. I think any soldier heals better if he has a good diet. Did your dietician training have any thing about parasites?"

I stopped listening.

Major Sykes dour mood inclined me toward avoiding him as much as possible. Helping Pvt. Stilley seemed the best way to avoid him since I couldn't really walk very far away from him here in this high desert. I served the coffee after Pvt. Stilley poured it into the metal cups we had brought. Though the sun was beating down, everyone relished fresh hot coffee. The view across the valley to Mauna Loa Mountain at this elevation was spectacular. It provided sufficient reason to contemplate and avoid talking. Besides, we could see that the fog which appeared at dawn on the coast had disappeared. We had somehow missed the most direct sun so nobody was complaining of sunburn.

The drivers parked the jeeps outside the new Volcano House and we went inside. The huge fireplace, made of lava rock in the front parlor was very impressive. We could hear plenty of noise coming from the bar. There were uniformed men everywhere it seemed, especially sailors. Most of them were smoking cigarettes. Though we were not in uniform, the staff seemed to immediately know that we were Army. Somehow, these doctors commanded deference even without their uniforms. Perhaps they had visited here before.

It was late afternoon, so we imbibed only of tea and coffee in the café. However, we were lucky enough to get two tables near the big window looking out over the crater.

The women we saw sitting with the sailors were not in uniform and they looked like they were from Hawaii. Their hair was black. Their skin was naturally darker than mine, not as if they had been out in the sun more than me. We were all wearing slacks and these local looking girls sitting with the sailors were in lovely dresses. We four "Caucasian" women got plenty of glances from the fellows in uniform but it was obvious we were not free for flirting as the doctors and Pvt. Stilley stuck close to us.

The sun had disappeared in the clouds behind us as we rounded the turn by Pszyk Road and drove through Mountain View Village.

CHAPTER 31

Where is He?

When the jeeps drove up in front of the nurses' cottage, Major Sykes leapt out and gave me a hand to exit the jump seat in the back. Then he ordered Pvt. Stilley to assist Cassie as well though she was already half out.

With half the patients gone, the Hospital on the Hill seemed quiet when we got back. This gave us all a chance to recover from our beach outing. Luckily we had not really had time to get a good sunburn except on our faces from riding in the jeep and all our swimming had been when the sun was low. We had not been out in the sun at midday when most folks get sunburned as we had been covered up with long sleeved shirts and slacks most of the time. Besides Cassie and I probably wouldn't have sunburned anyway. None-the-less, we were fatigued and needed some good sleep to recover from the long hours in the bumpy jeeps.

Next morning when I went first down to the Section 8 Building to see how many of the "battle fatigue" patients were still in residence, I learned from the nurse in charge that Arne Erickson had disappeared. They radioed from the ship that he had been scheduled to be on the departing ship, but he had not been accounted for when they did a final count of patients. His bed awaited another patient. The temporary shelves he had made under his bed were still there, but empty.

He had not been put on the AWOL list yet as staff wanted to be sure he had not somehow been on the hospital ship by some counting error despite evidence to the contrary. He had been on the list to be shipped out with those patients but mistakes were sometimes made. A telegram had been sent to Letterman General Hospital on the Presidio Army Base in San Francisco where the ship was expected to dock on Wednesday to see if somehow he had actually been on board. Meanwhile we kept the information of his missing state within the hospital. We did not like to lose patients, for any reason.

A ship arrived on Tuesday from the South Pacific with more patients. We were so busy, that the status of Arne Erikson disappeared from our minds and concerns. When the ship full of new patients arrived from Australia, it was necessary to sort them into the different wards within the patient barracks for infectious diseases, for wounds, for surgery and for "battle fatigue." This took more than a whole day to get everyone to the right place.

On Thursday, a telegram came back from Letterman General Hospital that there had been no Arne Erickson on the ship though his name was on the manifest as was his service record. Now his name was put on the AWOL list and military police began asking local Mountain View citizens if they might have seen him. During the confusion of assembling the convoy to the hospital ship, he could easily have slipped away and gotten on a train to Hilo. If he was in civilian clothes, he should have been noticed since most haole men here were in uniform.

Meanwhile, Dr. Beving summoned me to his office in the school administration building down the hill to question me about what I knew that might help him learn where Arne had gone. I was leery of visiting him in his private office which was in an alcove shaped from some temporary walls in a former classroom.

"Lt. Brett, so we meet again," Dr. Beving started in a rather flirtatious voice. "What do you know that might help us find Sergeant Erickson? He might have told something to someone as pretty as you."

I felt myself blushing but doubted it showed on my ecru skin so I went on anyway, "I was as surprised as anyone else that he has disappeared. Though I found Sergeant Erickson challenging to work with, I could see that he was searching for a way to get back to himself."

As I sat across from him, I notice a stack of unopened v-mail and regular airmail envelopes on his desk. I tried to see the return address on the top one, wondering how he could bear not to open them since most fellows lived for the letters from home.

The doctor explained, "I had discussed the possibility with him of trying electro-shock therapy since nothing else seemed to get the results we were looking for. He saw how the patient Elmer Schmidt was when he came back after having a treatment. Maybe that scared him and caused him to go AWOL, and he probably knows that a soldier with conversion neurosis almost always gets discharged. They don't make good soldiers," Dr. Beving continued. "Of course, he could just be out hunting for girls."

The doctor seemed to be flirting with me even as he explained this. He seemed oblivious to me casting my eyes on the stack of letters. I noticed he still had not replaced his wedding ring on his finger. I managed to get away from Dr. Beving's office before he could make any unwelcome proposals.

Later Private Owen reported that he had had the opportunity to talk to one of the Japanese plantation workers who frequented the local gambling casino up the street from the Yamada Theater. The worker said he had given a red-headed soldier a ride down to Kurtistown in his plantation truck Saturday evening. He thought the soldier was just trying to find a little Saturday night fun as he asked where he could find a place to get a drink when he dropped him off. Rules of sale of alcohol had just been relaxed.

After a staff meeting by the doctors and Capt. Sullivan, we were informed that since he had not reappeared, he was considered permanently AWOL which some considered the equivalent of desertion of duty. However, we were now focused on the priorities of our new patients. None-the-less, Sergeant Erickson lingered in my mind.

More than a year had passed since the famous event when General Patton had cursed and slapped the soldier who said his diagnosis was "nerves", when the general was touring the 93rd Evacuation Hospital near the front in Italy. While it had happened half a world away, the story had by now made its way to Hawaii Island more than a year later. The general had called the patient "a yellow bastard" and a "whimpering coward." The patient had been afflicted with malaria, a fever and chills and had already requested to be returned to the front when the general exhibited his rage. The injustice of this had been discussed by patients and nurses who had expressed what they intended to do if such an officer threatened their patients.

Going AWOL, absent without leave, was another matter. This was indeed considered desertion. While military police searched, the nurses and I discussed our various hospital experiences with Arne. Though I was reluctant to share that I allowed him to use me as a portrait model, I decided under the circumstances

I must share about the disturbing picture with the threatening faces in the background.

"Was that wise, to allow him to be treated as special, Lt. Brett?" questioned Captain Sullivan.

I decided it was best to not defend myself and replied, "Perhaps it was not wise but he seemed to be much better when he was allowed to do art. Since he was a military artist, I was influenced to comply with his request for me to model, as my job is to help men return to work."

"Well, it probably doesn't have anything to do with his going AWOL. If he was flirting with you, he'd probably still be around."

The military police used the line of least difficulty when searching out AWOL soldiers, we learned. They questioned the storekeeper in Kurtistown who admitted to seeing the "red-headed haole. "I sold him some beer and when I went to lock the back door, the haole man was sitting down on the ground sharing his beer with a couple kanakas who live out in the forest." The storekeeper motioned to the south. "They plenty lava tubes where kanakas live out in da forest," he went on.

The military police knew better than to try to go searching for lava tubes. The island was perforated with them they knew and their chances of finding him were almost nil. So Arne just stayed on the AWOL list.

CHAPTER 32

As Husbands Go

The night of the play arrived. Pvt. Owen had gotten a couple of local girls from Mt. View to take the parts of the daughter and the maid in "As Husbands Go." He had approached the young Japanese woman who worked in the laundry to be an actress and to bring her girlfriend to take the maid's part.

Cassie remarked, "These Japanese girls are so cute that all the soldiers that work on the sets want to help them learn the few lines they have to say. I think that makes Wanda jealous."

"Don't you care," I asked her.

"Nah, I don't care what these soldiers think. I only care if they do what I tell them in physical therapy. Most of these guys are dimwits. I just feel sorry for their injuries."

None-the-less, she took her acting part seriously and gave a bravo performance along with the rest of the cast. The Yamada Theater was so small, that they performed the play two nights in a row so everyone who wanted could see it.

After the second night, Capt Sullivan and the doctors hosted a party for the cast and stage crew. Though I was not part of either group, I was invited. The Japanese girls, Umeyo and Mitsuko, in the cast had declined the invitation, we knew not why. I wondered if they feared they might not be safe so late in a military establishment but I did not ask. If they had wanted to come, I felt sure we could have made up a party of women and men to walk them home to the Ueyama Camp. They still declined to come to the cast party. This landing of a whole bunch of Caucasian military people in the middle of a mostly Japanese community was hard for them to stomach, I felt sure.

Because the party was held in the recreation room, I had used occupational therapy supplies to make some festive decorations with the help of some patients. Festoons of paper twirled across the room beneath the ceiling. A tarp covered the pool table where the hors d'oeuvres were spread. The first scene of the play had taken part in Paris. The recent Allied Army conquering of Le Havre, Calais and Boulogne had reinvigorated American Francophile feelings. So a French flag which a nurse who had transferred from the French front had brought and an American flag were draped over my bulletin board. The cooks had prepared French fries, deviled eggs from the many already boiled eggs that they received in the food shipments, peanut butter cookies, and punch from local Hawaiian fruits. The cooks had put red food coloring into it to make it look like French wine.

It was against regulations to serve alcohol in an Army hospital but people slipped outside and shared the liquor they had hidden in the nearby forest. By midnight, almost everyone was intoxicated to some degree including me. We all agreed that Pvt. Owens should be reassigned to our unit rather than being sent back to fight. His job should be in recreation since he was so good at it.

When Cassie, Wanda and Beatrice got back up to the nurses' cottage, Lt. Shirley Thompson, who had replaced Nurse Wagner, had just come in from her noon to midnight shift. She informed us, "Sergeant Erickson, the patient who went AWOL, had been brought back to the Section 8 Barracks by the military police from Hilo."

Where was he all this time?" I asked. "And how did the military police from Hilo find him?"

"Well, you can probably get the whole story from him tomorrow. But the MPs reported that he had been picked up hitchhiking in the village of Kurtistown and taken to the brig in Hilo. They said they were only returning him to us since he had been a patient in our hospital," Lt. Thompson explained.

Despite my curiosity about his recent whereabouts, the few drinks I had ingested helped put me right to sleep.

Next morning, after two cups of coffee with milk and some buttered toast, I was able to drag myself to the recreation room first to make sure that the corpsman was properly supervising patients there. Then I walked down the gravel path to the Section 8 barracks. I found a rather belligerent Sergeant Erickson sitting on his bed doodling on a newsprint tablet. His face had several shaving nicks which looked red and raw on his pale "red-head" skin. He was dressed in Army hospital pajamas.

"I missed you Sergeant Erickson," I said. "Sometime, I hope you tell me about this adventure."

At first, I got only a grunt in acknowledgment of my request. Then, he said, "I just needed to see more of this island and I figured this was my only chance."

"So you chose the confusion of moving patients to sneak away, yes? Did you think of it as going AWOL?" I asked.

"I didn't care. Being in a Section 8 building already made me a creep. Being AWOL didn't seem any worse since I was already an outcast." Arne's head hung glumly so I just barely heard his words.

"Well I haven't had much of a chance to see much in Hawaii either. Maybe you'll tell me what you saw?" I encouraged. I was curious and did not intend to share whatever Arne said with Dr. Beving, whom I distrusted.

He perked up a little as he said, "This is just for you, not for my service record, OK?"

Knowing I'd have to tell the others on the staff if he said anything too out of line, but also knowing he wouldn't tell me unless I convinced him of my trustworthiness, so I nodded my head, and said, "Well, I don't think Dr. Beving will give you a grounds pass to come to the recreation room after you just went AWOL, but after I finish up up there this afternoon, I'll come down here while the other patients are eating dinner and you can tell me then, OK?"

CHAPTER 33

Lava Tube Living

"Well, I brought my lunch to eat while you tell me about where you went and what happened," I announced as I drew up a chair near the foot of Arne's bed.

The section 8 patients without grounds passes had already eaten their noon meal before I arrived. The nurse and the corpsman were stacking the cart which held the serving pots with the used dishes and cutlery, ready for it to be rolled down the boardwalk ramp and back to the kitchen. All the patients seemed to be watching me to see what I was going to have for my lunch.

Arne slid down until he was sitting near the low metal foot of the bed. There really was no true privacy in a hospital ward but he lowered his voice so his fellow patients would have to struggle to hear our conversation." You already know I went AWOL, but I did get out for a while," he grinned. Mostly, he didn't care whether or not other patients heard him, it seemed. In fact there was almost a bragging bravado quality to his story.

"Well did you get to see some of the Island of Hawaii, like you wanted to?" I asked.

"The part I saw is probably not what you would have wanted to see. When I realized how crazy it was going to be here when they started moving patients, I figured I wouldn't be missed for a while so I got as much of my stuff as I could carry, dressed in my civvies and walked down to Mt. View train station and waited for the next train. It took so long to come, that I got tired and walked back to the village where this Jap worker picked me up in a plantation truck."

"Weren't you afraid of being recognized?" I questioned.

"Well, there was always that chance but I figured I'd never get another. Besides, everybody was busy over here. So I got in this guy's truck and asked him if he was going to Hilo but when he said he was only going as far as Kurtistown, I decided it might be better to just go there. Hilo is where the MPs would expect me to go, so I was glad to get off in Kurtistown at the Sako Store. That's where the guy dropped me."

"Did you stay in Kurtistown this whole time?" I inquired.

"Nah, just that first afternoon. I bought a few bottles of beer since I hadn't had any for months. I had thought about setting up a still out in the jungle and making banana wine but never got a chance. There's always somebody watching here in this barracks."

I acknowledged his account with head nods and grunts to let him know I was listening while I ate my cheese sandwich and apple.

"I went out behind the store to drink them beers because I was afraid if I sat in front by the road, somebody from the hospital might see me and turn me in. The convoy was just leaving I figured. There were a couple kanakas out there drinking their own beer so I sat down with them. At first they acted kind of unfriendly, but after I offered them a couple of my beers, they became more friendly and pretty soon, they asked me to go in and buy some more. Then one of them picks up his ukulele and starts singing a Hawaiian song. They try to teach it to me, but I don't know no Hawaiian. Well pretty soon, I started teaching them 'Home on the Range' and some other American songs. We git friendly. Then they invite me to come with them to their cave in a lava tube. This was the Hawaii I'd been wanting to see, so I agreed. I bought some more beer and by the time we got to their cave by walking through the cane field and down a gulch, we were all feeling pretty good. They told me their names; Koma and Lopaka. When we got to the cave, there was a Hawaiian woman there. She was sitting on a pile of lumber which looked like it had been stolen from a building site. She was cooking something over a campfire just inside the cave. They told me her name was Kamila."

"Was she living in the cave, too?" I was thinking that this had turned out to be quite an adventure for this Minnesota boy.

"Well, none of them were actually living in there permanently. They would just come and go. They told me there were plenty other caves around where people could sleep out of the rain if they got tired of the company in one cave. The cave was not high enough to stand up straight in it. The bottom of the cave was kind of rounded like a tube. Old blankets and quilts were thrown on top of a pile of lava rocks stacked back where the lava tube narrowed. They threw them back there to keep them away from the constantly dripping ceiling. The floor was damp. It had some of these rock icicles hanging from the ceiling. Outside, there were piles of rubbish all around the edge of the campsite, tin cans and bottles."

I made sounds of acknowledgment though my mouth full of sandwich and I nodded encouragingly for him to continue.

"Pretty soon we were all pretty drunked up including the woman. Lopaka keeps playing and singing Hawaiian songs and the woman starts doing a hula dance right outside the cave near the fire. By now it's dark. Before you know it, Koma's up there dancing the hula with her. She comes over and grabs me and pulls me up to dance too. Koma didn't like that and he swung at me, but he was too drunk and missed and fell down and did not get up. Then the purple stuff she was cooking was finished and the three of us ate some on plates made out of leaves."

Curious about the woman and the food, I asked, "What was the purple stuff? Was the woman wearing a grass skirt?"

"Nah, she was wearing blue jeans and one of those shirts like the Japanese women wear. Dresses don't go good out there in the jungle. Not even grass skirts, I guess. The purple stuff was sweet potatoes, purple sweet potatoes!" He seemed slightly irritated that I had interrupted his story. "After we ate and finished the beer, Koma woke up and pulled the boards inside the cave to cover up the wet floor and then grabbed the blankets and fell asleep. He had forgotten all about trying to punch me I guess. I joined him in the lava tube. Lopaka took the woman off into the jungle for a little hoochy-koochy and Koma and me fell asleep there inside the cave." Arne glanced at me to see my reaction to his reference to sex. I simply nodded in acknowledgment not wanting to interrupt his story again.

Arne went on with his story, "When I woke up, I was thirsty but couldn't find no water. We'd drunk all the beer so I wandered off toward where I heard running water. I drank from my hands and headed back to the cave, but it was so thick and dark in the jungle, even though the sun was up, that I got lost until I heard yelling and followed the voices. Koma had woken up and went to get more beer. We ate the rest of the sweet potatoes left over from the night before. When Koma got back, Lopaka took two beers, one for himself and another for Kamila and then Koma got mad and swung at Lopaka. Before you know it, Koma cracked his beer bottle against a rock and takes off after Lopaka who ran into the jungle with the woman yelling and following and here I was left all alone."

Imagining myself in his shoes lost in the jungle, I asked, "What did you do? Did you have any money?"

"Nah, we'd spent all my money on beer." He became quiet for a few moments as he relived the scene in his head. "I figured they'd be back sooner or later, but nobody showed up so after a couple hours, I decided to follow a path that led downhill. When I could see the sun above me through the jungle, I figured out that I must be walking south since it was almost November now, though I hadn't been keeping track of the days. When it was about noon by the position of the sun, I heard some voices and started heading toward them. It was a cane field and there were a bunch of Japs sittin' down at the edge, eatin' out of these little metal boxes. At first I thought they were the enemy invaders but then I could see that they didn't have no weapons except machetes. I couldn't hardly understand them, but they motioned me to sit down and a couple offered me rice balls from their boxes. They had bottles of tea and they let me have a drink. By then I was plenty thirsty having walked several miles on a rocky trail in wet muddy boots. Besides I was still feeling last night's drinking."

"Have you ever meet Umeyo and Mitsuko, those girls from the Ueyama Camp?" I asked, wondering if he had ever met any Japanese people before.

"There weren't any women in this group. Nah, I never met any Japanese girls or men before. These guys seemed friendly enough but pretty soon they went back to work. I went around the edge of the field hiding back in the cane about this high when I saw this guy on a horse," Arne held his hand above his head to show how high it was. "He looked like he was the boss and I didn't want to get caught by him. So I ducked back in the cane until he was gone. Then I tried to find the trail back to Kurtistown. I just kept going toward the mountain I knew was on the north."

"My lunch recess is over," I said reluctantly. "I have to go back up to the recreation hall to show a fellow how to use the ceramic kick wheel," I explained as I stood up. "I'll have to hear the rest of your story later. I'll be back later this afternoon to work in the garden if the rain stops." I knew that men who went AWOL usually went to the brig, but since he was a psychiatric patient he would probably just be given a dishonorable discharge.

CHAPTER 34

Newspaper Boy

Tadashi, the little Japanese boy who called himself Tom was in the recreation room when I got there. For the fourth year in a row, since the Army had taken over their school, students in Mountain View had been attending classes in haphazard classrooms in homes and Sunday school rooms. The schools had suffered greatly during the war as many teachers and other school staff had joined the military services or civilian government services. These teacher shortages sometimes resulted in children being squeezed into crowded rooms or being released from classes early. Older students were often recruited from classes to work in the fields especially during harvest. This September, there was an especially large Kona coffee crop which had been delayed due to excessive rain. Even teenagers from Mountain View were recruited to coffee camps on the other side of the island of Hawaii.

When eight year old Tadashi showed up with his newspapers, we were never sure whether he was a truant, or whether his class had been dismissed. Since it was now after one o'clock in the afternoon, I assumed his classes were over.

Tadashi parried with the soldiers as they taunted him, "So what are the Japs doing today, planning to bomb Hilo?" or, "Are you related to Hirohito? Are you sending messages to General "Yamashita?" or "Tell Tojo to watch out!"

"I'm American. I'm born in Hawaii. I ain't no Jap!" he responded. "Look here. The 100th guys home on furlough. They been fightin' for the Allies!" He held up the headlines over the photo of the famous 100th, or at least they were famous in Hawaii.

"Oh, those guys just came home to spy on us," taunted one of the pool players as he dug a nickel out of his pocket to pay for the paper.

Tadashi simply ignored the taunts and tended to the sale of his papers.

The pool player continued his badinage with, "Get me a date with your sister and then I'll believe you are not a spy yourself."

"My mother no like soldiers. She tells my sisttah 'No go with haole soldier'." Tadashi replied easily and laughed. It was apparent that he was used to this kind of interchange. Tadashi's reply made it obvious that the soldiers and the boy had a warm relationship.

Captain Sullivan had told us that she had written an article for "The Defender", the section published once a week of the daily Hilo Tribune Herald to report on what was happening in the different military camps and services." The Defender" had jokes, cartoons, articles by service members, and schedules of the various USOs. Some of the jokes were pretty silly such as:

"Well Doctor, How's Thompson this morning?"

"Coming along nicely! This morning he took a turn for the nurse."

The chief nurse of the Hospital on the Hill was requested to write an article once per month. This was Captain Sullivan's first article so we were all eager to read about ourselves through her eyes. The article she wrote was about the performance of "As Husbands Go." She had told us that she had praised the community for their support and participation for the entertainment of the sick soldiers. I wanted to read it and report back to the others in the nurses' cottage later so I brought out my nickel and handed it to him. He handed the paper to me and as I unfolded it I saw a note folded inside. As soon as possible, I went to my desk and read the note while hiding it inside the newspaper.

The note said:

Major Beving wants to take you to the Annual Football Frolic this Sat. at the Waiakea Settlement Gym in Hilo. He says nobody will know you there. I

told him you would go. He will pick you up at 1900.

The presumptuousness of Woodrow made me angry. He had not even signed his name knowing I would know who sent this note. I quickly wrote a response and handed it to Tadashi Tom with another nickel to bribe him to deliver it to Woodrow. I wrote:

Tell the Major I do not date married men.

I did not sign mine either, as Woodrow would know who sent it, and I did not want anyone else who might inadvertently read the note to know who sent it.

CHAPTER 35

Threat

I felt so worried that I consciously had to distract myself by concentrating on my work; my patients and their problems such as, that the wheel chair ramps from the boardwalk to the doors of the barracks and recreation room were all too steep. I worried that patients on crutches would fall or wheelchair patients would be too weak to keep from rolling off the edge. I promised myself to get a duty detail to fix this problem.

The note said that I got back from Woodrow which was carried by Tadashi:

You go or I'll tell:

I did not have to guess what he would tell. I wondered what Dr. Beving held over Woodrow to force him to do this. He would cause both of us to be discharged or at least be transferred to black units. I felt trapped. It felt so unfair to be in this compromising position. I did not like Dr. Beving, let alone want to spend an evening with him. Even if he were single, I would not have wanted to spend time with him. He seemed sly and seemed to enjoy others' discomfort. He reveled in the idea that he as a doctor had power over his patients. But wouldn't keeping my position in the nurses' corps be worth sacrificing the one evening that he seemed to be asking? I wouldn't have minded being blackmailed to go to a dance if it were Major Sykes, I thought.

I asked Tadashi, "Would you come back and get a note later this afternoon?"

This little boy had a winning personality and readily agreed. As I considered what I would write in the note so it did not sound to Woodrow like acquiescent or agreement to any further demands, I also wondered what I could give to Tadashi as payment for his courier services. I decided a proper payment would be to offer to teach him how to make a canvas sling to carry his newspapers. I had the materials and had instructions in the Army manual for occupational therapists. Meanwhile I struggled with the wording of my note.

Just this once, **BUT ONLY ONCE** will I help you keep your promise to get me to go with him. I will walk to the motor pool. I do not want him to pick me up.

On Saturday, after I left Pvt. Stilley in charge of the Recreation Room, I hurried back to the nurse's cottage. Because it was between change of nursing shifts, nobody was awake when I got there so I was able to change my clothes without any observation.

I decided I would wear my one really nice civilian outfit which was pale blue rayon gabardine. It had a bow tie at the throat so there was no need to wear a blouse under it. The only times when I had been in Hilo before had been during the day and it had been too hot to wear that many thicknesses of clothing but now it was getting slightly cooler. I had not been in Hilo at night, so I had to use my best judgment about what to wear. I decided to wear my Army cape over it as a sort of way to be more anonymous now that Hilo was such military town with all the training camps nearby. As I walked across the road toward the motor pool, I enjoyed the silky feeling of the rayon compared to the white cotton uniform I usually wore. None-the-less, I dreaded the evening ahead, knowing I would have to use all my wiles to keep Major Beving's hands off me except during dancing.

I arrived at the motor pool just a few moments before 15:00. I could smell the mechanical smells of gasoline and oil as I approached the fenced yard where the vehicles were parked off the road. Major Beving was sitting in the jeep already but he leapt out and ran around to assist me into the passenger seat. He had put the canvas cover up over the jeep for which I was grateful. Even if there was no rain, there was almost always heavy dew in the nighttimes. Also, the cover made me less visible to passersby.

As we drove down the hill with the lights off, we fortunately met almost no traffic. The ones we did meet had engines working hard to climb this mountain and thus we could hear them coming even without lights. At this time of year, it was dark even as we started our descent.

I had dreaded any conversation as my feelings toward him were so defensive, but he took off discussing different bands and musical styles. I merely had to give murmurs of acknowledgment of his observations about musicians. He told of having played in his high school band. My Knox High School had had no money or tradition of a school band so I had nothing to reply with in this realm. I tried to discuss Arne Erickson with him hoping to keep this on a professional basis but he refused saying "This is time for fun. Forget about the patients!"

The smell of the ocean blew over us as we parked in the marshy grass near the gymnasium. We could hear the band playing as we crossed the road toward the gym. It was obvious to me that Major Beving was already familiar with this place. I realized he must have brought other girls here. As we mounted the board walk which led to the door of the gymnasium, I could hear them playing the foxtrot "The Fleet's In." American flags draped the walls even though this was really just a high school dance. National patriotism took priority over school loyalty. The dozen or so members of this first band looked as if they were all of the Caucasian race. They looked like they were just boys from our troops though they were not in uniform. Local high school students of all the spectrum of races living here on Hawaii Island lined the first row of the bleachers while a few brave couples moved around the area of the gym used as a dance floor. When I looked more closely, I could see that the different racial groups clustered together. The Japanese boys clustered in one corner looking shyly at the girls. The Portuguese girls grouped together, touching each other's hair and helping adjust each others' dresses and earrings. The Japanese girls also clustered together bracing each other's courage. Occasionally, they glanced longingly at the Japanese boys or enviously at the glittering Portuguese girls. They were more casual and modestly dressed than the flashier Portuguese girls who wore more jewelry and lipstick. A variety of styles made up the clothing of all the girls as rationing had severely restricted what was available to sew. The military uniform needs had come before civilian clothing for several years by now and girls had had to innovate, remaking old worn-out dresses.

Major Beving took my cape and checked it with the hat-check boy at the door. Girls could not do that hat-check job as all girls were needed to dance with the men. In addition to the high schoolers, there were soldiers and sailors here as well. Then Major Beving swept me unto the floor to the sound of the fox trot "Sentimental Journey." He held me out so he could see my face, but gradually, his arms relaxed and seemed to be moving me closer in toward him. I offered some slight resistance as he tried to bring me closer to his body. Realizing my non-cooperation with his clutching attempt, he allowed me to keep my distance. Soon the music changed to the more rapid rhythm of "Juke Box Saturday Night" which allowed me to keep my distance through the vigor needed to maneuver for the fast steps. I did not have to try to talk or respond to Major Beving. Anyone who might have cut in looked at the major's brevets and passed us by. Obviously most of the men there were not officers. Few of the high school boys looked brave enough to cut in on the soldiers. Besides I observed that most of them stuck with their racial group when choosing dance partners.

When the band took a break, a Hawaiian band took over. Major Beving bought two fruit drinks from the concession stand and pulled a flask from his pocket. I just had time to cover my paper cup with my hand before he could pour some of the clear liquid in it. I made a joke of it about needing to be fresh to work tomorrow forgetting that it was Saturday night. He did not press me anymore at that time.

We were soon back on the dance floor dancing ballroom style to the Hawaiian music. Suddenly, I saw Dr. Sykes and Dr. Zukoski from the corner of my eye. They stood on the side while the Hawaiian band played and sang some Hawaiian song. The lead singer played some songs none of us knew on a slack-key guitar but we danced anyway until the leader announced that a hula was to be performed by two local Hawaiian girls. The lead singer announced that they were Hilo High School students. We all watched in fascination. The soldiers and sailors appreciated the sensuous movements and applauded loudly and made catcalls. Tension arose in the room seemingly as the local high school boys seemed ready to protect their girls from insult. Wisely, the lead singer called for another break. The temperature in the room seemed to cool and after the break and the band of Caucasian musicians took the stage again.

Suddenly, Major Sykes was tapping Major Beving on the shoulder to cut in. "You sly fox," he said to Major Beving as he swung me away.

Then as we swirled around the floor to "The Anniversary Waltz", he said, "You know he's married, don't you?"

"Oh, yes, I know," I said without explaining because I didn't know what else to say. However, I did realize that my body became more relaxed and I began to enjoy dancing. After a few minutes, I did think to ask, "So are you married, too?"

Major Sykes, gently pulled me closer so my face almost lay on his lapel as he said, "No, I was engaged before I went to medical school, but while I was away, she married somebody else. So I've nobody at home waiting for me."

By this many years into the war, I had heard enough stories of jilting and other unusual pairings or disjoining, that I was not surprised. So I responded in what I hoped was a proper therapeutic response, "That must be painful for you?"

"Oh, I'm over her long ago. My surgical training and medical work has absorbed me so much, I haven't had time to think much about it." His hand slipped up behind my neck under my hair and pulled me closer to his chest. "But now maybe its time to change that."

The band began to play the foxtrot "I'm Beginning to See the Light." Major Sykes sang along in a low voice as we moved a little apart to be comfortable with the faster steps. After the words "now that your lips are burning mine," he pulled me to him and kissed my mouth. My lifelong reticence about men's desires was quelled as I gave into and enjoyed the feeling.

Suddenly, Major Beving was beside us tapping Major Sykes on the shoulder, "May I cut in?"

Being the gentleman that he was, Dr. Sykes gracefully allowed me to be swept out of his arms and away. "Later" he mouthed a whisper to me.

It was a constant struggled to keep Major Beving's hands in the proper place on my back. He did his best to slide them against my breast when we twirled or to allow his left hand to slip down unto my buttock. This behavior was giving me the willies as I dreaded the ride back up the hill. Fortunately, Dr. Zukoski broke in and saved me. I wondered if

Major Sykes had sent him to do that.

When the band next took a break again, I excused myself to find the girls' restroom while Major Zukoski went to get more fruit juice. I told him, "Please just get water for me." I was grateful he offered to get me a beverage as I did not trust Major Beving to do it. I suspected Major Beving would lace a fruit drink with liquor if I were not watching. It would be harder to conceal liquor in plain water in case he tried to do it behind my back. I'd smell it immediately.

As I exited the girl's restroom, I encountered Major Sykes who seemed to almost be waiting for me. "Looks like Major Beving is giving you a difficult time. What are you going to do to make him behave on the drive back to the hospital?"

"I don't know," I said desperately. "If I could find another ride up the hill, I'd probably take it even though he would be mad."

"Well I have to work with him too so I don't want him mad at me either," said Dr. Sykes, "but maybe I can suggest that we convoy up the hill on the drive back. He will have to search hard for a reason not to do that."

When Major Zukoski handed me my paper cup of water, I sipped it sniffing to make sure he had not laced it with vodka or gin even though I had no reason to distrust him. Major Beving soon found me. Before the dancing resumed, Major Sykes came over to us and suggested, "Let's drive back up the hill in convoy. That will be safer for all of us in case the MPs stop us."

This was disingenuous as we all knew that MPs would give doctors the slip despite the recent order from Major General Henry Burgin of the Central Pacific Command who had just ordered that GIs that were driving drunk should be arrested. But the married Doctor Beving could hardly say he had plans to despoil me and riding in a convoy would hinder that, so he agreed. Major Beving and I took the lead while Drs. Zukoski and Sykes followed in their jeep without lights. I was glad as Major Beving seemed to keep a grip on himself and on his driving on this narrow road. He did not, it seemed, want the colleagues behind us to know he was drunk.

We delivered the jeeps to the motor pool and since we all walked in the same way up the hill to the nurses' and doctors' cottages which were next door to each other, I was not forced to be alone with Major Beving again that evening.

CHAPTER 36

Holloween Party

Next morning, Pvt. Stilley and I began our preparation for the Halloween party that I had gotten permission to arrange for the patients.

I enlisted Pvt. Earnest Owens to ask the Japanese girls, Umeyo and Mitsuko, with whom he had become quite friendly during "As Husbands Go" if he could get them to come to the Halloween party to increase the number of women in attendance as that usually cheered the patients up considerably. Mitsuko and Umeyo appeared to me to be even shier than the Japanese girls I had seen at the Football Frolic. I also extracted promises from all other female staff to attend if they were not on ward duty on Saturday night October 28th. The night before on October 27th, there was to be a Halloween Carnival at the Waiakea Settlement House, which I had learned about at the Football Frolic Dance. I did not want to compete with public events like that as most citizens patriotically welcomed all the soldiers and I knew some of them would want to attend that one as there would certainly be more girls in Hilo Town. Even the ones in wheelchairs liked to watch from the sidelines. An ambulance had been engaged to take a few patients and their wheelchairs to the Waiakea Halloween event the night before our party.

I asked Pvt. Stilley to ask Umeyo and Mitsuko where we could get some pumpkins to make jack-o-lanterns. He and Mitsuko came to the recreation room carrying baskets full of huge not-quite-ripe almost orange papayas on the morning of the 27th. We got knives from the kitchen. I enlisted several patients to help carve jack-o-lanterns from the not-quite-ripe papayas.

From the laundry, I borrowed several sheets to make ghosts to hang in the corners of the recreation room. The kitchen had promised to make some cake with orange frosting and to get some apples for bobbing.

Mitsuko was so sweetly shy when I asked her if she could find some other local girls to come and visit with the hospitalized soldiers at the party. "Maybe," was all she would promise.

Apparently Major Beving had not seen the notices about the occupational therapy Halloween Party. He sent a note via Pvt. Woodrow Minter.

Come to the movie in Hilo Saturday night. Gaslight has Charles Boyer, Joseph Cotton and

Ingrid Bergman.

He did not sign it, but instructed Woodrow to tell me who it came from. I had immediately recognized his handwriting anyway from looking at his notes in the patient files. I handed Woodrow one of the mimeographed fliers that I made and had posted in all the barracks and cottages as well as at the village bakery and laundry. There was no way I was going to sit with that lecher in a darkened theater. I was so glad I had a legitimate reason to refuse him. I was beginning to think it might be easier to just defy Woodrow and get discharged for lying about my race.

I took it back and quickly wrote a reply on the flier:

That is the night of our patient Halloween Party.

Sorry.

The corpsmen brought as many wheelchair-bound patients to the party as the room would hold. In fact, they had to bring some and then return them to their barracks and bring others so that most patients who wanted to could spend at least an hour in our festive rec-room. Using flashlights, they began bringing the patients about 1800. Pvt. Owens, whom we had gotten reassigned to our unit, had persuaded a wheelchair-bound soldier from Tennessee to sing and play the guitar that Owens had bought at a pawn shop in Hilo. He played songs that men knew and could sing along such as

"Shine on Harvest Moon", "Hail, Hail, the Gangs All Here", "Red River Valley", and "There is a Tavern in the Town." I had many things to be grateful to Pvt. Owens for in making the party a great success. We were all so glad he had not been sent back to shoot at Japs. The candles inside the papaya jack-o-lanterns made a flickering light on the walls. I had not bothered to use blackout curtains as this rule was seldom enforced now that the Japanese Navy was almost destroyed. The wavering light of the papaya jack-o-lanterns felt just right.

I had borrowed a wash-tub from the laundry for bobbing for apples. For the soldiers too disabled to bend over into the tub, I attached string to the apple stems and hung them from a hook in the ceiling. The length of the string was adapted to each soldier's capabilities. Some soldiers who had never before appeared in the rec-room seemed to have the most fun. Because Arne Erickson had gone AWOL, none of the Section 8 patients had been allowed to come to the rec-room by order of the commander. I did not agree with this edict but was compelled to follow it.

Umeyo and Mitsuko had been able to convince four of their friends to come. With Cassie, Wanda, Beatrice, and me, there were ten girls. I had persuaded our female staff members to dress in costume but I had been unable to get that message to the Japanese girls so they were clad in skirts and blouses. Cassie dressed as a cowboy while Wanda had made herself a cloth fishtail from a sheet and came as a mermaid while wearing her swimsuit. She was a hit. Beatrice, whom I knew less well, even though she was my roommate, dressed as a princess with a crown made from cardboard wrapped with copper foil from here in occupational therapy. She had used the occupational therapy sewing machine to whip up a long white princess dress from sheets.

I instructed all the girls to circulate, to please move around and talk to different men. Because the corpsmen kept rotating the men in wheelchairs, there were different men to talk to all evening. The Japanese girls seemed to have more difficulty terminating a conversation with the men, but those of us who had been working with the patients had developed kind ways to end conversations quickly. A couple of the Japanese girls were just high school students. The girls were all quite tolerant of the soldiers when they called them "Japs." It was a first time for many of these young men to meet anyone that looked like the "enemy" in a normal social situation. Because we were not allowed to serve alcohol and it was difficult for wheelchair patients to go off campus to get any from a bootlegger, we avoided the usual drunken fights that a group of young men often enjoyed.

I had not expected the doctors to attend but toward the end of the party about 2200 hours a group of the doctors did appear though they were in their white doctor's coats, not bona-fide costumes, including Sykes, Zukoski and Beving.

Well, now I knew that Beving knew at least that I had not been lying about the Halloween Party. I was not pleased to see him though I was glad for the patients that their doctors had joined us. This would encourage esprit de corps.

I had found a record player and a couple records and before the evening closed, Pvt. Stilley and the other corpsmen, pushed aside the pool table and we had a little dance floor in the middle of the room. The men who were ambulatory were not shy about asking us girls to dance. A patient in a wheelchair took over the record player and replayed "When the Lights Go on Again", "You'd Be So Nice to Come Home To", and "That Old Black Magic" over and over as they were the only records we had.

As the party ended, I asked the three doctors with whom I was familiar if they would walk with me to take the Japanese girls back to the Ueyama Camp where the girls lived. I did not feel it was safe for the girls to be out walking at night when there were so many marine training camps in the area. The girls were still under curfew as were all Japanese so I did not want them to be arrested either. I knew with the doctors in attendance there would be no chance of that. And I did not want to allow Beving to have a chance to get me alone, nor any of the Japanese girls either. I no longer felt like using the name of his rank when I thought of him. He didn't deserve it.

Leaving Pvt. Stilley to clean up, we seven girls

were accompanied by Doctors Zukoski, Beving and Sykes. We passed the Stable Road. It was the dark of the moon, so Major Sykes led with his flashlight. Because of Mt. View's unpredictable weather, I carried an umbrella just in case. We passed several plantation workers' homes. Most were quiet and dark. Music floated out from the steps of one where a fellow was singing to an ukulele.

Before I realized what was happening, Beving was dropping back further and further preventing Mitsuko from keeping up with the group. I didn't want to go back and chide him possibly making him think I was jealous but I couldn't allow such a man to intimidate one of these nice girls who had helped us more than once. She did not know that he was a married man.

I decided to stay with the group and ask Dr. Zukoski who also had a flashlight if he could go back and encourage them to keep up. "Major Zukoski, I'm afraid that Mitsuko and Major Beving are too far back. I'm responsible for getting her back to her camp safely. Could you go back and hurry them up?" I asked.

Major Zukoski, being one of the most agreeable white men I had met despite being a Southerner, nodded to me and slowed his step to fall back with them. "We don't want to lose you folks. Should we slow down or can you catch up?"

"We were just having a nice conversation," said Beving excusing himself. By this time, all of us Army folks knew his ways. Major Sykes realized what was happening and slowed his pace as well. With Umeyo leading the way with Dr. Sykes, we turned downhill at the next road. We walked each girl home to her worker's cottage. Umeyo was the first one to depart our small company. Each girl giggled, bade us goodbye, semi-bowed and thanked us, though I was the one in their debt. Mitsuko was the last one to leave us as we turned back up the hill on the Stable Road. Beving was obviously trying to hang back to talk to her after the rest of us headed up hill. Major Sykes aimed his flashlight back toward Beving's feet. Seeing this, Beving reluctantly turned up toward us.

As we walked, Beving began to expound, "Those Japanese girls love American soldiers. I could tell that one wanted to talk to me more."

"Major Beving, you are a married man," protested Major Zukoski. "Leave these girls alone."

"But Zukoski, my wife will never know and I don't believe she'd care if I get to know some local girls," said Beving. "I could tell from the way that girl looked at me and danced with me, she likes American men. It would be a waste not to get to know these girls better."

Major Sykes voice dripped with sarcasm as he said, "Beving, I'm sure your wife won't mind, but these girls might mind that you have a wife already."

Now the four of us women were almost back at the hospital. I saw that the lights were out in the rec-room and decided to leave checking it until morning. The doctors' cottage was next door to the nurses' cottage so I did not have to be alone with Beving. The three doctors left us on the boardwalk by the cottage.

As the men walked away toward their own cottage, I could hear Major Sykes recommending, "Beving give yourself a 'hand job' or go down the 'The Mango Tree' in Hilo and buy yourself a woman but leave these young innocent girls alone." Major Sykes was his superior officer; that I knew, but apparently he was reluctant to make it a more direct order.

CHAPTER 37

Conversation

Pvt. Stilley brought me a note next afternoon from Dr. Sykes as the corpsman wheeled a patient up the ramp and into the recreation room:

Give Cpl. Givens something that uses his arms. He is healing from bone infection. Please come and discuss his case with me.

Major Sykes

I recognized his blunt printing immediately from having read notes he had made about patients in their 201 Files.

I asked Pvt. Stilley to carry a note back to Major Sykes and to leave Corporal Givens with me. Sitting down at my desk, I scrawled a quick note:

After the rec. room closes at 1600 hours, I will come

to the surgery.

Lt. Brett

After handing my note to Pvt. Stilley, I went to evaluate Cpl. Givens. Some papers hung in a pouch on the handle of his wheelchair. I took them out and read them. He had received his leg injury during the landing of the 77th Infantry in the Battle for Guam, July 1944. A Japanese sniper had shattered his leg with one shot. He had been dragged ashore. Through the quick thinking of one of his soldiers, the bleeding was stopped with a tourniquet, he had been treated at a front-line aid station and moved onto a hospital ship and then transferred to the same ship that had just brought more patients to Hilo and thence by ambulance to Mountain View. Dr. Sykes had cleaned the suppurating wound and administered some of the new wonder drug penicillin.

I had treated similar patients already here at the Hospital on the Hill and wondered why Major Sykes felt the need to talk to me about this particular patient as his treatment seemed clear to me. I asked him to raise his pant-leg so I could examine the bandaged leg wound. The wound was halfway down the calf. It was his tibia that had the infection.

At my request Corporal Givens extended his knee and then flexed it as much as the wheelchair would allow. He grimaced in pain.

"Can you put any weight on it yet?" I asked.

"Nah, I can't stand up on it. But I can walk a ways on crutches. Major Sykes assures me that I'll walk again if I keep on with my physical therapy. But I'm getting so bored. He thought you might find me something to do."

I began to question him about what had interested him before he was drafted. He was a nice looking though very thin young man with brown hair in the regulation Army haircut.

"Well, since you can't put any weight on it right now, let's try to find something interesting for you to do with your hands. Those fellows over there are playing checkers. Does that interest you?"

"How about pool? I see that guy in the wheelchair can play pool. I used to be pretty good. I wonder if I can do it sitting down," he replied.

I followed him as he maneuvered his chair up to the rack and selected a queue. He slid his hands up and down it as he watched the game going on. When the winner was declared, he did not wait for an introduction from me to get himself into the game.

Since there was already one wheelchair patient playing, he did not apologize for his condition. His confidence was bound to set off competitiveness.

I left the table to that day's corpsman, a Pvt. Gonzales, and went back to teaching another patient how to lace leather. This fellow, also in a wheelchair, sat on the lacing pony held between his thighs which clamped his leather wallet in position for him to pull the lace and needle with what remained of his right hand, his left hand having been amputated.

At the close of OT clinic at 1600, I helped Pvt. Gonzales clear up and put away the tools and supplies that we had been using. We stored the patients' unfinished craft projects in a cupboard near my desk. The corpsmen came and holding umbrellas, and wheeled away the patients who were unable to manage the distance from the recreation room to their hospital barracks which was not far away though the boardwalk was slippery with rain. It took me about five minutes to walk up the hill to the surgery. Remembering the last time I had entered this door, I paused before knocking. Folding my umbrella I leaned it beside the ramp.

A female voice answered my knock "Come in." Lt.

Shirley Thompson was clearing up the surgery. She held an armful of wadded sheets.

"I had a note from Major Sykes summoning me up here," I explained.

She waved her empty arm toward the area behind a folding screen. I followed the direction of her gesture. There, I found Major Sykes seated on a stool next to a wooden counter writing on some document.

"Major Sykes, you sent for me," I said in a questioning tone in order to get his attention.

"Oh, yes," he said turning briefly. "Wait just a minute while I finish this note," as he went back to his writing.

I used this time to look around the surgery now in the daylight. The school gymnasium had just had a slap-dash make-over by the Army to make it usable for surgery. The hardwood floor had not been changed but the walls had been painted white and the overhead lights had been lowered on long cords to bring focus of the light closer to the surgery tables. The metal folding screen frames were covered with white percale cloth to divide the large gymnasium space into smaller areas so that more than one surgery could be performed at a time. Most surgery were performed during the daytime when more light came in from the high windows.

Shortly, Dr. Sykes, stood from the stool and said, "Let's go sit over here at my desk," leading me behind another folding screen on the other side of the room nearer the door. He indicated the straight-backed chair beside his desk while he hung his white lab coat on a nearby coat rack and then sat in the office swivel chair behind the desk.

"You wanted to talk to me about Cpl. Givens?" I remarked while I awaited his instructions holding my hands folded in my lap.

"Oh, yes, that was so I could finally get you up here alone to talk to you," he said sotto voce. "We can wait until Lt. Thompson has finished and gone." He seemed slightly embarrassed to be saying this. "I have a thermos of coffee here, would you like a cup?"

"That would be nice. I was just thinking about the last time I was up here in surgery."

"Oh, let's forget about that. I could tell that Beving was trying to get to you, too. He just can't seem to behave like a married man. I don't want him asking me to solve his problems again. Besides I wanted to protect you from him."

This was the most I had ever heard Major Sykes say at one time. It left me almost speechless, but I knew he wanted a response so, "Yes, he is a pill. I feel sort of sorry for him except I bet his wife is glad he's over here where she doesn't have to know about what he does," I said.

"Well, I guess we should talk about Cpl. Givens and get that over, but then I'm hoping we can make a date so we can get away from this place and get to know each other better."

I should have known something like this was about to happen when he said, "I could finally get you up here alone to talk to you" but I was so unaccustomed to flirtations except for the crude remarks from the patients or Beving, that I struggled to respond. "Well, what did you have in mind?"

"I'm usually booked for surgery most mornings except Sunday. If I get a jeep, maybe we could take a ride to Hilo and then take the 'rail bus' excursion to Pa`auillo and back. How does that sound? I've heard that's a nice afternoon's adventure."

While the rec-room was open for games on Sunday, usually, the corpsmen supervised things. I had no reason not to go with him. I had felt that the opportunity to see anything of this exotic place was difficult to come by. "I think that would make a lovely outing," I replied after a moment of consideration.

"Wonderful!" he said and went on, "The jeep is too noisy for us to have much conversation but we should be able to talk on the train. Could you meet me at the motor pool so we can avoid as much gossip as possible? Be sure and wear your regular WAC uniform so other service folks will give you some respect." He gave a secretive smile. Uniforms had made all of us feel more powerful as they protected us from criticism and any other sort of assault.

I was glad he did not care to advertise such an adventure to our colleagues in the 148th and I gladly agreed. "I'll ask the mess to make us some lunch but I'll let them think it's for a nurse's outing," I offered. "Let's get an early start to be sure to be there in time at the Hilo Railway Station. Is 630 hours too early for you?" he asked.

I nodded my acceptance. We both stood at the same time and I hurried out of the gymnasium hiding my excitement.

When I finally lay on my bunk, I realized part of an excursion with the Major meant that he would want to know about where I came from and why I joined the WACs. This was the fateful time in all my relationships, when I must manufacture another childhood for myself. I had made up stories for Cassie and Wanda so I realized I must use the same stories lest I be discovered in a deception later. I remembered having accidentally told Cassie I was from the Black Belt of Alabama so I decided I needed to continue this fiction. I fell asleep designing a different childhood for myself in Montgomery, Alabama. That was far enough away from Selma for anyone to be able to discover my fakery. Dr. Zukoski was from Birmingham so Montgomery was far enough away from that city too, for him to know many people.

CHAPTER 38

Rail Bus

Woodrow was working on one of the jeeps when I slipped into the still almost dark, fenced motor pool area. When he saw me, he wiped his hands on a rag he pulled out of his pocket. Coming forward toward me, he said, "Did you hear about the race riot at Camp Claiborne in Louisiana?"

I wished I could forget about race as it reminded me what I had to lose if I were discovered to be passing. None-the-less, I was still interested in such race events. I was just glad I was not part of them. "Tell me about it as fast as you can, because Major Sykes is meeting me here to drive to Hilo and take a train ride," I explained in a low voice that I hoped could not be heard by the other two mechanics I could see working on other vehicles in the motor pool.

"The colored soldiers in Camp Claiborne, Louisiana got tired of the German POWs getting better tents and better everything than them. The Northern Negroes disrespected the white officers. Then some of them white officers lynched a colored private. All hell broke loose." He spoke as fast as he could meanwhile he acted like he was polishing the jeep nearby.

"How did you learn that?" I asked as I had seen no Negro soldiers near Mt. View, and there certainly were no colored newspapers here since there were supposedly no colored soldiers.

"It wasn't in the white newspaper but I got a letter from a buddy and he told me the particulars." Woodrow's face changed so I knew someone had come through the gate behind me.

"Ah, I see you are here already," came the deep voice of Major Sykes. "Have you got a jeep ready?" he said to Woodrow who was saluting.

The jeep made too much noise for conversation. Major Sykes needed all his attention to drive the jeep on the curving road as daylight arrived. Rather than leave the jeep on the street, Major Sykes drove it to the motor pool area near the airport in Hilo and got one of the mechanics to drive the two of us to the Hilo Station. We walked into the station which was full of uniformed men. Major Sykes stood in line with me beside him to buy our tickets. All this mob of men inclined me to stay within the protection of this tall doctor. The ticket seller looked Japanese but I realized I couldn't really tell the difference between Chinese and Japanese. Because the Japanese had lost many important jobs after Pearl Harbor, I guessed this man was probably Chinese.

Out on the covered boarding platform we could

see the rail bus sitting on the second set of tracks between the station and Hilo Bay. The bus wheels had been replaced with train wheels. There was a cow catcher in front of the engine.

The rail bus was quickly filling up with passengers so we hurried across to get a good seat. There were nine rows of seats and half were already full. Major Sykes ushered me into an empty pair of seats on the mountain side of the bus. It was indeed a strange contraption with a section of three rows of seats having been added to the original bus so it looked like the two segments had been welded together. Soon it was full with almost all passengers wearing uniforms. I saw that I was the only woman on bus. I was glad of the protection that my uniform gave me as I tugged the skirt down over my knees. "Thank you Major," I said as he placed the lunch hamper in the luggage rack.

Major Sykes said to me as I addressed him by rank, "Please, now that we are away from the hospital, I want you to stop calling me Major and call me by my given name, Paul."

I knew this was going to be a struggle for me as I had adhered rigidly to Army standards in this regard so far with all males including patients except for Woodrow. But at least since we were both officers, it was not forbidden for us to "consort."

Once we crossed the Wailuku Railroad Bridge the passengers became quieter as they became absorbed in the scenery. Their cigarette smoke drifted out of the open windows. Major Sykes was careful to make sure that the other men on this bus knew he was my escort by putting his arm over the back of the bus seat.

"I've wanted to get to know more about you ever since we first met," Major Sykes studiously avoided mentioning Miss Wagner's abortion.

I wanted to delay telling my falsehoods for as long as possible so I said, "Well, I think you should tell me about your previous life first since you thought up this outing." I said this with an arch look sideways at him where he sat between me and the aisle.

He had seldom known me to act flirtatiously before so he seemed surprised but took it in good humor. "Well you already know I was born near Lake Erie. Also I told you about being jilted while I was in medical school. What else would you like to know?"

"Did you have any sisters? What did you father and mother do? Was your mother a homemaker?" Now that I got started I found I had a long list of questions but decided this was good enough for a start.

"I had a sister and two younger brothers. Mother was a school teacher before she married Dad. Dad's father had immigrated from Scarborough in Yorkshire, England before the turn of the century. Dad's father was a fisherman and Dad worked as a fisherman on Lake Erie, too. Now it's your turn to tell me something about your family." He sat looking and waiting for me to speak.

Just at that moment I heard the two men behind me discussing fliers' chocolate. Pretending to be curious about it, I used this as a distraction to delay telling my lies. "What's fliers' chocolate?" I asked.

Major Sykes was glad to explain "Fliers chocolate" is chocolate with amphetamines which pilots use to keep themselves awake on long flights. It's also called "tankers' chocolate" when those cavalry guys in Africa and Europe make long tank trips." He briefly listened to the conversation in the seat behind us before returning to his questioning. "And what did your parents do?"

I knew there was no way to further divert him without arousing suspicion so I launched into my made-up family history that I had constructed. "I grew up in Montgomery, Alabama."

"Well you certainly lost your Southern accent. What happened to it?" he questioned.

"Oh, I worked hard to get rid of it after being teased a few times." I had decided that anything that occurred in my life after leaving Selma and getting to Chicago I could simply just tell the truth about my nurse's training. "In the Nursing School at Henrotin Hospital in Chicago, I learned right away to talk like a Yankee." I said this in a light-hearted way while smiling to cover my nervousness about the upcoming lies.

"Well, what about your family? I haven't known too many Southern girls before," he commented.

Before I lost my nerve, I said, "I was an only child and my parents were killed in a car accident when I was just five. So my grandparents raised me and they are already dead, too." I had figured out that if I said all my relatives were dead, I would never have to promise to let him or anyone else meet them. Besides, it was near the truth, except for Uncle Edgar and Aunt Phyllis.

His faces immediately reflected sympathy for my misfortune. "That must have been a kind of lonely childhood."

I had already decided that my story would not include any cousins or aunts and uncles or someday he might want to meet them, too. "Sort of, but I got used to it. Grandpa and Grandma died right before I went to nursing school so I didn't have much time to miss them." Part of me felt badly about the lies I had made up but the other part of me was glad these lies seemed so plausible.

Again the conversations going on around us were a distraction. We were using voices only discernible to each other but the other men on the bus were shouting over the clacking of the wheels on the rails so it was hard not to hear their conversations.

"Did you hear about the attempted massacre of a Jap village up by Honey Cow?" A red-faced sergeant who looked like he had been out in the sun too much asked this question of those sitting near him but we could all hear his blaring voice. I knew that soldiers had nicknamed the town of Honoka`a on the northeast coast of the island "Honey Cow."

Heads turned toward him as he recounted, "A Marine who was visiting a bar in 'Honey Cow' heard about this village full of Japs who spoke only Japanese and was probably a whole bunch of spies. Well, he went back up to Camp Tarawa and got a big bunch of guys to head back to 'Honey Cow' to get rid of them, but somebody squealed and the MPs and local cops met em halfway back to 'Honey Cow' and turned 'em around."

His audience was truly surprised and entranced by his story. "Too many dirty Japs on this island," one soldier slurred as he slipped his flask out of his pocket. I shuddered as I had heard too many similar remarks about "niggers" while growing up in Selma. We were all surprised as none of the others on the bus-train had heard the story either. A discussion ensued about how this could have happened and how many Marines were involved. Realizing the whole thing was hearsay, Major Sykes, I mean Paul and I returned to our own private conversation after Paul remarked, "Bigots!" This remark gave me hope, hope of exactly what, I did not define to myself.

However, I used this distraction to turn the conversation back to Paul. "Tell me about going to medical school."

When we arrived in Papaikou, I excused myself to go to the restroom before we set off to find a place to have our picnic before the bus train turned around to return to Hilo. As I entered the restroom in the station, I remembered the colored and white restrooms in York, Alabama where I had changed races. Then I shut off the dread that accompanied this thought when I pushed from my mind the possibility that I might ever have to confess this to Paul, to Major Sykes.

Most of the men on the bus train turned toward the

small Pa`auilo town center. Paul and I walked the other way until we found a ledge of lava rock a short distance off below the road. Paul climbed down and I handed him the hamper. Then he took my hand, helping me as I stumbled down to the ledge. There was only one tree between us and a full view of the Pacific Ocean. It felt a little safer to have something between us and a drop off over the edge of the ledge. Down below on the side of the hill beneath where we sat, were sugar cane fields and an isolated looking clump of small houses. This ledge had been used for picnics before we realized by the small pile of bottles and cans at one end.

Paul spread an Army towel on the ledge between us and took the food out of the hamper; Spam sandwiches, bananas, canteen cookies and two cokes. He pulled a bottle opener out of his pocket and popped the tops off the cokes. I relished this full view of the ocean. Since Mountain View was so far from the ocean, it was an unusual treat. I had only seen the ocean from Hilo and Punalu`u except for when we were in Honolulu and the five days spent on the troop ship. I had seen the Potomac River while in Washington, but they kept us too busy to take an outing to see the Atlantic Ocean.

CHAPTER 39

Return Trip

The ride back to Hilo was uneventful except that the fog rolled in so that some of the views we had seen on the way up the coast were now hidden. Paul seemed to be aware of my reluctance to tell more about my childhood so he seemed to compensate by trying to build my trust by telling more stories of his own youth.

When we finally got back to Hilo, the rain was pelting down so Paul had me wait in the station while he went and got the jeep. When we got back to Mountain View in the dark rain, he drove me right to the door of the nurse's cottage. He opened a GI umbrella and walked me to the door, kissing me with one arm round my back while holding the umbrella over us with the other, before returning the jeep to the motor pool.

"I hope you enjoyed this trip enough to come with me again sometime. We could ride to Pahoa.

They don't have a rail bus, but we could just ride the caboose. I hear there are lots of farms down there. Next time we could try riding the train from Mountain View Station to Hilo and not take the jeep. It's so noisy we can't talk anyway. Do you know how to drive?" he asked as an afterthought as he released me. I confessed that I did not. "Would you like to learn?" he asked.

Taken by surprise by this offer, I said, "Let me think about," as I went inside.

* * *

In the morning, at breakfast, I learned from the other staff members that a ship had left with a number of patients on their way to San Francisco where Cpl. Erickson was slated for dishonorable discharge. I felt badly that I had not had a chance to say goodbye to that sad man. I wondered if there was a way to get his home address, but the expectation of an influx of new patients, pushed it from my mind. However, when I got to my desk, there was an envelope with a note from Arne Erikson.

Lt. Brett, thank you for your kindness while I was here. I know I was no model patient but you helped me anyway. Not too many folks in the Army I'd ever care to hear from, but if you feel like writing, I would answer. Look me up if you ever get to Petersburg, Minnesota. Arne

In the lower corner he drew a little sketch of me like the portrait he did of my face in the ferns but this time, he had not added the fiendish faces.

Complicated thoughts came into my mind as I looked at a list trying to familiarize myself with the new patients I would expect to meet tomorrow. I was still pondering the good feelings that I had experienced while with Major Sykes, whom I seldom remembered in my mind to call Paul. There was enough stress being around all these fellows in occupational therapy trying to get my attention without trying to sort out feelings about Paul, and now Arne asking me to write to him. If I thought only of Arne as someone who needed kindness, it would be OK but I remembered the electric feeling he had conveyed to me when he tipped my face up while drawing my portrait.

* * *

When I returned to the barracks before the evening mess, Cassie was sitting on my bed across from the bunk of Lt. Thompson. She looked flustered and breathless as I burst in without knocking as this was my room and I knew that Lt. Thompson would not be sleeping yet. Neither of them, Cassie or Shirley, spoke. It was odd. To relieve whatever this tension was about, I asked if either of them had seen Arne before he left. He had lost his rank when he went AWOL so I just called him Arne. Because of his AWOL debacle, he was well-known enough to all the nursing and allied staff, that there was no need to even say his last name.

Both Shirley and Cassie seemed relieved to have

something to talk about. I wondered if they had been talking about me and so my suspicion level went way up. It wasn't possible for them to know for sure anything about where I really came from but maybe they had been discussing my ringlet hair or café olé skin. Despite all the rain, the occasional sunshine had darkened my skin, I knew. Even if they suspected, I doubted either would be brave enough to bring it up with me, but they were also loyal enough that I doubted they would turn me in or try to investigate further. So I gave them an account of my ride on the rail bus.

* * *

November 1944 was a busy month for our soldiers. They celebrated that President Roosevelt had been re-elected on November 7th. They knew that the cooks in the mess were preparing a special Thanksgiving meal for November 23rd. And the deadline for posting Christmas greetings to the United States was fast approaching though Thanksgiving was not yet past.

I set about preparing supplies for patients to make their own Christmas cards from Hawaiian materials. There could be nothing in the cards to identify the soldier's location in words but if we used Hawaiian vegetation or flowered cloth, it might pass the military mail censors. I made a trip by train to Hilo to the S. Hata Dry Goods store and chose several half-yard pieces of colorful Hawaiian print cloth. The Japanese cloth had disappeared from the shelves though the young woman who helped me by cutting the lengths of cloth explained the necessity for removing Japanese merchandise after Pearl Harbor.

I had watched a friendly Hawaiian woman weaving Lauhala leaves sitting outside her tiny house in Hilo. It gave me the idea to try to weave some of these leaves that the English call Pandanus into little Christmas wreaths to be glued unto the front of the Christmas cards. She had explained to me how to treat the leaves to make them pliable enough for manipulating into the wreath shapes. We glued sequins to represent berries on the wreaths.

When the patients assembled to work together on constructing the Christmas cards, they found partners whose disability complimented their own. The one-armed soldier worked with the man blinded by an explosion telling him how to weave the leaves. The paraplegic cut out the cloth in the shapes of Christmas trees handing them over to the man with the burned face and neck to glue the shapes unto the front of the cards. I thought of Arne and how much better the shapes might be if he had drawn the patterns rather than me. Nonetheless, the cards turned out to be quite beautiful. We made so many cards that there were extras left over after the patients had chosen the ones for their family and friends so that we sold the others to the staff and doctors to make money to buy more craft materials for occupational therapy. What the higher ups did not know would not hurt them. I was supposed to account for all material costs.

I began to make arrangements for the local school children to come before Christmas to sing Christmas carols to the patients. Tadashi introduced me to his teacher so I could solicit her cooperation. Miss McNairy agreed to have her students who were meeting in the front room of one of the Japanese homes, to prepare some Christmas carols to sing during the special program at the Yamada Theater. Since they no longer had the classrooms with pianos, she used the Yamada Theater to practice. The program would be on Saturday, December 23rd. Pvt. Earnest Owens was still posted to Mountain View Hospital so I asked him if he would be willing to choose a Christmas play or skit for the patients and staff to perform. I had found a play titled "Christmas High Jinx" which promised laughs for these poor injured soldiers far away from family and friends. Pvt. Owens chose patients and staff for the parts and play practice began.

CHAPTER 40

Major Paul Sykes

The month of November was passing rapidly. The holiday preparations occupied me so much that I was taken by surprised to have another invitation from Major Sykes so soon, to take a Saturday walk. I continued to have difficulty calling him by his given name. He typically performed most of his surgeries on Tuesdays, Wednesdays and Thursdays, using the other days to prepare the patients and himself and the nurses for these complicated operations, but often he had to do surgeries everyday. Many of these damaged patients required a series of surgeries so when he finished with one, he was not really finished. He followed his patients' progress and worked closely with Cassie to get the patient up and walking even if it was with crutches or to get them to maneuver their wheelchairs themselves. Although he had a busy schedule he found time to send a message to me almost daily now. As often as we could make our schedules work, we began to take walks outside the hospital grounds along the Pszyk Ditch or along the railroad track toward Glenwood.

No surgeries were scheduled for Thanksgiving Day so we planned a hike down to Kukui Heights immediately after the noon Thanksgiving dinner to see if we could see the ocean from there. Most of the time, because of all the marine training camps in the vicinity; we decided it was safest to wear our uniforms to assure our safe passage. There had been more than one rumor of marines attacking local people, especially women. I usually chose to wear for our walks, the new slacks uniform which had been approved for WACs as I could never predict when I might be climbing almost straight up a hillock of an old lava flow. We both wore our uniform hats and carried GI umbrellas. I needed the umbrella to keep me from tanning even more deeply and Paul need to wear his hat to cover the bald spot on the top of his head. Of course, rain came often without warning and umbrellas were also good to use as walking sticks when climbing embankments.

We did not sit together during Thanksgiving Dinner as neither of us was willing to appear to be part of an exclusive couple right yet. I probably felt this more than Major Sykes. Perhaps his rank intimidated me. I had never been part of a couple, except casually in a group of others. We simple paid attention to when the others arose from the meal in the doctor and nurses dining room and went to our quarters to get ready. We met behind the bakery near the theater in the village.

I thought about how this surgeon had more empathy for his patients than Dr. Beving the psychiatrist. Nurses usually expected the opposite of these two categories of doctors. Major Beving had seemed to be the only staff member to pay attention to the frequency with which Paul and I went out walking. Lately though, he seemed preoccupied with leaving meals quickly so I wondered if he had some other woman besides his absent wife, as a conquest. I sincerely hoped so at it meant he was not interested in badgering me through Woodrow.

Paul and I were silent until we were far enough away from houses of the Kiyabu Camp to feel our voices probably would not be heard. This silence seemed to be by common consent. Eventually, Paul took my arm and broke the silence by saying, "I remember a Thanksgiving when I was a boy was great fun as my American grandparents lived nearby. Mom would roast the traditional turkey but always cooked the special fish Dad would bring in for this holiday."

My own mother and I seldom celebrated Thanksgiving because for Negros who worked in the hospital or worked as maids in white homes, it was not a holiday. I searched my memory for things from Sunday dinners we shared with Uncle Edgar and Aunt Phyllis for something to use as a story to reciprocate. "Well in the South it was usually roasted pork, rather than turkey. We most often had greens cooked with ham-hocks, biscuits, gravy and sweet potato pie."

Paul continued to reminisce, "Mother usually invited neighbors or people from church. When I got into high school, she allowed me to invite a friend over if I wanted."

Struggling to keep up my end of this conversation, I lied, "My mother let me invite a friend also. I had Glenda over once," using the name of that white girl from up north hoping that it gave no hint of my background. Even though I had changed the city of my birth, I needed a name that I knew was not a particularly Negro name. Then I really let my fantasy take over when I lied again, saying that, "The Negro maid cleared the table and washed the dishes afterward while my friend Glenda and I went up to my room to listen to the radio."

I wondered why I said that last sentence which I felt denigrated my own mother, but the lie was already said. My whole life was a lie anyway so what was one more, one more bigger one?

Paul struggled up a hillock and then turned to give me his hand to assist me in climbing it also. As he grasped my hand, I looked at our two skins and compared the color; his was whiter than mine but not much. It was hardly noticeable in the November light.

After crossing the railroad tracks, we came to the edge of the recently planted cane-field which we skirted lest even the new short half-grown sharp leaf edges could cut us. The cane-field workers almost always were covered in clothing from head to toe to protect themselves from these vicious leaves.

Paul asked as we walked away from the threat of the sugarcane, "What do you think you'll do after the war?"

I had not given this much thought though the topic came up sometimes in the dining room. Most of the last few years had been so occupied with study and work and the Army, that I had not given it much consideration. I spent much of my contemplation time before sleep in confirming my efforts to conceal my parentage. Now, having to think quickly, I said, "I am sure there will be lots of jobs in the United States for occupational therapists. There will be so many wounded soldiers who still need care and work. How about you?"

"Well at Thanksgiving dinner today, I was thinking how nice it would be to have children at the table like we always did at home. I think I'd like to get married and raise a family. Of course, I will probably want to go back and open a surgery office near the hospital in Erie, Pennsylvania."

The idea of going back to Alabama gave me the chills. I knew if I ever went back there, eventually, I would meet someone who knew me in Selma. So I quickly made something up. "I've always wanted to find out more about California after staying at Letterman Hospital in San Francisco for those few days."

"Do you want to stay alone or is there someone

waiting for you that you haven't told me about?" Paul asked.

At least this time, I would not have to lie. "No, there isn't anyone waiting for me." I did not explain further.

"Don't you want to get married sometime? You don't seem like the 'old-maid' type to me," he commented.

Because my own family experiences were not enviable, I seldom had thoughts of a normal family as the kind the movies showed us. I did not know how to answer him so I made a flippant answer, "I'll think about that after we beat the Japs."

He took my answer in the way I had said it and gave me back a flippant salute without further comment until we climbed Kukui Heights and looked out at the view of the ocean far below on the coast.

Despite having eaten a big dinner, we were soon thirsty and hungry and glad to eat the cookies and drink the coffee that the mess-cook had packed for us. We took off our jackets as the walk had warmed us up considerably.

While we were sitting on a log, enjoying the view, Paul slipped his arm around behind my waist and pulled me toward him and kissed me. Until now, our bodily contact except for the goodnight kiss after the rail car ride, had been only a brief touching of my hand or arm during assistance to alight or ascend. The rush of feeling surprised me as I returned his kiss. Without real effort, we both arose and continued to kiss, clinging together until breathlessness made us separate our lips.

"See, I told you that you didn't seem like the 'old-maid' type," he said as he held me out at arms' length and stared at me.

CHAPTER 41

Christmas 1944

Ola`a Sugar Plantation had contributed four Cook Island pine Christmas trees to the hospital. The plantation workers had cut them from one of their wind-breaks. I had the job of celebrating this holiday with the patients so I decided to put the biggest one in the Yamada Theater for the Christmas program. The smaller trees were put into each of the patient barracks with the smallest of all in the rec. room. I persuaded the patients to make decorations.

For those patients that could manage with two hands, I taught them how to cut paper snowflakes, how to make paper chains, and how to form and paint paper machè balls. I was able to obtain a purchase order to buy electric tree lights at the Post Exchange in Hilo. Things such as this were gradually becoming more available again in stores as the country realized the Allies were finally winning both wars, the one in Europe and the one in the Pacific.

I had spent several hours after the scheduled occupational therapy sessions, to sit down at the sewing machine and make dozens of small cloth draw-string bags to hold candy for Santa to distribute. Some ladies from the Ueyama Camp donated some draw-string bags as well. I had enough for one bag for each patient and all the school children.

On Saturday, December 23rd, before Pvt. Owens directed his play "Christmas High Jinx" the children of Mountain View School sang "Jingle Bells" and "Silent Night." He had discovered that even the Buddhist children knew these songs. Miss McNairy had persuaded several other teachers to practice these songs in their classes under the houses as well, so the children's choir had several dozen children singing along with her and the theater piano which was played by a pretty young Hawaiian school teacher.

Dr. Zukoski, dressed as Santa Claus in a costume that I had run up on the sewing machine with red fabric from the S. Hata Store, passed out the small cloth bags of hard candy. Miss McNairy and I led the whole audience and choir in singing other Christmas Carols. I was grateful for the practice I had had in Knox High School to speak and sing before audiences. The program was quite a success I decided after a conversation with Pvt. Owens afterward. We congratulated ourselves on making it as close as possible to what might have happened in the home towns of these patients.

The next night, Christmas Eve, all the nurses not directly serving patients, gathered at the recreation room and practiced Christmas carols for a few minutes. Then we walked slowly in a column through each patient barracks singing those traditional songs. Each of us carried a flashlight with red cellophane over it held on with a rubber band. Captain Sullivan led this parade. We started with "We Wish You a Merry Christmas", then "Dreaming of a White Christmas" followed by the usual non-denominational carols; "Silent Night', "I Heard the Bells on Christmas Day", "Deck the Halls with Boughs of Holly", and "God Rest Ye Merry Gentlemen." The patients applauded our off-the-cuff efforts and in jest, asked us for celebratory non-alcoholic drinks.

On Christmas morning, the men in each hospital barracks received the various gift boxes that had been sent from home which we had placed around the small decorated trees in their respective barracks. Cassie and I went to each barracks to make sure that each man got something from us even if he had not received something from home. We had assembled some bigger cloth drawstring bags with cigarettes, shaving soap, razors and razor blades for the men whose boxes had not arrived. Of course there were some patients with no families to send them gifts. These were my special concerns.

The cooks had made a special effort for

Christmas dinner; ham, candied sweet potatoes, mashed potatoes, red eye gravy, Waldorf salad, yeast rolls, mince and apple pie. It was quite a feast compared to the usual "shit on a shingle" which was creamed gravy with shreds of dried beef and sliced boiled eggs on toasted bread. Nonetheless, because it was served on the usual mess compartment trays, it reminded us of our Army status while celebrating this Christmas while in service to our country.

Paul had invited me to join him again in a long afternoon walk. We met beside the Kato Store in the village and walked uphill toward the Up Camp. We walked behind the Ochiai Camp and the nearby chicken coops and outhouses. After three years of war, we had begun to feel it was possible to contemplate peace and to truly feel the wish of the Christian Savior for "Peace on Earth,"

Since the walk Paul and I had made on Thanksgiving when he asked me what my "after-war" plans were, I had begun to contemplate the possibility of him proposing marriage to me, as it was such a common occurrence among soldiers. Every nurse had stories of proposals. I had helped patients who had little writing skill compose proposal letters to their sweethearts back in the United States. Men had shared their sense of loss with me when they received "Dear John" letters as well. Pin-up pictures of actresses over men's bunks in the barracks inspired comments from them such as, "I'm looking for someone like her for a wife."

Talk of love, marriage and proposals was ubiquitous. Consequently, I had tried to formulate in my mind what I might say if Major Sykes proposed to me as we had become much closer. Having had very little experience of a marriage except seeing Uncle Edgar and Aunt Phyllis, who did not seem all that happy, my ideas of marriage came mostly from movies such as "Gaslight" and "Jane Eyre" and magazines like Glamour. The magazine and movie marriages seemed lovely but so elusive.

Some WACS I knew of, were freer with their affections. I was constantly surprised to learn of affairs I would not have dared to contemplate. Miss Wagner's dilemma was just one such situation. Remembering the betrayals of the red-headed banker who was my real father and also of the marriage of Mr. and Mrs. Creston for whom I had worked as a maid in Selma, they all seemed rather off-putting as models for family life. My romantic emotions had not been stimulated to the point in my life to overcome my calculations about what was possible. I suppose others, especially men, saw me as a very guarded person. My usefulness as an occupational therapist who kept up the spirits of my patients seemed a more valuable role than ideas of how to be a housewife. And could I be happy doing just that? Some of the other nurses and WACs seemed to know exactly what to respond to proposals as we discussed it often enough. It was easy for them to predict whether they would say yes or no to particular men's marriage proposals. I had no such ready response. Previously, I had protected myself from such situations.

I anticipated that Major Paul Sykes, being raised in a "normal" home, would have expectations I might be reluctant or unable to fulfill. Maybe I was borrowing trouble even thinking he might be planning to propose to me.

After such a meal, it was a challenge to force ourselves to walk rather than take a nap. We were quiet for the first mile or as our digesting food competed with our efforts to walk uphill. Eventually Paul said, "I didn't feel as lonely as I expected today being this far from my family. I suppose we have almost become a family here, the corpsmen and doctors and nurses."

"I've been too busy to have time to feel lonely this Christmas. Making decorations and making sure all the patients had gifts really took my mind off thinking about previous Christmases," I replied. "Besides with the war almost over, I hope, I realized I probably will never have another Christmas like this one in Hawaii."

Paul immediately took up this theme. "Where will we all be Christmas 1945? I hope I'll be near where you are so we can continue our walks."

Fearing what he might say next and knowing I was unready to answer if he proposed, I stumbled ahead around a huge koa tree trunk calling, "Oh, look at the view from here." I gestured out toward the newly-harvested cane-field which gave us a beautiful view of the mountain Mauna Kea and its wreath of clouds.

With unusual frustration in his voice, Paul said, "Will you quit running away from me? You know I'm trying to talk seriously about whether we have a future together."

Was that a proposal? I was unsure though that I knew what Paul was implying in these words.

Most concerning of all was my mother's race. I had learned about Mendelssohn's Sweet Peas during the biology lessons in nursing school. The chances of my ever bearing a Negro baby were one in four. It sounded from what Major Sykes said that he expected to have children. I could never marry him knowing that I might surprise him with a Negro baby sometime in the future. He would probably suspect that I had had sexual relations with some black man, rather than the fact that I was considered black for the all years of my life spent in Selma. With these thoughts going through my mind, I responded slowly, "Exactly what are you saying?"

CHAPTER 42

Secrets

"Please don't play dumb. You've heard most of my story about my family. I want a family like the one my parents had, love, kids, trust, enough money to not worry, and to feel like I'm doing good work." This was what Doctor Major Paul Sykes said he wanted.

"And where am I in this?" I wondered aloud. "I hear what you want but I don't hear what part I play in that plan."

"I know I'm better at surgery than I am at expressing myself. It's my clumsy way for asking you if you are interesting in discussing whether we might become a permanent couple and get married." He held his hands out in front of him as he said this to demonstrate where he thought his skill lay.

"Well if it is to discuss our interest in the subject, I am willing to have such a discussion," I said as I reached out and took those hands in mine again noticing the color difference as I did so.

"Well, that's encouraging," he laughed sarcastically. "I'll start," he went on. "Lt. Brett, I find you a wonderful walking companion and good train travel partner. Do you think you could carry these good traits over into a marriage and family?"

I actually appreciated his rather calm realistic approach rather than a highly charged emotional display. "Paul, you know I haven't had regular family experience like you have so I am not sure I'd be good at that. All I had ever really planned for was my career in occupational therapy. I certainly care enough for you to want to make a try at it." I had pulled his hands around behind me so I was in his embrace as I gave this confusing answer.

He stood a moment assimilating what I had said before lowering his face to kiss me. After separating his lips from mine, he said, "Well that gives me some hope. I suppose this means we should get to know each other better before we tell anybody what we are discussing. Besides, I have some secrets I want you to know before we tell anybody else."

Why did I think I was the only one with secrets? I was not ready to share my secret right now so I managed to delay such a confession by saying, "It's going to get dark by the time we get back to the nurses' cottage. Maybe we can postpone the secret telling session till after Christmas Night." I held his face in my hands as I gazed up at him with conflicting emotions, both love and fear.

We walked back down the hill in silence, our arms encircling each other's waists. It was a warm pleasant feeling even though the rain began to fall. Paul opened his umbrella and we snuggled together under that arch in our little new world of contemplations.

When we got to the door of nurses' cottage, I invited Paul to come into the hallway rather than to try to kiss me goodbye under the umbrella on the slippery boardwalk. "Please don't stand out in the rain while we say our goodbyes after this serious discussion." I smiled slyly up at him, an invitation in my eyes to kiss. "Man in the hall," I yelled out the warning as it was protocol to warn nurses to wear bathrobes as they headed for the bathroom because occasionally, a woman might walk down the hall wearing just her slip or even less.

Paul shook the rain off the umbrella and stepped inside, closing the umbrella and standing it in the big dishpan we had put by the door to catch the drips. There were several other umbrellas both wet and dry keeping it company. The overhead light reflected off his bald spot as he bent over removing his hat.

"I'm not inviting you in my room, but I was wondering if yours looks like ours. Let me show you how big it is for four people." I turned the knob but nothing happened. I gave it a little push and it still did not open. With a little more force, I tried to push it open and realized something seemed stuck against the door. This was strange so I called out,

"Shirley, the door's stuck,"

There was no answer. I put my ear to the door and listened and could hear nothing. These doors didn't have locks as they had to be ready for inspection all the time. I wondered if perhaps there had been an earthquake we did not feel outside during our walk and it might have knocked something against the door. We had earthquakes so often here that I had ceased to be alarmed when the building began to shake. "Well, I guess I'd better go down to the recreation room and get a screw driver to take the hinges off rather than try to break down the door."

"I'll walk with you. It's dark now and not safe for you to be walking around here unaccompanied." He retrieved his umbrella and we went out into the rain again, actually relishing this additionally time together. We crossed the road and walked down the boardwalk between the patient barracks and the recreation room. I quickly got one of the OT screw-driver kits from the cupboard. We turned out the lights and headed back up the boardwalk and across the road to the cottage. Paul followed me into the hallway. I decided to try the door one more time before starting the work of unscrewing all the hinges. It swung open as if nothing were wrong. I switched on the light and saw that Shirley Thompson was not in her bunk which had the Army blanket smooth and tight over it. It was after time for her shift to be over. There was nothing near the door that could have been blocking my opening it.

The other bunks were empty as well.

"That's a puzzle!" I understated my mystification. "What do you suppose happened?"

"It is very strange. I wonder if somebody was playing a trick, trying to see if we would try to sneak into your room. Whatever or whoever did it must be having a good laugh making us go out into the rain again."

"Well we had the last laugh on them anyway," I said as I reached up to give him one last kiss before sending him on over to the doctors' cottage.

I had just hung up my damp clothing on hangers to dry and climbed under my Army sheet and blanket when Shirley opened the door and came in. She switched on the light which I had just switched off. "Where have you been?" I asked as I noticed she was not wet from outdoors.

"Oh, I've been playing cards with some of the other nurses and Cassie," Shirley explained.

There was a sitting room here in this cottage so I assumed it must have been there that the card game occurred. "The door was shut so I couldn't get it open when I got back. I couldn't figure out what was keeping it closed. After going to get a screw driver to take the hinges off, it was OK. Very strange! Oh well, Merry Christmas," I said as I turned over in bed to sleep.

CHAPTER 43

As the war rumbled on, we began to receive injured soldiers from the December 1944 Leyte battle in the Philippines as well as from Okinawa, the most southern Japanese island. Some patients, rather than having to endure weeks on a hospital ship were being flown to Hilo. This meant that many were sicker or earlier in their recovery period than previous patients who had come by ship had been. Every bed in the patient barracks was full despite attempts to move recovering patients back to the United States hospitals. Many patients just seemed grateful to have been injured and sent home rather than being captured and spending the rest of the war in a Japanese prisoner of war camp. Stories of frightful treatment of prisoners had begun to circulate through the Army gossip circuit. When we prepared patients for the next stage of their journey on the Navy ships from Hilo Harbor back to San Francisco, we had to be more careful of our paperwork as the Navy nurses on these ships were known for their pickiness and strictness about the paperwork.

We medical people were even busier than previously so Major Sykes and I had less time to spend together. The recreation room had increased the number of hours per day it was open. That meant that either I or Pvt. Gonzales had to be there all the time. We opened our door immediately after breakfast and did not close it until 10 o'clock at night. I was able to get the corpsman, Pvt. Owens more or less permanently assigned to occupational therapy. He had such a therapeutic personality. All the patients responded to his gentle but firm ways. I had seen him develop into a real leader and I intended to recommend him for promotion. I was glad that he had not been either sent back to the battle front or sent home to the United States. Because he had been wounded himself, the men really trusted him and discussed many things they were reluctant to discuss with the women.

Finally, one Sunday afternoon in January, Paul Sykes and I were able to get away for a walk.

"My dear Clara, anticipating spending time with you and finishing our discussion is one of the things that has kept me going during this flood of patients in surgery," Paul said as we followed the railroad tracks toward Glenwood. He carried the always necessary GI umbrella under his arm as we stumbled along the raised railroad bed behind the plantation store.

Near the railroad bridge across the Pszyk Ditch, there was a rock that provided a good seat. "You said you had a secret that you wanted to tell me." I started hoping to get by without revealing my own big secret.

"I had told you that I was engaged when I started medical school, remember?" he said.

Nodding my agreement, he went on, "Well when I went back to Erie for Christmas in 1942, she told me she was pregnant and asked me if I still wanted to marry her. We had never had sexual relations so I knew it wasn't mine. I asked her why she would still want to marry me if she had slept with someone else. She said she knew I'd be a better father."

Astounded at the nerve of his former fiancée, I asked, "So what did you tell her?"

"Well, I thought about it for a couple days. She wouldn't tell me who the real father was. I found out later that it was a one-nighter that she met at a party where she got really drunk. I tried to forgive her but after a couple days; I realized I would never be able to look at the kid without remembering her betrayal. Besides, I realized she wasn't as interesting a person as I had thought she was. I decided a life with her would not be happy. She asked me to do an abortion on her." He paused.

"So did you do it for her?" I asked.

"No, I found I couldn't bring myself to do it for

her. Besides I knew I could never make love to her again after doing that surgery on her. I broke it off."

He went on, "She offered to go to Mexico and get an abortion. I told her if she wanted that I'd help her find someone to do it but that our engagement was over. I asked around at the medical school and finally, found somebody that would do it anonymously if she went to a certain hotel down in Pittsburg. I guess she did it. I was disappointed enough that I couldn't bear to find out," Paul explained further.

"Was it hard to do one on Lt. Wagner then?" I could not contain my curiosity about how he would have been able to do it on Nurse Wagner if he couldn't do it on his fiancée.

He struggled on with his explanation, "Well after that experience, even though they didn't teach abortions in the surgery classes, I went to the library and studied the book on female surgeries before I finished medical school. I realized that it could sometimes be the best option for some women or girls, especially thinking of girls like my younger sister."

"Did she get pregnant?" I asked.

"No, I was just using her as an example. If my younger sister Ella needed one, I would have helped her, but it never happened so far as I know."

"Was the one you did on Lt. Wagner the first," I queried.

"Yes, it was. I was nervous as hell, fearful she'd

start really bleeding and then somebody would figure out it was me that did it. Are we still good friends, now that I've told my secret?" he asked.

"Of course we are still friends. Will you promise to keep my secret absolutely to yourself only?" I said knowing that if he didn't, I'd be discharged, probably dishonorably discharged if the brass found out I was actually Negro. Let alone what he would think, say or do when Major Sykes found out he'd been kissing a colored woman.

"Of course! Haven't we become friends enough for you to trust me?" His casualness was about to be shattered.

"I'm not sure that trust is enough for what I'm going to tell you," I said.

"Well, don't keep me in any more suspense. It can't be much worse than the secret I already told you or the secret we share about the abortion." Laughingly he said "Out with it!" as he slipped both hands together in a clasp behind my back.

Inwardly, I felt myself gulp as if I were about to plunge out of an airplane, not knowing whether or not the parachute would open. "I'm a mulatto. My father is white and my mother was Negro."

I waited for his response but there was no immediate change in his demeanor except his hands clasped behind my back slowly fell apart. He seemed otherwise frozen so I went on, "I know if the brass knew this I would be dishonorably discharged.

So I hope, even if you hate me for this, that you'll help me keep my secret because I love this Army. I love working in this hospital as an occupational therapist."

"You don't look Negro," This was his first simple reply. His face began to morph into a sort of shocked look as he examined me. "I haven't known many Negroes. I've never even had a Negro patient. I don't know what to think. It's going to take a little while for me to absorb this but you have my promise that I won't tell. I guess we both have secrets to hold over each others heads that could get us discharged."

We were both silent as we walked back to the cottages.

CHAPTER 44

Anxiety

I immediately began to consider what to do next. I couldn't resign as I had not even finished the two years of enlistment for which I had signed up. I would not go AWOL as Arne Erickson had done. Should I request a transfer? I was really needed here. After a day in the recreation room these are the thoughts that occupied me as I lay on my bunk after returning exhausted to the nurses' cottage. I was able to avoid thinking about it while working with the patients but not when I was alone.

I was disappointed not to hear from Major Sykes. As each day went by without a note from him, I came to believe that he realized we could not be a couple anymore even though he was the only one besides Woodrow Minter who knew I was an impostor. I had not told him that Woodrow knew so he was having his own struggle, not particularly in relation to what other people might think of him because of my race but rather about race being more important than our closeness.

In thinking of my future, I realized I would have a much better chance at continuing a fulfilling career in occupational therapy if I completed my enlistment in "this white man's Army." I knew that there were Negro women's nursing corps but I had done so much to make myself white, I could not face being Negro again. I would not want to compete with these women after the war for the limited jobs for Negro women. Besides, this war was almost over. It was accepted knowledge that by now the Allies were winning on both sides of the world.

The other women in 148th General Hospital corps seemed to share with each other their emotional struggles and thoughts about men. I, on the other hand, having been a solitary individual my whole life, had no one in whom I felt free to confide, not even Cassie. I wished I knew Umeyo and Mitsuko better as they might understand my dilemma more than any of these other women. I could not risk telling anyone anyway, so I struggled with the anxiety that somehow I would be exposed when I least expected it, or whether there was any action I might take to neutralize the situation.

Knowing about the depth of racial feeling in the United States and its territories, I did not expect to hear from Major Paul Sykes, though I dearly wished I would. I had begun to have real feelings for that man. At least, I did trust that he would keep my secret. I knew he was trustworthy. I was not bitter because most of America was leery about Negroes. I knew that. I was just unlucky enough to be caught up in this American delusion. I was more White than Negro I knew, even though Mother never told me about my white ancestors. Her skin had been light enough for me and all Negroes to know that there had been some white person in her bloodline.

Cassie seemed to discern something different in my demeanor." You seem quieter," she said to me one day as we pulled on our uniforms before going to breakfast. "Has the good doctor abandoned you? Or maybe you are just hiding your doings from us."

"Oh we were never that involved," I lied. "He's just not my type." I continued my lies. I would not give her any further excuse to question me. "Besides, I don't see you spending any time with any particular man either."

"Well, you seem a little sad. I was just wondering." She changed the subject to one of the patients she knew I was working with also. "Did Shepherd give you an excuse about why he isn't doing his exercises?"

Relieved to have another subject introduced, I gladly reported that "Pvt. Shepherd doesn't have any trouble limping up to the pool table during recreation."

After breakfast, we headed off in different directions, she to the surgery to consult with Major

Sykes about a patient, and I went down to the recreation room. I felt a little jealous knowing Cassie would be talking to the quiet man I cared about, but I gave no hint of that feeling to her, or so I thought.

I got to the recreation room just in time to intercede in a scuffle that resulted from one soldier accusing another at cheating in poker. My little bit of officer training and occupational therapy training had educated me about how to calm down soldiers with too much energy and limited ability to use it up. I persuaded the friends of the adversaries to remove each of them to different part of the room and one went outside to cool down. Many of the men were disappointed that the fight was averted as they had little excitement here unless we had a special event such as the Halloween party or the play. I decided it was time to find some event here at the hospital to divert them and their overflowing energies.

We began to plan a talent show at the Yamada Theater. I canvassed the patients who came to the recreation room as well as those in the Section 8 barracks. We found patients with skills we had never suspected; musicians, poetry reciters, singers, story tellers, jugglers and even wrestlers. However, the physical injuries that the wrestlers had sustained prohibited them from this particular activity. I asked Umeyo and Mitsuko about sumo wrestling, thinking perhaps we could get some local wrestlers to put on a demonstration for our patients, but all the Japanese boys were pretty much gone to the Army, they explained. So we planned our talent show for mid-March as this would give us time in case we needed to make costumes and borrow a guitar, and a microphone. Several of the patients had purchased ukuleles from a local musician whom we had had in for short Hawaiian music concerts in the mess hall. These patients were eager to show us what they had learned.

By the end of February, we had gotten news of the Yalta conference between Roosevelt, Churchill and Stalin. We heard of their plans to make separate protectorates in Europe when the war was over. This made us hopeful that the Pacific War might end soon as well. Since the Asia war was not over yet, we in the 148th worked on diligently caring for our patients. Reports of the U. S. flag being raised over Mount Suribachi on Iwo Jima gave us heart.

By mid-March we had heard of the Superfortress bombers over Tokyo. Finally in April we learned of the Army landing on Okinawa.

CHAPTER 45

Several hospital ships had brought deliveries or pick-ups of patients. Each time a ship departed with some of our patients, we lost some budding artists who had been on our talent show line-up. Pvt. Owens, now that he was assigned to the rehabilitation unit was able to take these changes in stride. He finally felt that his performers were ready for the show near the end of March. A last few rehearsals in the theater were scheduled since places for practice were few and far between in the Hospital on the Hill.

I attended the rehearsals as often as I could since I was charged with such tasks as making a western vest costume for a guitar player, and with finding books of readings and sheet music as well as other theater props for performers.

Late one afternoon as I ran over to the nurse's cottage to change into slacks before going to the theater for a last go-through before the big night, I grabbed the door and flung it open planning to dress shielding myself behind the door and leave quickly. I stopped in my tracks as I realized two people were trying to untangle themselves on Lt. Shirley Thompson's bed. It was still light enough that I had not reached for the chain to the bulb hanging in the middle of the room. It was absolutely forbidden to bring men into this cottage without announcing "man-in-the-hall," let alone "man-in-the-bed." It took but a moment for me to realize that both bodies were women's bodies and that they had their slips pulled down to their waists. I was tempted to just turn around and go back out into the hall and try to forget this.

"We were just wrestling for fun," Cassie sang out.

I decided to try to ignore this breech of all rules of love and war. I said, "I just need to change into my slacks." I grabbed them where they hung over the end of my bunk and turned my back on the women on the bed who were tugging their slips back into place. Pulling off my stockings and garter belt, I struggled into the slacks while holding onto the doorknob with one hand. Without another word, I flung myself back out the door while buckling my belt.

Outside on the boardwalk, I stopped to gather my wits and to catch my breath. While the other woman had not spoken, I realized it was Shirley Thompson. It was her bed across from mine where the two had been. That person seemed to have hidden her face but all the little clues one sees but does not consciously register, after sleeping in the same room with her for a couple months, told me it was her. She was usually on a noon to midnight shift at this time. It must be her one afternoon off. With these thoughts came the realization that these two women could be immediately discharged if they were reported. I felt like both were my friends, especially Cassie whom I had known since the train from Chicago to Washington over a year ago.

Knowing I could not spare more time to think about this unusual situation, I rushed back across to the village center and the Yamada Theater. We had more than twenty talented people, not all patients in our program, which I promised to print out on the mimeograph machine to be ready for tomorrow evening. We had invited the local people to attend. This was a way of thanking them for their support through providing us with fresh food and letting us use their theater and store. We did not expect many to attend fortunately, as the theater wasn't that big. Also, most of them had to be back in the cane fields early in the morning.

I did not have time to think about Cassie and Shirley until late that night as I lay on my bunk looking at the bunk above me. They were all asleep when I came in from rehearsal or so it seemed as their breathing seemed regular. I questioned myself about what to do; should I discuss it with Cassie?

Should I just try to forget it? Should I ask Wanda if she knew of anything unusual happening in our room? I realized I could put off all this until after tomorrow evening's talent show. That was my priority. I was finally able to sleep.

The Talent Show went off wonderfully. The mimeographed program listed each performer's name and talent. It started at 1900 and ended at 2100. I had had Pvt. Owens ask Dr. Sykes to get two other doctors to help be the judges. The three doctors arrived just a few moments after 1900 just as Pvt. Owen was announcing the first performer, a piano player and vocalist singing and accompanying himself on "A Nightingale Sang in Berkeley Square." One of the walking patients acting as usher immediately rushed the three doctors to the reserved seats in the front row.

The next was a trio singing and acting out the song "Der Fuehrer's Face" from the Walt Disney cartoon film by that name. They were hilarious and the crowd loved their antics. Even though the European war was far from the battlefields of the Pacific, everyone seemed to know the lyrics and soon everyone was singing along.

The next performer was a patient in a wheelchair who quickly changed the mood of the audience when he recited from memory the World War One poem by Lt. Col. John McCrae "In Flanders Fields." The theater became very quiet as they were reminded of the fields of poppies covering the graves of the dead and perhaps other more recent graveyards of their buddies.

The program progressed with another wheelchair patient who juggled empty coke bottles, and then a man with a stump on his right arm playing Ravel's "Concerto for the Left Hand."

I tried to keep from having to talk directly with Major Sykes but when it came time to ask the judges for their decision about who got first second and third places, Pvt. Owens was busy with moving the microphone. So I bravely grasped my inner self and walked to where the three judges sat in the front row of seats.

"Have you judges made the decisions about who the first, second and third place winners are?" I asked trying not to look Dr. Sykes in the face.

He held out a paper which I judged must have the names of the winners but he held it so I had to move closer in order to grasp it. I did so without comment. When I got back to the stage steps where I intended to hand the list of winners to Pvt. Owen to announce as it had really been his show, I discovered a second sheet lay under the winner list. I saw it was addressed to me. Not wanting to have anything distract me from ending this show with a hurrah, I tucked it into my uniform pocket.

Other bunk mates were all sleeping soundly when I returned to the nurses' cottage after helping Pvt. Owen put the Yamada Theater back to rights. Like the gentleman that he was, Pvt. Owen had walked me back along the dark roadway. We had praised each other for the success of our endeavor. With the satisfaction of knowing the Talent Show had been even better than anticipated, I lay on my bunk to read the note:

Lt. Brett, please come to the surgery.
I need to consult with you.

Major Sykes

With two things now to worry about, what to do about Cassie and Shirley and what Dr. Sykes might want with me now, I found it hard to sleep. I did not want to lose my best friend Cassie here, which I would surely do if I discussed what I had seen with anyone. Also, I did not want to ruin someone else's career. Cassie had indicated she might like to stay in the Army after the war ended. While I knew Shirley very little, I was also reluctant to cause trouble for a roommate, but I could not pretend I had not seen what I had seen. This brought me to the decision that I must get Cassie alone and ask her what she was planning and see if there were some other explanation.

But for Dr. Sykes command to consult with him could be about a patient but since he passed me the note in a most secretive way, it probably meant he wanted to tell me that he wanted to formally end whatever we had had between us.

Finally, fatigue won out and I slept.

CHAPTER 46

The next afternoon, I used the excuse of returning some bed-sheets used in the stage backdrop at the Talent Show to walk uphill to the surgery. I did not want him to think I was his to command.

By now on Hawaii Island, though there were less apparent seasons than there were in the United States, it seemed like spring with only a few clouds and flowers in abundance. The patients' flower garden looked lovely beside their barracks. When one patient who had worked on it left, he usually made sure someone else would keep it weeded. It had geraniums, petunias and morning-glories which had begun to grow up the wall of the barracks.

Paul Sykes was sitting at his desk looking through a medical journal when I entered the surgery after knocking to make sure I was not interrupting an operation.

He closed the journal and stood. "The Talent Show was a great idea! The patients have been discussing it. Being a judge was also fun. Sit down,"

He said as he dragged a chair away from the wall by his desk.

I told him as I sat down that, "I appreciated your help but that isn't why you asked me to come, is it?"

"No," he said reseating himself. "I have thought a lot about your secret and since I have orders to return to the United States next week, some other surgeon will be taking over here, I wanted to say a proper goodbye and ask if we can write letters after I leave."

"Of course we can write letters. I would enjoy that very much. Where will you be going, do you know?" I asked puzzled but relived and excited.

"During these weeks when I haven't been seeing you, I started studying some special orthopedic techniques to help keep my mind off of you. Well, that didn't work, but I did learn something about spinal fusion for intractable pain patients. We have plenty of them here and I'm sure there will be lots more after the war. I've been reading about the research at the Alfred DuPont Institute in Wilmington, Delaware, where they started doing spinal fusions a couple years ago. I asked for a transfer to some Army hospital near there where they are doing that surgery now so I could specialize after discharge."

"And so where will they send you?" I asked apprehensively.

"I am being posted to the Army Air Corps Hospital at New Castle Air Base outside Wilmington.

I figure if I am that close, I'll be able to meet some of the researchers and maybe they'll invite me to do surgery with them so I can learn the technique."

"When will you be leaving?" I wanted to get as much information as possible. He had not said anything yet about my race. So I asked, "And what about my secret? Does that matter?"

"Of course, I can't ignore it because if anyone ever found out, it would affect everything, where we could live if we were married, what my friends and colleagues might think, but as long as nobody knows, I guess it doesn't matter. It certainly hasn't made me care less for you."

That was what I wanted to hear, that he still cared for me. "Does writing letters mean anything more than that we are special friends?"

"I want to have plenty of time to discuss this and to write about it. I see so many folks in the military getting married so quickly and I wonder if they are going to be happy. I want us to be happy. So taking more time to be sure is a good idea, I think," he finished.

Since he was the first man I had ever let myself have these kinds of feelings for, I was very pleased to anticipate a possible future. "I will be so happy to write to you and we can learn more about each other that way. It makes me happy that you care still for me." I wished he would reach out for me but he stayed seated behind the desk. The overhead light bulb glanced light off his shiny bald spot. We parted in this ambiguous situation. I felt anxious but still hopeful.

I was tempted to ask his opinion about Cassie and Shirley, but felt restrained by knowing that I would not like him talking about my secret with anyone. So I struggled on with my dilemma.

Out of loyalty to my friendship with Cassie, I decided I must discuss it with her. If she were like me, she would be worrying about what would happen if a higher up found out about her.

Rather than face her personally, I left a note on her bunk the next morning after breakfast asking:

> Would you like to walk up to the stables sometime and look at the horses with me?
>
> Clara

I did not receive a reply from her that day but the note was gone when I came into the room that afternoon before supper. Cassie and Shirley were already seated waiting for the mess line to start, when I went into our dining room.

"Shirley has never been up to the stable," said Cassie. "I was thinking maybe she could go with us when we walk up there."

Knowing it would be too difficult for me to ask the kind of questions I needed to ask if Shirley walked with us, I forced myself to say, "I was hoping to be able to have just you and me because I need to ask you something private."

Cassie's face reflected fear as she waited a moment before replying, "Oh sure. When did you want to take that walk?"

I wanted to get this over with but I was no longer sure of what schedule Cassie was keeping with her patients so I suggested, "Let's do it Sunday morning." I figured Shirley would be sleeping after her night shift and many of the patients might be in church then so it was unlikely we would meet anyone else walking then, and it would mean only one day to wait and worry for Cassie, and also for Shirley. Cassie would probably tell her everything we talked about anyway. I didn't want to torture them by making them wait to see what I had to say about witnessing their "wrestling match."

Shirley sat immobile as if she had not even heard our conversation. The rain pelted down outside and was audible through the open windows. Someone had placed a single pink hibiscus in the middle of the table.

"Ok, let's go right after breakfast," said Cassie, "unless it is raining too hard. If it's raining then, let's go down to the administration building where most of the doctors have their offices. We can sit in the hallway. There's usually nobody around down there on Sunday morning."

Our plans agreed to, all three of us got into line for breakfast. We were unusually quiet during this meal. Fortunately, other nurses carried on lively conversations around us so it was not uncomfortably silent in the dining room. Consequently, I did not feel conspicuous in my silence as I did not know what to say in this situation. I needed to clear this up with Cassie.

Sunday, immediately after breakfast, Cassie and I grabbed our umbrellas, though it was simply misting as we walked the trail between the gymnasium which is the surgery now and the closed Japanese school. This way, we did not have to go by the rubbish dump. We had the Stable Road to ourselves. On one side it was pasture with cattle and on the other, sugar cane.

"Well, I guess I know what you want to talk about," Cassie started.

"Yes, when I surprised you and Shirley the other day, I figured out what happened those other times when the door was blocked shut. I was hoping you could talk to me about it," I responded. "You and I have been friends almost two years now."

"I never really knew why I didn't feel crazy about boys like other girls," she said. "Being in the WACs I began to realize that there were other women who didn't give a hoot about flirting with men, being with men."

"Was Shirley the first woman you've been that way with?" I asked curiously. I'd heard of lesbians but not given it much thought. They were obviously some sort of aberration. That designation for women had been briefly discussed in our psychiatry class at Walter Reed Army Hospital at the same time as male homosexuality was defined as a sickness. Now I was interested in Cassie's story more than I was in trying to figure out what to do now that I knew.

"I had only brothers. I had six older brothers but when my mother had me, she decided she had her girl and she wasn't going to have any more. She didn't tell my father when she got the doctor to tie her tubes after my birth." Cassie spoke with her head down, not looking at me as she talked. A mongoose chased another mongoose across the trail in front of us. Cassie didn't even seem to see it.

I gave a sort of positive grunt to encourage Cassie to keep talking. The problem of what I should do about it could continue to wait for me to decide. I needed to hear Cassie's story.

"In seventh grade when the other girls were starting to refuse to play with the boys yet wanted to dance with them, I discovered that I did not want to dance with boys. Instead, there was this other girl in my class, Celia, who didn't want to dance with boys either, so Celia and I would dance together. My mother let me invite her to stay overnight at my house since she went to the same catechism class as me and since I didn't have any sisters. She knew Celia's parents from church. Celia and I would wrestle in bed and it was great fun but I didn't have a name for what we did or what I felt." Cassie continued to talk, all the while looking at the dirt track right in front of her feet.

Another of those encouraging murmurs from me provided me with the time to think without having to give a clearer response to her story. This was confusing to me as I had never stayed over night alone with another girl at her house.

"Then in nursing school, I didn't have much time for anything except an afternoon to go to visit my folks. I occasionally had an occasional warm twinge of feeling for one of the other nursing students but none of us had time for flirting. Besides, there were always other people around. The dormitory had four beds so the room was never empty like ours sometimes is here," she said giving me a sideways glance. She raised her closed umbrella and struck out at a fern frond bending out over the path.

"Well, when did you know what you were doing was considered deviant?" I asked with some trepidation for fear she'd be offended by the word deviant.

"I just knew I was different, that I didn't care about boys. I never thought of myself as 'deviant'. When I was in nursing school, I heard about homosexuality in my psychology class. That was when I realized I was considered abnormal."

"You know you'll be kicked out of the WACs if anybody finds out?" I questioned.

Well, it didn't say it anywhere in the papers

I signed, but I figured it out by gossip after one girl was dismissed from the PT training group at Walter Reed Hospital." She said this as rain started to pelt down just as we neared the stables door. It was locked. We stood under the eves to open our umbrellas.

"Let's go back by the Mamalahoa Highway," I suggested. "In this rain, the road will be easier to walk on than that trail."

The noise of the rain on our umbrellas precluded further conversation. The trail toward the highway was shorter than the Stable Road which was really just a track. When we got to the cottage and shook off the drops, I whispered to her, "What are you going to do now that you know I know? I don't know what I need to do. You're my friend and I don't want you to get a dishonorable discharge. Or Shirley either." I wanted to add "Why weren't you more careful?" but it did not seem like a good time to scold her.

"Both of us, Shirley and me, felt really scared when you found us together the other day. I told her that you were my good friend and wouldn't tell. I hope I was right because I want to keep on working in physical therapy for the Army. I know there will be plenty of jobs for me because there are so many injured soldiers who need my help."

CHAPTER 47

Could I, as one kind of outcast, betray Cassie, another kind of outcast? We were both doing important work for our country by helping heal these soldiers who had risked their lives for our county's freedoms. I knew that I deserved to continue my work. Patients had told me how much occupational therapy meant to them. Did Cassie and Shirley deserve less? Were our different aberrations a risk to our patients?

Inevitably, I began to wonder if I were also afflicted with their peculiarity. I had never had a boyfriend until Paul Sykes. Was I homosexual? I had admired Miss Norris, the homemaking teacher and also Miss Alcorn, the Tuskegee graduate nurse. Had those been homosexual feelings? When the Hawaiian woman came to teach us hula dancing at St. Louis College in Honolulu, I could not take my eyes off her and her body as she danced. Her face had been so beautiful and her body movements so graceful. Was I a lesbian because I loved watching her?

I had also loved dancing with Paul Sykes, loved it when he held my hand, loved it when he kissed me. Was there some other sort of aberration where a woman was attracted to both men and women? Or did my attraction to some women just mean I honored them for their beauty or intelligence? I could not remember craving to be in close physical contact with them. Maybe my watching hula was like when some men enjoyed watching wrestling. To me, most women were more fun to look at than men. Their clothes were more interesting and their faces showed more expression much of the time. This is what I said to myself.

Did the difference between Cassie and me mean she should be denied rights like I had been denied the right to use the Selma Carnegie Library? I was not brave enough to discuss these ruminations with Cassie or I might have resolved my inner conflict sooner. A flurry of transfers came down from headquarters. Major Sykes got his desired transfer to the Army Air Corps Hospital at New Castle Air Base outside Wilmington. I promised Cassie to keep her secret before she was sent to Letterman Hospital in San Francisco. More and more ships of patients sailed straight to the West Coast of the United States rather than stopping to drop their load of patients in Hawaii. Everyone saw that the war would soon be over despite the bombing that was still going on over Japan.

I walked with Cassie to take the train from the Mountain View Station to Hilo where she would fly to Honolulu and then take a hospital transport plane to San Francisco. I helped her carry her pack. Shirley did not get a transfer immediately and I assumed they had found some private place to say their goodbyes as she did not accompany us. Perhaps their relationship had just been a convenience. I was too shy to ask Cassie if this were the way it was. We promised to write though we had never had the deep discussion about sex that both of us desired but were unable to figure out how to start.

Major Paul Sykes on the other hand, could not leave until a replacement surgeon came. After the new surgeon did come a few weeks later, Paul got someone from the motor pool to take him to Hilo Harbor where he boarded a hospital transport ship on which he intended to help in the surgery on the way to the Port of San Diego. We had a private walk in the rain the night before he left, using the opportunity to confirm our commitment to writing to each other until we figured out whether or not we thought we could face a future together in what we expected to be a new peaceful world.

Dr. Beving got his just desserts or so it seemed to me. I heard it through Army gossip as I was receiving my discharge at Fort Sheridan. He was discharged out of the Army with the many other unneeded personnel after V-J Day. When he returned to his hometown, his wife asked for a divorce as she had taken up with another man while he was away. It was rumored that his 201 file reflected his philandering behavior and that he had a hard time finding a psychiatric hospital to hire him. He tried a private practice but without success and ended up taking a job in a new veterans' hospital.

The surrender of the Japanese at Manila on August 31, 1945 was the signal for me to begin to make plans for my own return to the United States. The bombing of Hiroshima and Nagasaki in early August had caused such uproar among patients as well as staff that I had not really taken seriously, the obvious signal that the war was over. Almost all of us at the Hospital on the Hill were unprepared for the suddenness of the surrender by the Emperor of Japan. We made a celebration parade two days later from the recreation room up to the surgery and residential cottages, down through the village and across to the hospital administration building which would soon return to its real purpose of a school building. Wheelchair patients used crepe paper to decorate the wheels on their chairs. Those that could march put on their uniforms and we sought out as many flags as possible. Those few patients who owned or borrowed musical instruments made up a small band and played the national anthem. As we passed the homes to which classes had been displaced, some of the children came out to join the parade. Patients demonstrated their hope that they would soon return to the United States.

I received orders to begin to wind down the recreation program as they transported more and more patients out of all the barracks and returned them to the United States military hospitals.

The Mountain View School and the cottages would be returned to the community after removal of most Army supplies and a thorough cleaning. Tadashi went back into the discipline of a regular school there in Mountain View. Before Christmas 1945, I returned to Fort Sheridan for discharge. The Hospital on the Hill closed a few months later. As I began my new life as a civilian, I realized that I too, was eligible for the GI Bill. I began to make plans to find a college in the north where I could further my professional education. Until then I found a job working as an occupational therapist at Cherokee State Hospital in Cherokee, Iowa.

Correspondence with Cassie Amari and Paul Sykes buoyed me up as I went from wearing the Army uniform to wearing a white uniform similar to the nurses at Cherokee State Hospital. In choosing that place to work, I felt it showed Dr. Paul Sykes that I was not chasing him by trying to settle too close to where he was working. Petersburg, Minnesota was close enough that maybe I could discover what happened to Arne Erickson someday though that had a low priority on my list of things to do as a civilian. My blackmailer, Woodrow Minter reenlisted in the Army and I lost track of him thankfully. I necessarily adjusted to the general population of psychiatric patients rather than a bunch of youthful injured soldiers.

THE END

Glossary of Hawaiian Words

Haole – White person

Kanaka – Human being or meaning a Hawaiian

Koma – Tom

Lopaka - Robert

Kamila – Carmilla

Hapu`u – *Cibotium splendens*, endemic tree fern

Haole Koa – *Leucaena leucocephalia*, name means foreign koa.

Punalu`u – Jump into the spring water

Kiawe – *Prosopis pallida,* the Algoroba tree has dangerous thorns.

Bibliography

Aynes, Edith A. (1973) *From Nightingale to Eagle*, Prentice-Hall Inc., Englewood, NJ.

Bailey, Beth & Farber, David (1992) *The First Strange Place: Race and Sex in World War II Hawaii*. The Johns Hopkins University Press, Baltimore.

Brown, DeSoto (1989) *Hawaii Goes to War: Life in Hawaii from Pearl Harbor to Peace*, Editions Limited, Hong Kong.

Christensen, Eric (1991) *A Proud Heritage: The American Occupational Therapy Association at Seventy-Five*, The American Occupational Therapy Association, Inc, Rockville, MD.

Fitts III, Alston (1989) Selma: *Queen City of the Blackbelt,* Clairmont Press, Selma, AL.

Hartwick Ann M. Ritchie (1993) *The Army Specialist Corps: The 45th Anniversary, Center of Military History United States Army,* Washington, D. C.

Litoff, Judy Barret & Smith, David C. (1991) *Since You Went Away: World War II Letters from American Women on the Home Front.* University Press of Kansas, Lawrence, KS.

Minear, Richard H. (1999) *Dr. Seuss Goes to War: The World War II Editorial Cartoons of Theodore Seuss Geisel*, The New Press, New York.

Monahan, Evelyn M & Neidel-Greenlee (2003) *And If I Perish: Frontline U. S. Army Nurses in World War II*, Anchor Books, New York.

Schryver, Grace Fay (1930) *A History of the Illinois Training School for Nurses 1880-1929*. The Board of Directors of the Illinois Training School for Nurses.

Warshauer, Kent (2007) *Riddle of the Relic: Memories of Hawaii*, Hawaii Plantation & Industrial Museum, Hilo, Hawaii.

Weatherford, Doris (2008) *American Women and World War II*, Castle Books, Edison N. J.

Winchell, Meghan K., (2008) *Good Girls, Good Food, Good Fun,* The University of North Carolina Press, Chapel Hill.

Wright, Mike (1998) *What They Didn't Teach You about World War II*, Presidio Press, Novato, CA

www.ingramcontent.com/pod-product-compliance
Lightning Source LLC
Chambersburg PA
CBHW070755190726
48292CB00002B/543